UNDERTOW

ELIZABETH HEATHCOTE

Quercus

First published in Great Britain in 2016
This edition published in 2017 by

Quercus Editions Ltd
Carmelite House
50 Victoria Embankment
London EC4Y 0DZ

An Hachette UK company

A CIP catalogue record for this book is available
from the British Library.

PB ISBN 978 1 78648 169 6
EBOOK ISBN 978 1 78648 167 2

10 9 8 7 6 5 4 3 2

Typeset by CC Book Production
Printed and bound in Great Britain by Clays Ltd, St Ives plc.

To Nev, Ben and Franny

Chapter 1

Paula had every light on in the kitchen. It was nearly June but gloomy, raining and cold, miserable weather even for England. She would have been happy to stay indoors all day, but the dog was getting restless and he'd have to be walked. She pulled on her wellies and cagoule and went back to the cloakroom for a scarf.

It was half-term and the children were watching TV, still in their pyjamas at twelve. Paula's dad was upstairs fixing the light in Cheyenne's bedroom. She shouted up to let him know that she was going and then put her head round the living-room door. 'I'm taking the dog out,' she said. 'Granddad's upstairs.'

The children were side by side on the settee, a blanket pulled over their knees, their bodies barely touching. They didn't look up.

'Hello?' she said.

'Shh!' said Charlie, her boy, his eyes fixed on the screen.

'Did you hear me? I'm taking the dog out and—'

'Mum! I heard.'

She tutted and closed the door, her lips spelling out what she'd like to have said as she searched for her keys in the pile of scarves and gloves and school books by the front door. Then she heard a shout. 'Wait, Mum, I'm coming!'

Cheyenne, her little girl, came running through.

'You want to? It's raining.'

'I know, Mummy, I want to come with you.'

'Get dressed quickly then.'

Cheyenne scrambled upstairs, still climbing on hands and knees at four. Paula smiled after her and picked up the dog's lead without thinking and of course Roxy heard and went wild, bounding into the hall and jumping up at her over and over again, barking and snapping with excitement. The next few minutes were chaos, trying to calm him and to hurry Cheyenne, to get her shoes and coat and hat on with the dog jumping round them. By the time Paula opened the front door she felt frazzled.

The dog tore through the yard and into the street, crazy for the air and freedom. The drizzle closed around him and drove him wilder, as though it harboured spirits that only he could hear. He twisted and leaped and snapped, then disappeared into the mist, around the corner and on to the beach.

Cheyenne ran after him, and Paula set off too, but then she realised she had forgotten the dog's ball. She paused for a minute, watching her daughter run ahead, but there was no road to cross, and Cheyenne and the dog both knew every inch of that beach, so she hurried back into the house to pick up the ball.

When she came out again the street was empty. She ran

2

round the corner, across the lane that served the old seafront cottages. No one was around so she took the short cut through one of the gardens, with its driftwood bench and tufts of dry grass clinging to the pebbles, then jumped over the low fence on to the beach.

Her steps were loud against the pebbles. She stopped for a minute, squinting through the drizzle for her daughter and her dog, and the weather shrouded her in a perfect silence. She couldn't see any movement, couldn't see anything more than twenty metres ahead.

'Cheyenne,' she called, and stepped forward. Her foot on the stones was too loud in the void where her daughter's voice, or someone else's, or anything normal should have been. She felt the stab of panic that came whenever she let Cheyenne out of her sight, that moment of terror she almost teased herself with before her daughter inevitably appeared again.

'Cheyenne.'

She pulled her hood off to listen better. Moisture gathered on her face.

'Cheyenne.' She ran a few paces. 'Cheyenne!'

The beach fell away here, from the high-tide mark, a slope of pebbles that got steeper in the winter storms, as the sea pounded it into a wall. Her feet sank deep into the loose shingle. She started along the top, not sure which way they would have gone, reluctant to drop down to the harder, sandier ground left by the retreating tide. She could move quicker down there but she could see further from up here.

She forced her feet on. 'Cheyenne!'

The tide was going out below her but the waves were winter waves, as tall as her daughter, crashing on to the beach and dragging everything they could find back with them. How could she have been so stupid? That bloody ball!

It was in her hand still. She was squeezing it tight. This was the last time she would let her daughter out of her sight even for a second.

'Cheyenne! Roxy!'

She heard a bark, to her left, not close. Oh thank God . . . She touched her fluttering heart, her breath slowed a little. How silly of her. She set off after the bark, moving faster through the shingle now so that she was quickly breathless. How could they have got so far so quickly?

'Cheyenne!'

Through the drizzle she could see movement, ahead and below her, near the waves. It was the dog – long and flat, down on all fours, then leaping in the air and dropping again. He was playing with something, the way he worried a bucket or a duster at home, a poor domestic substitute for some ancient memory of hunting.

There was no sign of her daughter.

'Cheyenne!'

She ran towards the dog and he bounded towards her, but stopped halfway and twisted around on his hind legs to run back to the same spot. There was something there, some piece of flotsam he was busy with. He was barking at it, calling her over to show her.

It's a person, she thought. Lying face down on the beach.

4

And for a moment it seemed perfectly natural that a person should be lying on the beach in the freezing drizzle, the most natural thing in the world. But something about the person, the leg, the angle, it wasn't right. And then a wave hit and nudged the leg more askew, and she thought it was a doll. And then she realised it was a body. Someone dead.

She didn't scream her daughter's name. The world screamed too loudly in her ears. She was running but she didn't know it. She was frozen, the muscles in her face and her mouth and her arms and her heart. She didn't breathe. The noise in her ears was deafening. Her brain had seized up. She felt rain again on her face. Her brain sent a message. The body wasn't a child. It wasn't Cheyenne.

She stopped ten metres away. She was shaking. It was a woman, black hair, blue skin, bloated. She had a red bikini on, ripped. She stepped closer. Part of the flesh on the arm was missing. Paula could see bone.

She turned away. How awful. But where was her daughter? 'Cheyenne!' she shouted.

The dog nipped at her hand. He wanted her to throw the ball for him. She was so dazed she did it, threw it up the shingle to the plateau at the top, away from the body, then she started after him, her wellies slipping on the pebbles.

'Cheyenne!'

Roxy disappeared over the brow after the ball, and then his head popped back up, and another dog was beside him. Paula was struggling to run up the steep shingle, digging her wellies in, her panic was slowing her, her tense arms and legs kept slipping back. The dogs ran past her, back towards the beach.

A man was standing at the top. He was middle-aged, she recognised him vaguely from around but she didn't know him. He had a beard. 'Have you seen a little girl?' she said, clambering up.

He didn't answer. He was looking beyond her. 'Is that a body?'

The dogs were circling the dead swimmer, barking and playing together, chasing each other around this strange totem.

'Yes,' said Paula. 'The tide must have brought her in. Please, have you seen a little girl? I can't find my daughter.'

He looked at her, as though he wasn't quite following. She was touching his arm, she realised. She pulled her hand away. He nodded over to the strip of grass and pebbles that lay at the top of the beach.

And there she was, Cheyenne, sitting down in all this rain, her pink hat bobbing above the grasses. She was staring at the ground, concentrating – playing with the shingle or looking for shells, oblivious.

Paula laughed, relief coursing through her. 'I'm so sorry, I thought I'd lost her. Oh, thank goodness.'

She bent over, exhausted now from running up the slope.

'We should call the police,' he said, and for a moment Paula didn't know that he was talking about the body on the beach, the poor woman down there. 'It'll be that woman who went missing.'

'What woman?'

'At the bank holiday. She went swimming. Hadn't you heard? A woman from London.'

Paula hadn't heard anything. She'd been in with the kids most of the week.

She went to sit with her daughter. She hugged her and praised the picture she had made out of shells. Thank you, God, she thought. Thank you, thank you.

When they got home, Charlie hadn't moved. Cheyenne pulled her wet clothes off and joined him in her pants under the blanket, her eyes fixed on the TV. 'Don't just leave those there,' said Paula, and picked up the wet clothes, took them upstairs to the washing basket. She emptied the pockets of pebbles and shells, and there was a bracelet that she hadn't seen before. Cheyenne must have found it on the beach – it was nice, good quality, made of metal discs and stones, blues and greens. The metal discs had rusted a bit – it was a shame. Paula decanted it along with the other bits and put it into Cheyenne's fairy jewel box.

Sometime around 2 a.m. that night, Cheyenne crawled into her parents' bed, in the middle. Normally Paula would have told her she was too old for this, but tonight she hugged her tight. Shaun didn't stir; he slept through anything.

'That lady on the beach was dead, wasn't she?' Cheyenne whispered.

'Shh. Yes.'

Her daughter lay in her arms. 'I was scared,' she whispered.

'It was a bit scary, wasn't it, the police coming?'

'Not then. Before you came.' Cheyenne started to cry.

It hadn't occurred to Paula that her daughter had seen the body before she had arrived. She'd just assumed Cheyenne had been at the top of the beach, skirted around it.

'What happened to her?' Cheyenne sniffed.

'She drowned in the sea.'

'Couldn't she swim?'

'I don't know, darling. The sea can be dangerous. You have to stay away from the waves unless Mummy's there. Do you promise me?'

Cheyenne nodded.

'She was cold,' she said.

'You touched her!'

Cheyenne started to cry again.

'Shhh, shhh, shhh,' Paula said. 'It's OK, you didn't do anything wrong.' She held her daughter closer. Would she be traumatised by what she had seen?

The woman's name was Zena and she was twenty-nine. There was a picture in the paper – she was very good-looking, slim with long glossy black hair, flawless ivory skin, in the photograph she looked like a model. Paula recognised her, had seen her before in the village. Shaun had pointed her out one day – he knew her a bit from when they were young, she'd grown up nearby and then moved away. Shaun had said hello to her, but she'd blanked him. He'd been stung by that, she could tell, but he'd laughed it off.

It turned out she and her partner had been living around the corner in Shell Road. The paper said that they'd bought it as a weekend place just a few months ago. Paula could see the house from her garden – an old lady called Iris used to live there and after she died it was empty for a while. Paula knew someone had moved in, but she hadn't seen them yet, she didn't realise it was the same woman. They were down for the bank holiday. The woman went for a swim late afternoon on the Monday and didn't come back. The paper said she had swum from the stretch of the beach next to the bungalow, which wasn't safe – she should have known that, growing up around there. It wasn't protected for swimming – jet skis and boats used that area, plus the tide was strong and there were big waves, an undertow that could be dangerous.

There was lots of talk in the village, about the dead woman, theories about how she had died, rumours that it wasn't just a simple case of drowning, that there was more to it than that. Shaun said it was all nonsense and Paula was happy to agree with him. St Jude's was a gossipy place, everyone liked to have an opinion.

Someone who knew the dead woman from way back said she was a strong swimmer, that she knew what she was doing. Sometimes, Shaun said, it isn't enough.

Chapter 2

Late May, three years later

Carmen dreamed that Nick was making love to her. They were away somewhere, hiding from life in a shabby hotel room. He said they could stay away for months and no one would notice, but that they should move around, he had places he wanted to show her. He was holding her naked body and she was much younger, a teenager again, her whole self moulded around him. She wanted nothing but to be with him, and that feeling of certainty was more powerful than anything in the dream.

She woke abruptly, sweaty, disorientated. The thread of the dream was slipping away already. She had no idea how they had got there, what had come before. Just the feeling was left, her certainty, her arousal.

God. She rolled on to her back. Where did that come from? Tom was asleep beside her, his back to her, clutching his pillow and dreaming his own dreams or more probably not dreaming anything at all, just oblivious after a long week at work. She pulled herself up so she could see his face, frowning in sleep, as though even here life was a bit of a struggle these days, and she felt the love twitch in her stomach. She felt bad about the dream. Had she betrayed him somehow? She told herself to stop being stupid – it was just a dream, a shadow from her past, stored away in some file in her mind, randomly accessed and mixed with another file and another. She and Nick had never been anything like that in real life, or if they had it was so long ago she couldn't remember.

The room was too hot. It was May, time to turn the heating off. Carmen pulled the quilt to one side. Tom was wearing only his underpants and the skin on his back was pale and smooth, no hair and no slack beneath, his muscles defined from the daily half-hour at the gym in the basement of his office. She rolled on to her side and ran the back of her fingers across his shoulders. He didn't stir, so she did it again, stroked the soft skin, and her desire flared up. May as well put it to good use, she thought, and pulled her cotton nightdress over her head. She lined her body up against his, pressed herself into him and snaked an arm around his body.

He grunted, half awake. 'What are you doing?'

'You want me to stop?'

He grunted again. Of course not.

When they woke for the second time it was nearly ten and they were running late. It was their weekend to have Tom's children; they were due to pick them up at noon and the drive alone would take two and a half hours. They shoved clothes into bags and Carmen emptied the contents of the fridge into a cool box, and they had to go. The forecast was good and they'd planned to stop over at the beach, the first visit this year. There was no time for breakfast, but Tom was starving and insisted they stop to pick up coffee and rolls from the deli on the corner before getting stuck in the Saturday-morning jams through south London.

'They didn't have any bacon,' Carmen said as she climbed back into the car. Tom was texting. 'Is that Laura?'

'Yes.'

Laura was Tom's ex-wife. He would be texting to tell her they were going to be late collecting the children. 'You are so gutless. Why don't you just call her?' said Carmen.

He laughed, there was no need to explain the obvious. 'What did you get then? Sausage?'

'They didn't have sausage either, nothing hot. Egg and cress, or egg and smoked salmon, which do you want?'

He wanted the egg and smoked salmon of course, but he said she should have it, but she insisted that she felt like egg and cress, and they laughed at their good manners and split them. 'We'll have to buy sandwiches for the beach too,' said Carmen. 'Annoying.'

'Why?'

'It's such a waste of money.'

He laughed and kissed her.

They crawled along. The traffic approaching the Blackwall Tunnel was as bad as ever but Carmen didn't mind. She liked this time, travelling side by side in Tom's Audi, catching up.

They listened to the radio and he told her snippets from his week, gossip from the office, little irritations and anxieties. Evenings were her time, when she told him details of her day, about the people she had spoken to, the stories they had told her, new ideas she wanted to follow up. 'Are you looking forward to seeing the kids?' she said.

He shrugged, yes, of course, but . . .

'What?'

'Laura wants me to have a word with Mel.'

'Why?'

'She stayed out all night without telling her.'

Mel was his oldest, a challenging fifteen. 'Where was she?'

'I don't know. She said a friend's, but for some reason Laura checked and she wasn't there and she won't say where she was.'

'That's not good.'

Tom handed her his empty coffee cup. Carmen slid it inside hers then dropped them down beside her left leg on to the floor, where Tom wouldn't see. He hated rubbish in his Audi, he could be anal like that. 'You'd have thought Laura would call you about something serious like that, not just text,' she said.

'Actually she mentioned it earlier in the week when she rang.'

Carmen had suspected that was the case and she was irritated by it. She remembered Laura calling – they had been watching a DVD in bed. She had paused it, and when he came back up she had asked him what Laura was calling about, and he'd said nothing important. Why hadn't he just told her at the time?

She was about to say something when he said, 'I suppose I'll have to have a word with her.'

13

'Of course you will, you can't have that.'

Tom looked gloomy. Carmen knew what he was thinking – he saw his children infrequently enough and he didn't want to spend the time telling them off. Mel was hard enough to get on with anyway.

She took pity on him. 'You only need to have a word, it doesn't need to be heavy,' she said more gently.

They cleared the northern suburbs at last and were on the M11, out in open country. It was a beautiful spring day and the blue skies were a balm after months of grey London drear. When they left the motorway they took small roads heading north-east, passed through unspoilt villages with pubs and greens. The skies widened as they crossed into Norfolk, until a few miles later Tom took his hand off her knee to make a right turn. 'Here we are,' he said unnecessarily.

They pulled through a gateway between high brick walls on to a circular drive and Carmen tensed the way she always did as the house came into view, the elegance of the double-fronted Georgian fascia, the stuccoed pillars supporting the porch. In a previous incarnation it had been a vicarage and Tom still referred to it as that, as the vicarage, not Laura's house. To Carmen it bore no more relation to her experience than a set from a period drama, but to Tom of course it had been home for more than a decade.

He pulled up in the gravel parking area at the side of the house, which provoked a volley of barking from Riley the Labrador, shut away somewhere out of view. Laura was walking towards them, immaculate as always in pressed jeans and a

Barbour, her short red hair blow-dried close to her head. She showed no sign of annoyance that they were more than an hour late, whereas Carmen knew that in her shoes she would have been fuming and unable to hide it.

Carmen sank lower in her seat. It was no good, there was something about coming here that just reduced her. All that history, all that substance, and Laura – she was such a grown-up. Carmen knew that in part the way she acted was for the children's sake – Tom had explained Laura's insistence that they show nothing but cordiality in front of them, that they always present a united front as loving parents. But everyone knows that you're meant to put the kids first in these situations – how many exes can resist having the odd pop?

Not Laura. Whenever they met, from the very first time, Laura had been meticulous in being polite to Carmen – she always came up and said hello, and how are you, and what are you planning for the day? Only this time she couldn't because Mercy was clinging to her leg with one hand and a fence post with the other and screaming 'I don't want to leave Mummy!' so that Tom had to get out of the car and prise her away. Carmen overheard his brief exchange with Laura – when he would drop the children off, a comment about a friend's wedding next weekend (God, did that mean Laura was going to be there too?) and then Tom was coaxing and pulling the little girl towards the car . . . 'You want to come to the seaside, don't you?'

'I want to stay with Mummy!'

'Don't you want an ice cream?'

15

'I WANT TO STAY WITH MUMMY!'

Jake shot through the front door as though he was spring-loaded and dived into his seat with a flick of his fringe and a shy half-smile to Carmen, the tinny overflow from his earphones filling the car. Mel was last out, dressed in skinny jeans and a low-cut lilac top that she must have known would annoy Tom. She pushed past him as he tried to strap Mercy, kicking and arching her back, into the booster seat, and slumped into her corner, her hands over her ears. 'Can't you stop her screaming, Dad?'

'I am trying. Do you think you could help?'

'She doesn't want to come, does she?'

'Thanks, Mel.'

Carmen felt better once they were away from the house and back on the road, but the atmosphere in the car didn't improve. Tom was artificially bright as they drove to the coast, asking Mel questions about school and her friends, but Mel was glued to her phone – she fiddled with her long red curls and was monosyllabic. Then as soon as they had laid out the rugs in a dip in the dunes Mel curled up and fell asleep and Tom's patience ran out. 'What's wrong with her?' he muttered to Carmen, and marched off with Jake to play cricket, leaving her to play with Mercy. Carmen didn't mind. She would have liked Tom to ask, Is that OK? but there was no room for these niceties sometimes. Besides, Mercy was a sweet child, just six, and how could you not feel sorry for her? She had been three when her parents split up – she would grow up barely able to remember a time when they were together. Carmen had heard Tom's friends say that it was Mercy's arrival that broke up the marriage – the unplanned third just as things were getting easier – and though it was never mentioned in Mercy's hearing of course, Carmen believed children can sense these things, be weighed down by them.

'You're not listening!' said Mercy.

'I'm sorry, sweetie, what did you say?'

'The fairies are *over there*!'

'Come on then, show me.'

They played beside Mel's sleeping body until Mercy got absorbed in digging. Carmen leaned back in the sand. There was warmth in the sun for the first time that year and it was delicious against her skin. She wished there had been time to make a flask of coffee; it was so peaceful, just the sound of the spade tapping against Mercy's bucket, the breeze in the dune grass. Out of sight, below on the sands, she heard Tom calling to Jake, 'That was five yards wide!' She leaned forward until she could see the top of his head below her, poised, waiting for Jake to have another go. There was something about the way he was standing, eager for the ball, willing his son to get it right, that tugged on her heart. 'Line your left hand up with the stumps,' Tom shouted. She watched the crown of his hair dip back and forth in anticipation of the shot, impatient for the chance to show off his skills to his son. Why did she find that so attractive? What was it? His lack of self-consciousness? He was so at home in the world, so sure of his place, so confident. It all came so naturally to him – children, marriage, a great job, a nice home, money, the trappings of a good life. He never questioned that all of this was his entitlement, and he really had no idea it was different for other people. He laughed at her wonder still, that she too could have all of those things.

Soon Mercy got bored and said she wanted to paddle, and Carmen roused herself and they scrambled down the dune. 'We're walking to the sea,' she said to Tom. 'You want to come?'

'I do,' said Jake, and dropped the ball.

'What about the cricket?' said Tom.

'I want to go in the sea, Dad.' He peeled off his shirt and threw it up on to the grass.

'You can at least pick this lot up before you go.'

But Jake was already on his way. Carmen raised her eyebrows at Tom – it must just be something about me – and set off after him with Mercy. When she looked back Tom was brushing sand off the stumps. 'You should have helped him,' she said to Jake.

Jake shrugged.

The sands were vast at low tide, wet and shimmering in the spring sunshine. They walked in silence. Jake was thirteen, on the cusp of adolescence, taller than Carmen already, striking with his mop of red hair, lean and muscular and shy. She felt shy too – she got along with him by teasing him when they were with the others, but when they were on their own she never really knew what to say. He started playing with Mercy, swinging her and then lifting her into the air. Mercy loved it of course, and laughed, and Carmen laughed too and he threw the little girl higher, swung her harder as she came down. 'Careful,' said Carmen. Then Mercy cried out – he'd tugged her arm, he was pulling too hard. 'Stop, Jake, you're hurting her,' said Carmen, but he did it again, threw her even higher, and Mercy started to cry.

'Jake!' said Carmen.

She saw him waiver, ready to ignore Carmen and carry on, but then he put Mercy down, a little too hard. 'Baby!' he said, and ran his awkwardness off into the distance.

By four, the young sun had lost its warmth and they gathered everything together and clambered back through the dunes to the car park. Everyone was tired and they drove in silence around the coast road to St Jude's, where they would spend the night. Tom parked outside the mini-market on the village green and without discussion they all piled out of the car and scattered across the shop. Tom and Mercy went in search of milk and eggs, Jake headed for the sweets and Mel for the magazines. Carmen crouched at the far side of the checkout to look over the front covers of the Saturday papers. A middle-aged woman, overweight and wheezing, hefted a basket on to the counter. 'How are you, Nim?' she said to the guy serving.

'Fine, Mrs B. Sick of these roadworks.'

'I know. What is the story there?'

The barcode reader beeped as the man checked items out of the woman's basket into a plastic carrier, and their chatter went on, but then there was a pause in the flow that felt unnatural and Carmen found herself sneaking a look at the pair. They were locked in unspoken dialogue, the woman indicating with her head to the other end of the shop, where Tom and the children were now clustered together. Then, as the little group turned and moved towards them, Carmen stood up and the shopkeeper and the woman looked embarrassed.

For a moment Carmen felt angry, then she felt unsettled. It wasn't the first time something like this had happened. What were they talking about? She told herself they were probably just being judgemental about them coming from London, second-homers. She wasn't used to the tight spotlight of a place like St Jude's.

They paid for the groceries, piled back into the car and drove the hundred metres to the bungalow. The children went into the front room and the TV blared into life. Tom carried the bags in while Carmen set to work in the kitchen. She had unpacked the chiller bag and the groceries and was pouring boiling water into the teapot when he came up behind her and nuzzled her neck. She turned her body into his arms and they kissed, softly at first and then properly, tongues caressing. She was the first to pull away, conscious of the children next door. 'Later,' she said. 'We need to eat. What do you fancy? I could do some pasta.'

'How about fish and chips?'

'Really?' She smiled. He always wanted fish and chips when they came here.

'I'll get them in a bit,' he said.

'No, I'll go now.'

'You sure?'

She nodded. 'I fancy the walk.'

St Jude's had not been gentrified like some of the villages on this stretch of coastline, it was a bit of left-behind English seaside and Carmen felt she could breathe here. The sea was at the end of the road and she walked that way back to the village. It was getting late and night anglers were setting up their gear on the shoreline, sinking into camp chairs with blankets and flasks and cans of live bait, waiting for dusk. She dawdled watching them, enjoying being alone. Then there was a queue in the chip shop so that it was three-quarters of an hour before she got back to the bungalow, the hot food bundled inside her jacket.

She knew something was wrong as soon as she walked in. She could hear the TV but the living-room door was closed, which it never was. She stepped further into the hall and saw Jake in the children's bedroom, sitting on the bottom bunk. She went in – Mercy was squashed up beside him. She had been crying.

'What's going on?' Carmen said.

'Daddy went mad,' sniffed Mercy.

'What do you mean? Jake, what happened?'

'Him and Mel had a row,' said Jake.

'Where is she?'

'I dunno. She stormed off.'

'Where's your dad?'

He indicated next door.

Carmen walked through to the living room. Tom was lying on the sofa, a bottle of beer in his hand. He sat up when she came in and smiled as though everything was fine.

'What the hell happened?' she said.

'What do you mean?'

'The kids said you and Mel had a row.'

'I just had a word with her.'

'Mercy said you went mad.'

Tom pulled a face – oh please. 'I just did what you said, told her off, and of course she didn't like it.'

'What do you mean, what *I* said? You're her dad.' But Carmen could tell he was upset, masking it. 'Did you hit her?'

'Of course not!'

'But you shouted?'

'A bit. I had to tell her. I am her father – she needs to know she can't do this. I just told her that, and of course she didn't like it.'

It was true of course, Mel did need telling. 'Where's she gone?'

'I don't know. She'll be sulking somewhere.'

'It's getting late.'

'She'll be fine.'

'It's dark out there!'

'She's fifteen, Carmen, she'll be fine.'

He was right. Mel was fifteen, nearly a grown-up, and a pain in the arse. But Tom's temper – he didn't lose it often, but when he did it was sudden and noisy and she didn't like it. She didn't like the way he seemed out of control. It was frightening, even for her, but worse for the kids.

'Jake and Mercy are really upset.'

He got up. 'I'll go and talk to them.'

She sat down on the sofa. She could hear his voice in the next room, and then they filed back through, the children

22

still subdued. Carmen fetched a rug and ketchup and they ate the fish and chips with their fingers, out of the polystyrene trays and paper, sitting on the floor. Tom made jokes and the atmosphere lightened till by the end of the meal the children were laughing.

Later, when they were all settled in front of the TV, Carmen heard the door, but Mel didn't come into the living room. 'Leave her,' said Tom, but Carmen couldn't do that. She slipped through to the children's bedroom. Mel was lying on the bottom bunk.

'Are you OK?' Carmen said.

Mel didn't answer.

'Where have you been?'

Mel shrugged slightly.

'What happened?'

Mel didn't answer.

Carmen sat on the edge of the bed. 'Mel, he's your father,' she said gently. 'He has to discipline you sometimes.'

'Not like that.'

'Not like what?'

Mel rolled over, turned her back to Carmen.

Carmen tried again. 'He loves you,' she said.

'You don't know what you're talking about,' said Mel.

Carmen caught the train back to London the next morning. Tom would spend the day with the children, then drive back early evening. That hadn't been the plan, but Carmen's friend Kath had texted late on Saturday to see whether she fancied meeting up. Kath's husband, Joe, was a police officer and he worked irregular hours and often weekends. Kath found it tough, especially with a baby, so Carmen decided that for once she would say yes. It was only two hours on the train. She would have lunch with Kath and then have supper waiting for Tom.

Tom was fine about it, said she should do what she wanted, but she still felt bad as she kissed him in the car outside the station, as though she was abandoning them, which was silly of course because everything was fine with the kids again. Even Mel seemed to have forgotten that she was meant to be in a sulk. Still, as Carmen queued for her ticket, she felt a weight lifting from her.

She bought a coffee and a newspaper from the kiosk and walked out on to the platform. The timetable they had at the bungalow for the coastal branch line was out of date and it turned out she had a forty-minute wait, but she would connect with a faster London train at Diss so it would work out much the same. She found a bench in the sun and was quite content. She licked the chocolate from inside the lid of her cappuccino. The top story was a murder, a woman and her children stabbed to death at their home. A man believed to be the children's father was in custody. It was a grim tale and one that was becoming more common. How could you explain it? How could anyone do that?

As she read Carmen was conscious of someone sitting down beside her. He kept shuffling, and she sneaked a glance – it was a young man, a teenager, wearing a hoodie over black trousers. Her London radar scanned him in a fraction of a second – no threat. He caught her eye and she smiled as a reflex, then regretted it because it encouraged him to strike up a conversation.

'You had your head stuck in that paper,' he said, as though she should have been talking to him instead.

She smiled vaguely and looked back at the page.

'Must be an interesting story. What's it about then?' He looked over her shoulder.

He clearly wasn't going to be put off. 'A man killed his wife and children,' she said.

The boy pulled a surprised face. 'Why did he do that then?'

Carmen shrugged. Who knows?

'Maybe she was sleeping around.'

Carmen's irritation surfaced at that. 'Are you serious? Do you think if she had slept with someone else then that's OK? To kill her? And his children?'

'I wasn't saying that. I was just saying that perhaps that's what happened.' He shifted in his seat. 'I wasn't saying it was OK.'

Carmen turned back to the paper, pointedly this time. The boy probably wasn't as stupid as he sounded, maybe he just didn't know the right things to say, but she had no more patience for him.

He was undeterred. 'It does happen though,' he said. 'It happened here – a man killed his girlfriend a few years back and people reckon that was because she was shagging around.'

She didn't reply. She kept reading.

'He got away with it too. He made it look like an accident. He was a lawyer from London – that's why he got away with it, we all reckon. He must have known important people.'

He had Carmen's attention now, she was looking at him, and he was obviously pleased by that.

'It's true. He still comes here – he's got one of those bungalows by the beach. He comes for weekends with his kids. Everyone around here knows about it. He's got a new wife now. I reckon she needs to be careful.'

Carmen's heart was thumping. 'What was her name?' she said. 'The woman who died?'

'I don't know, but she was good-looking. She had a weird name, I think it began with a Z. Zara . . . something like that . . .'

'Zena?'

'That's it. Do you know about it then?'

Carmen got up and said something about needing the loo. She gathered the paper under her arm and walked back out to the ticket office and asked for the toilet, but there wasn't one so she walked out into the car park and across to the field on the other side. She leaned against the wooden fence.

It's just gossip, she thought. I should have just laughed it off – told him who I was, that would have made him blush.

There were two horses in the field, two sturdy bays, scruffy with the remains of their winter coats. One kept looking her way to see if she was there to offer him a treat. The field was thick with mud from the winter, a quagmire, not picturesque at all. She willed the horse to come to her – she wanted to

26

touch it, to put her arms around its neck, but it had lost interest in her.

The station tannoy announced that her train was coming. She walked back across the car park and up the platform, away from the boy, who was still sitting on the bench. She knew he was watching her, but she kept on walking towards the back of the train and boarded there.

Sometimes when Carmen met someone new and explained that she had three stepchildren, that her husband had three children from a previous marriage, she would feel self-conscious and say, 'I have to add here that Tom and his wife had split up already when I met him,' and they would all laugh.

And if she got to know the person better, then at some point she might explain that actually there was more to the story – that there was another woman, a whole relationship, between the break-up of Tom's marriage and the first time that he and Carmen even met. Another relationship. Another love. Not a little fling with someone unsuitable whom he quickly moved on from, but much more. An affair that had started while he was still with his wife, but unlike all the affairs that you read about where the man never leaves his wife, Tom did leave Laura and their children to be with this woman.

And then, six months later, she died, drowned swimming in the sea, while they were staying at their holiday bungalow here at St Jude's.

Her name was Zena. Tom had told Carmen all about it in those first days and weeks after they met – how he had fallen in love with this young woman, how they had bought the bungalow as a base for seeing the children, how one afternoon Zena left the house to go for a swim and never returned. How days later her body had washed up a mile along the coast.

He'd told Carmen all of that over the course of their first few dates, more than two years ago now, but they had rarely talked about it since. No one talked about Zena any more, no one they mixed with anyway, and the children never mentioned her.

But, it seemed, there were plenty of people who did.

Chapter 3

Joe, Kath's husband, answered the door. He gave Carmen a half-hug and kissed her cheek. 'I'm just off,' he said. 'She's upstairs.' He was dressed for work, in jeans with a shirt and tie.

'Can I bring my bike in?'

'Of course.' He took it from her. 'Go on up.'

Carmen prised her shoes off and left them in the hall. Kath was fussy about these things and her stair carpet was pristine as a result, not grubby like Carmen's. 'In here,' called Kath.

She was in Lily's room, changing her nappy. Lily smiled up at Carmen from the mat. 'Hello gorgeous girl,' said Carmen.

'Not so gorgeous last night. I got about three hours' sleep, didn't I, lovely?' She pulled a face.

Carmen suspected that Kath overemphasised the tougher sides of motherhood to protect her feelings, in case she felt sensitive about not being pregnant yet. In the same way, when Carmen was single, Kath used to emphasise the challenges of marriage.

They talked about Kath's life for a while, how she was

managing, how she was finding being back at work. Then they carried Lily and some toys down to the kitchen and fixed her into her high chair and Carmen found herself telling her friend what the boy on the station had said, and about the way people whispered in shops.

'How awful,' said Kath. 'Aren't people awful? They're just bored, living in that shitty little place.'

'It's not shitty.'

'Well, you know what I mean. Just ignore them.'

Carmen was laying the table. There was a pizza in the oven for lunch. It had felt strange to her relaying those conversations, saying the words out loud somehow made them more real. Carmen realised how upset it had all made her.

'Poor Tom, being talked about like that. Honestly, how do they dream these things up?'

Carmen shrugged. Who knows?

'Surely it was clear what happened. Wasn't there an inquest? They must have made it clear then.'

'I think that's the thing – no one really knows,' said Carmen. That's what Tom had said to her in those early conversations, when she'd asked him why? How? Why did Zena drown? How did it come about? He'd said that no one had been able to tell him for sure, that he would never understand exactly what had happened. He'd said the stretch of sea where Zena had been swimming was hazardous, with waves that could knock a person off their feet and hidden currents. Plus jet skis and boats used the area without restriction, so there was always the possibility there had been a collision. He'd almost implied that Zena was to blame – swimmers were meant to use the main village beach half a mile away, which was sandier and protected, but she refused to walk round there. She had swum from this stretch of coastline since she was a child.

Carmen felt a chill pass through her. 'Kath, you don't think there's anything in it, do you?'

Kath pulled a face. 'Are you serious? Carmen, you're so suggestible.'

Carmen felt embarrassed. 'I'm sorry, forget I said that.'

Kath fetched the pizza out of the oven and divided it up. She put some on Carmen's plate, but Carmen wasn't hungry any more. She nibbled at a corner – she could feel Kath's eyes on her.

'You're really bothered about this, aren't you?'

'No . . .'

'Carmen, honestly, what do you think? That he killed her?'

'Of course not.' Of course she didn't, it was absurd, especially hearing Kath say it. But still she was unsettled, disturbed inside. 'I'm just – it was a horrible thing to hear.'

'Horrible.' Kath reached over and touched her friend's hand. 'What does Tom think about it?'

'I haven't told him. It only happened this morning.'

'Are you going to?'

For some reason it hadn't occurred to Carmen to do so. 'I don't know. What do you think?'

'Maybe you shouldn't. It will make things awkward when you go to the bungalow.' She blew on a small piece of pizza and handed it to Lily. 'To be honest, I think you should just forget about it.'

After lunch Carmen cycled home, up Crystal Palace hill and on to the small road that led to her estate. Her flat was on the top two floors of a low-rise council block, nothing to look at, stained concrete, but the rooms were big, the view from the front was over trees and though the odd noisy tenant came and went the estate was a relatively peaceful one. She owned the flat, or rather the mortgage company did – she'd bought it with a tiny deposit when that was still possible. Before Tom had come along she'd always had a tenant to help meet the bills, but of course that was no longer necessary. The plan was to move on soon, to somewhere bigger, smarter, a house in a better area.

She knew how lucky she was. Joe and Kath were desperate to buy a place of their own, but it was impossible in London now, even with two salaries. Instead they saw almost half their income go out in rent every month, and Kath had no option now she was a mother but to go back to her job as a primary-school teacher full-time. Carmen felt guilty about her good fortune sometimes, aware of the gap that was widening between her and her friend, but what could she do?

She changed into sweatpants and a T-shirt and chopped vegetables for a casserole, threw in some lamb from the freezer. Then she boiled the kettle and carried a mug of tea up to the spare bedroom. It used to be the lodger's room; now there were bunks crammed in for the children when they came to London for the weekend, plus for the last few months, since she'd started working from home, a desk and filing cabinet too. She went around the house collecting laundry from the radiators and folded it into two neat piles – hers and Tom's. Then she pulled out the big, comfortable swivel chair from the desk and sat down to drink her tea.

She felt tired. It had been a long twenty-four hours, first the row with Mel, then what that boy at the station had said. She felt silly now, for having got worked up about it, but Tom's past could be overwhelming. The whole ex thing – she knew she should be more mature about it, but she found it threatening, confusing. It was bad enough with Laura, who was a constant presence because of the children, but it was almost worse with Zena. Tom had left Laura, but Zena had died when they were still madly in love. Zena was a ghost.

Carmen sipped her tea. She thought about what Kath had said, that there must have been an inquest after Zena's death. She was right, there must have been, but Carmen didn't know anything about it. When Tom had talked to her about what had happened, early on in their relationship, he hadn't gone into minute detail, and she hadn't cross-questioned him. He'd obviously found it painful to recall and the truth was that Carmen had found it painful to hear.

Zena died less than a year before they met, and while Carmen had known he must still be in mourning, and accepted that as right and natural, her approach to dealing with it was pragmatic. The last thing she had wanted to hear from the mouth of the man she was falling in love with was how hard it had been for him, or how much he still loved Zena, or what a brilliant person she had been. She didn't want to see the pain on his face as he remembered her. She didn't want to know about Zena, for her to become real and take shape in her imagination, it wasn't necessary. She wanted to look forward, into a future that belonged to her and Tom, and so did he.

But perhaps that had been a mistake. Or maybe it had been right at the time, but now, now they were married and settled and the past was becoming a memory, maybe she needed to go back and look properly. A ghost had tripped her up today, she didn't want it to happen again.

As she sat there, she realised she was looking straight at his past. Stacked at the back of the room, against the wall, were boxes of Tom's stuff, untouched since the day he moved in. He'd unpacked the rest but said these were full of old junk, that he'd deal with them when they moved to a bigger place. Carmen had wondered about them from time to time but respectfully left them alone, but maybe now the time had come to look. She pulled a chair over and stood on it.

They were still sealed with removers' orange tape, but the adhesive had worn down and the tape was coming away. Carmen lifted the top box – it was heavy but she managed to manoeuvre it to the ground. She opened it up. On top were hardback books, nice old volumes without their dust jackets, a Shakespeare primer, a dictionary, a couple of law books. Underneath were papers and notebooks and a jumble of random objects.

Carmen pulled everything out so it was strewn across the floor. There were letters, some still in their envelopes, some clearly junk mail, all addressed to Tom at the Vicarage. There was an unused contacts book, a paperweight stamped with the crest of Tom's Oxford college, a pen tidy with the contents still in it, including discarded pencil shavings, a desk diary from several years ago. These were the contents of a desk, or maybe even just what had sat on the top, not sorted, just shoved into a box. Packed in a hurry. By Tom as he left? Were these the items from the desk in his study in the home he'd shared with Laura and the children?

Carmen gathered the loose papers together and looked through them, opened envelopes. There was a dental reminder dated June of the year he and Laura broke up, which supported her theory. There was a birthday card from the office, a picture of a rabbit drawn in a babyish hand, a sports review cut from a newspaper, a pension statement. A gas bill, a school newsletter.

But as Carmen worked through the papers she found items from the months after Tom had gone, as well as before – he must have returned for these things later on. Tom left in the late autumn – Carmen remembered him saying how much worse it had made it, leaving the children just before Christmas – but there was a postcard from a college friend living in Greece, dated January the following year. The friend sent love to Laura, so he obviously hadn't heard.

There was a school letter from February about an appointment for Jake to see a psychologist, asking both parents to come along. Carmen remembered Tom had told her about that too, that Jake had had some issues at one point and been given counselling for a while. She hadn't thought about the timing before – that it tied in with Tom's leaving – but of course. Poor Jake. There was another dental reminder, from March this time. In Tom's preoccupation with Zena he had obviously neglected his teeth.

Carmen guessed that Tom had collected these boxes months after he first left. Laura, conscientious, respectful even at that point, must have added any post that arrived to the stack already on his desk. It was a small detail of their break-up, but it heightened Carmen's compassion for Laura, made her feel more warm towards her composure, which could feel chilly. She also surprised herself by how angry she felt towards Tom. It made his betrayal very real.

She repacked the box and lifted another one down. It was heavier, packed tight with ring-binder files, notes from law school by the look of them, and university. The next box held more of the same. Surely he should just chuck these out, not carry them from home to home. Why did he bother?

She opened the fourth box. Again it had been packed carelessly, with items that seemed to bear little relation to each other. A photo album from Tom's childhood. Some tools. A biscuit tin filled with oddments. It seemed like random junk.

In the last box were pictures in frames, lined up and crammed into place with an old laptop and some law journals. The first was a school photo of Tom, dressed in what looked like a suit rather than a uniform, which said a lot about the sort of school he went to. The date was printed on it – he was fourteen years old, and he was a boy still, skinny, but he was already smiling his best professional smile. They laughed about it now, when he switched it on. He did it to amuse her – look at me, Tom Cawton, a fine Englishman, you can trust me. So he was doing it even then, already trained to conceal his true feelings, to put on a veneer. He did it sometimes with her, she would feel the mask slipping into place and it always annoyed her and she would say, 'Don't even try that with me.' And he would laugh and tell her that she didn't let him get away with anything.

She thought about keeping the picture out. She would show him later on, they would laugh about it, but then she wondered, Will he mind that I've been through his things? And she thought, yes, probably he will.

She pulled out more pictures – a flyer for a May ball at uni, some beer mats, all framed – bloody idiot. There was a picture of a young Mel and Jake, sitting side by side, stiff and awkward in school uniforms that included braided blazers and for Mel a felt hat. Next was a studio shot of the family – Laura, Mel and Mercy, with Jake standing behind them, deliberately casual, all laughing, three redheads and Mercy, the only one to inherit her father's brown hair. At first glance Carmen was confused because they looked so much as they did now, but no, the children were younger. Mercy was still little more than a toddler, on Laura's knee. It must have been taken shortly before the break-up. Jake was almost as tall as his mother even then, and Mel almost a teenager, but sweeter, fresher faced, happier.

She turned the picture over. There was a date label on the back – it was from the year Tom left. His affair with Zena had lasted in secret nearly six months before his marriage ended –

he was probably already sleeping with her when this picture was taken. Maybe he was already planning to go.

Carmen put the things back in the box. She'd had enough. There was such a sad story here, and it was unsettling too. It felt like an act of cruelty that he had betrayed this happy smiling family, these people who loved him – Carmen couldn't bear to think of Tom in that way. She stacked the boxes back in order, checked the tape was in place so he wouldn't notice, then she sat down at the desk.

She had found nothing of Zena. She'd assumed there would be mementoes of their relationship – photographs, gifts, cards. Tom had shown her a snapshot once, when she had asked early on, but she hadn't seen it since. It must be tucked away somewhere, but what about everything else? Had he kept nothing to remember her by? Wasn't that a bit callous?

She pulled herself up – she wasn't being fair. If there was nothing of Zena here, it was more to do with Tom being sensitive to Carmen's feelings than anything else. When he'd moved into her flat, Carmen had said it was fine if he wanted to put a photograph of Laura on the shelf, for when the children came to stay, but he'd said no, I know you won't like it and it's not necessary. And the truth was that she'd been relieved.

No, she wasn't being fair. Tom had been devastated by Zena's death. That's what he'd told her and that's what Flora had said too, when she was encouraging Carmen to go out with this old university friend of hers. Carmen had had reservations – it was all so recent – but Flora had said, go for it, he's better now, he was devastated at the time but men get over things quicker. She didn't say, better grab him quick before someone else does, but that was the implication.

They were married a few months later. How quickly life swallows up death, Carmen thought. But then perhaps that's the way it should be. Just as long as you're one of the survivors.

Tom got home at seven after a clear run. He was starving, so they sat down to eat the casserole straight away. He was in a good mood, sun-kissed from another afternoon on the beach. 'How was Kath?' he said.

'Fine.'

'And the baby?'

'Very sweet.'

He squeezed her hand. 'You next,' he said.

They'd stopped using contraception several months ago, but nothing had happened so far.

'Was Joe around?'

'Just for a few minutes – he had to work,' said Carmen. 'It's hard for Kath, she does get lonely, especially at weekends.'

'You should go over more.'

'We should have them here. We're getting lazy.'

'Fix something up.' Tom shovelled lamb and potatoes into his mouth. 'This is really good Carmen. Can we have it again?'

Carmen smiled, always pathetically pleased when her cooking got a good response. 'Kath's back at work next week. She's not looking forward to it,' she said.

'I'm sure.'

'Did Laura find it hard going back?'

Tom thought about it. 'I can't really remember. I think if anything she was quite relieved. Although maybe that was after Jake, when she had the two of them.'

'Didn't she like being at home with them?'

He thought again. 'I think she did, but she was very into her job. There was less maternity leave then – only a few weeks, I think. Maybe she did find it hard. I honestly can't remember.'

'But she gave up work completely after Mercy.'

'Yes, you're right. I don't know. Is there any more?'

He was eyeing hers. Carmen was picking at her own food, still not really hungry. She pushed some on to his plate. It wasn't Laura she was thinking about. 'Did Zena want kids?' she said.

'Zena?'

'Yes, remember her?'

The edge in her voice took him by surprise, she saw it just for a moment. 'I don't know,' he said.

'You must have talked about it.'

'You're right, we must have done, but I can't remember.' He looked at her. 'Is that awful?'

She felt deflated then. 'No,' she said. 'No, of course not.'

He stabbed at a piece of lamb. 'To be honest, I'm not sure I ever really knew what she thought.'

'What do you mean?'

He put his fork down. 'Why are you asking about Zena?'

'Would you rather I didn't?'

He shrugged. 'I don't mind, I just wondered why.'

'No reason. I just feel like there's loads I don't know.' Carmen walked over to the sink, poured herself a glass of water. 'Actually there is a reason. I met a guy at the station in St Jude's today and he said something horrible.'

She turned round. He was looking at her.

'He said that people there think you murdered Zena.'

Tom pulled a staggered face. 'Are you serious?'

'Yes.'

He started to laugh. And then he stopped. 'You are serious.' He looked astounded. 'Who was he?'

'I don't know. A teenager. He said they talked about it in the pub.'

'Oh for God's sake. And you took it seriously?'

'Of course I didn't . . .'

'Thanks a lot, Carmen!'

'I didn't! I already said that! But it was a horrible thing to hear.'

He came over and hugged her. 'Of course it was. Bloody idiot.'

She nestled into his embrace. 'It just made me think about how I don't know anything about her. About what happened.'

'You do. I've told you.'

'I know but . . . there's no trace of her. You don't have any pictures or anything – it's like she never happened.'

'You want to see some photos? You want me to keep one in my wallet?'

'No of course not, it's just that . . . would it be like that if I died? Just nothing left of me?'

'How can you even say that?' He stroked her hair. 'I adore you, you know that.'

'But you loved her, didn't you?'

41

'It's different Carmen.'

'How?'

'It just is.'

'Didn't you love her?'

'I did, but . . . it wasn't the same. Carmen, I don't want to have to pull it apart like this. Can't we just leave it?'

So Carmen went upstairs to have a bath and Tom went off to the living room to watch the sports highlights on TV. While the water ran, she took her clothes off and wrapped herself in the giant towelling dressing gown that Tom had brought her back from some work trip or another. She lay on the bed and read a book – the bath would take ages. They had talked about updating the boiler, getting a combi that would boost the pathetically low water pressure, but they kept putting it off because the plan was to move anyway, to buy somewhere bigger. But they kept putting that off too, waiting for things to improve in the City, for the big bonuses to come back. Plus Tom wanted to move to north London, which would shave an hour off the drive up to Norfolk and the children, whereas Carmen wanted to stay in this area, which was home.

After a few minutes Tom came up and sat with her. He put his hand on her leg. 'You're cold,' he said. 'We should get a new boiler.' He smiled and so did she. He stroked her leg, then reached inside her dressing gown and slipped his hand around her waist. She pulled herself up on her elbows and kissed him, gently at first, then properly, sensually. Tom was a great kisser, his tongue and lips were soft and sensitive and, unusually for a man, he really loved kissing. She pushed him on to his back

42

and started to pull his clothes off. She was often the one in a hurry, taking the lead and moving things on.

Afterwards he lay on his back and she curled up in his arms. He turned on the TV and flicked channels until he found some comedy reruns and they were laughing together when he said, 'Don't imagine things were perfect with me and Zena, that's all I'm saying.' He pushed the hair out of her eyes. 'I know it must be hard for you, that I have all this history.'

'I have history too.'

He laughed. 'I know. I'm very jealous of that guy, I've forgotten his name again . . .'

Carmen smiled. Nick, her ex, was an actor, a struggling actor all the years they were together, then soon after they'd split up he'd landed a role in an American sitcom that was popular in the UK and finally, now, his career was taking off. They saw his picture on the side of a bus once and she knew Tom found that sexy – in small doses.

She remembered the dream she had had about him the other night . . .

'I just don't want you to imagine that it was this perfect love,' Tom said.

He understood about jealousy. She smiled at him, grateful for his sensitivity.

'To be honest, I'm not even sure if things would have worked out.'

'With you and Zena?' Carmen felt for the remote and turned the TV down. 'Are you serious?'

'Are you sure you want to talk about this?'

43

'Yes,' said Carmen, although she wasn't sure.

'She could be quite difficult,' he said. He put his arms behind his head.

'Go on.'

'That's it really.'

'What do you mean, difficult?'

He thought about it. 'She used to wind me up.'

'So? I wind you up.'

'Not like you. You're funny when you do it, you're just teasing me but she . . . wasn't. I remember once, at dinner in a restaurant, she started picking away, talking about things . . . I don't know . . .' He stopped. 'Winding me up.'

'Darling, you're not explaining it very well.'

'I guess I'm just saying that it is possible that it wouldn't have lasted. I mean, I hadn't thought of it like that before, but since you brought it up . . .'

'Was she a bit of a princess? Is that what you mean?'

'I don't think it was that. I think she . . . I don't know, it was like, if things were just going fine, she'd just . . . cause trouble.'

'Start a row?'

'Just wind me up.'

'Why?'

He shrugged. 'God knows, I don't know, she was just like that.'

'Was she insecure?'

He shook his head. 'I don't know, maybe she just got bored easily, I don't know.'

'It doesn't sound like you understood her particularly well.'

'I didn't understand her at all – that's exactly it. I couldn't predict how she'd react to things. Maybe that was the problem. We were just different, I didn't know . . . There were times I thought . . . It's hard to explain.'

'What?'

He shook his head.

'But you left Laura for her, you must have thought she was pretty amazing.'

He looked pained – he didn't like being reminded of what he had done. Then he rolled over to face her. 'Carmen, I'm just so glad I'm with you,' he said, and pulled her close to him. 'In fact I know this is a terrible thing to say, but I think maybe everything worked out for the best.'

It was what Carmen had wanted to hear, and yet what she felt was revulsion. She got up and put on her dressing gown. She felt conscious suddenly of being naked.

'Are you OK?' he said uncertainly.

'Yes,' she said, although it wasn't true. 'I'm going to have my bath, it'll get cold.'

As she went out of the room she looked back. He was reaching for the remote.

Chapter 4

Tom had an early meeting and was up at six. Carmen dozed as he showered and dressed, moving back and forth between rooms. 'Lucky you,' he said as he kissed her goodbye, and she put on a smug smile for him, but it wasn't how she felt – she would gladly have changed places. When she and Tom met she'd had a good job that she loved, writing interviews for a local paper, but it had closed down six months ago, another victim of the Internet, the recession. She was freelance now, and it was taking time to adapt to the lack of structure, the lack of company. The lack of work.

She slept in till eight, then took her time getting dressed and making coffee before she settled down at her desk. She read through the news online and sent a couple of emails, but she had no commissions at the moment so after that there was really nothing to do.

She typed Zena's name into Google. It wasn't the first time she'd done this, but today she felt more determined. A page of Zena Johnsons appeared – an artist from Atlanta, a teenager from Penzance, a social worker from Lambeth, all LinkedIn and Twittering and Facebooked. The first reference to Tom's Zena came only on the fifth page. Each time Carmen had searched over the past couple of years the references had slipped further down the page list. Death happens by degrees in cyberspace. How long would it take for her to slide out of view altogether?

Carmen switched to Facebook and looked up Zena's page, again not for the first time, and unsurprisingly there was nothing new to see – nothing much at all in fact. Beyond a couple of out-of-focus, arty profile shots and a generic cover pic of a city skyline, Zena's page – her friends, posts, photographs – was blocked from Carmen's view. Zena must have set her privacy settings so that her information was restricted, which in itself intrigued Carmen – no one she knew bothered with any of that, so why had Zena? Was she a particularly private person? Paranoid? Carmen thought about trying to get a foothold on to her page via someone else's contacts list, but the only person she knew who knew Zena was Tom, and he had yet to sign up for twenty-first-century social mores. LinkedIn for work of course, but that was it.

Next Carmen googled *Louise* magazine, where Zena had worked. It was a strange coincidence that they were both journalists, though working on very different material. The magazine's home page appeared and Carmen typed Zena's name into the search window. Again, this was not the first time she had been here, and again she got the same result, which was zero. She wanted to see articles Zena had written, but nothing came up. *Louise* was still holding out against letting readers view their magazine content for free online.

In the past Carmen had let her nosiness end there, but today she persisted. She still had access through her last job to a specialist archive for printed material. She tried to use it sparingly because she didn't want anyone to realise that her login still worked and cut her off, it was such a useful resource, but needs must. She logged into it now and searched there for features by Zena.

Bingo. A list of headlines appeared, with issue dates. The most recent was 'Beautiful berries'. Carmen laughed out loud, not nicely – she was snooty about Zena's brand of journalism. There was a PDF – she clicked on it. It was standard lifestyle stuff: 'Blueberries are full of antioxidants, the anti-cancer genies that love your skin'. What a load of nonsense. Then she realised that the date of publication was after Zena's death – the magazine must have gone to press before she died and been published afterwards – and she felt bad for being so mean.

She called up another – 'Do women still want to have it all?' There were case studies, successful women talking about their lives and how they managed – 'Martha, 27, runs her own beauty business while raising her two children'; 'Vanessa, 32, a PR executive and mother to Ben, 3'. Carmen found herself absorbed in their stories, they were surprisingly honest about the daily struggle. But why no surnames? Were these Zena's friends, whom she'd interviewed for the piece? Carmen wondered about Zena's friends then – did she have many? Were they all there, hidden from her sight on Facebook? Tom had never mentioned anyone – there was no one he kept in contact with from that time. Was that strange?

She ran through a few more titles – 'Starter marriages', 'Too much of the white stuff', about sugar, 'Smart love', about how dating companies hone their matches. She clicked on an article titled 'Domestic violence – it could happen to a woman like you'. The piece said that internationally, domestic violence was the biggest killer of young women. Could that be true? How shocking if so. There was an interview with a woman, her face concealed in a moody photograph. Her partner had always been a bit jealous, she said, but after they moved in together as teenagers he started to control who she saw and where she went. Then the violence started. First he slapped her round the face during a row, then one night when she didn't feel like sex, he forced her. On both occasions she felt upset and disturbed, but he was so sorry afterwards and she had already got into the spiral of believing his behaviour was partly her fault, so she didn't leave. Then he came home drunk one night and beat her into a coma. Her face was unrecognisable. It was a miracle she survived.

It was a terrible story. It was also completely different to any-thing else Zena had written. Why was she researching domestic violence? Was it just an assignment the magazine had given her or was there more to it? Did she have a personal interest in the story? Had she experienced domestic abuse, or had someone she knew?

Next on the list was a report on an awards night the maga-zine had organised for inspirational young women. Carmen called up the PDF and there she was – Zena, photographed in a long strapless gown, on stage with the prime minister's wife and a couple of minor celebrities. Beside these other women, photographed professionally, Zena looked like a model. A dazzling smile, brown eyes shining against ivory skin, long gleaming black hair. Her dress was a sheath of pale grey silk, stunningly simple on her tall slender figure. She looked like a film star.

Carmen went downstairs and put the kettle on. She looked at her reflection in the toaster. She was still in pyjamas even though it was eleven o'clock. Her thick, curly, black hair was bundled into a messy black knot on the top of her head and she had no make-up on – this was hardly her best, but still. How was she meant to compete with that? She wasn't skinny – she had her mother's native curves. Her features were generous, which meant she had a big mouth and nose. People said she looked warm, friendly. She smiled at her reflection – she was attractive enough, she knew that, and when she made an effort she could get men to pay her attention. But Zena was beautiful.

Carmen pulled a face at herself, scowled. It was her own fault; she had gone looking for Zena's articles and she had enjoyed feeling snooty – maybe that was even why she had done it, so that she could feel superior. Well, it had backfired on her.

The kettle boiled and Carmen made a mug of tea and wandered back to her laptop. She clicked the image of Zena away. What was she even doing looking through this stuff? When did she get so insecure?

She had too much time on her hands, that was the problem.

She was used to working hard, not sitting around the house all day like this, and it was affecting her confidence. She should have tried to get another job straight away, when it became clear they were all going to be made redundant. It wouldn't have been easy – all around her publications were laying off staff who had a lot more experience than she did – but if necessary she had been prepared to go back into admin, which is what she'd done for years before she got her break. It was Tom who had said there was no need, that since they could manage the mortgage on her flat on his salary alone why not take some time out, find some freelance work or sign up for a course, be home when he got in at night. Set herself up for a life that would work better with a family.

She'd never had an opportunity like that before. She'd always worked, ever since she left school. Maybe he was right, maybe she could carve out a freelance career, or look at courses, even go to university and study for a degree – she'd never felt she had time for that before, even in the days of grants and free tuition it had seemed like a luxury she couldn't afford.

The freedom felt like an unimaginable gift. But a couple of weeks spent thinking about what next had drifted into months, and she had nothing much to show for it. She felt as though she was in limbo – killing time until the inevitable happened and she got pregnant.

Why did that thought, right now, make her heart sink?

Did it mean that somewhere, deep down, she wasn't sure about having a baby?

But she was, she really was – towards the end with Nick, she would have said it was all she wanted. It had seemed impossible for them. In his thirties Nick was still living like a teenager, scraping by on minimum-wage jobs between bits and bobs of acting work. They didn't even live together properly. How could they think about a baby?

In the end it wasn't why they split up. Other things happened. But still she remembered the feeling of explosive relief when she realised it was going to work out with Tom, that at last it was possible.

And now she could have it all, and would, just as soon as nature played ball. A family, without any of the financial worries that made it tough for Kath and Joe, supported by a man who knew what it took to be a good dad . . .

But as soon as she had these thoughts, the doubts clouded in. And end up feeling like this all the time? Having Tom's dinner on the table every night? Watching her independence and confidence slip away?

A phrase came into Carmen's head: *Wait for no man.* It was what the girls she went to school with used to say, the tough cookies in the playground, when someone had boy trouble – wait for no man. The faces of those girls came into her head and shored her up somehow.

There was an email from Tom, saying he'd be home on time tonight, did she fancy the pictures? Yes she did, she emailed back, and could they have dinner out as well please, because she was too busy working to cook.

Pathetic.

Her mind wandered back to Zena and she found herself

logging into the press archive again. She typed in her name but without the magazine this time. She was looking for reports of her death.

She found one in the *Norfolk and Suffolk Recorder* – 'St Jude's drowning – woman named' – and clicked on the file:

A woman whose body washed up on the beach at St Jude's on Wednesday was named by police last night as Zena Johnson, 29, a magazine executive from London.

According to the police statement, Ms Johnson was staying at her holiday bungalow in Shell Road with her partner, Tom Cawton, 38, a lawyer. She went for a swim around 5.30 p.m. on bank holiday Monday and Mr Cawton raised the alarm when she did not return. Her body was found by dog walkers on the main beach two days later at low tide.

It is understood Ms Johnson swam from the stretch of beach beside Shell Road, south of St Jude's main beach. Her death will raise new questions about management of this area, which is not patrolled by lifeguards. There have also been concerns about the uncontrolled use of speedboats and jet skis here.

Five years ago, St Jude's resident Jeremy Dwyer, 18, died from injuries sustained in a collision with a jet ski, and his family have since called for tighter controls. They were not available for comment last night.

Carmen moved on to the next entry. It was from the same paper, a report from the inquest held a few months after Zena's death. So there had been an inquest.

The coroner at the inquest into the death of Zena Johnson, 29, whose body was washed up in St Jude's in May, has confirmed that she died from drowning. But according to evidence from the police pathologist, she may have been rendered unconscious before death by a blow to the head, possibly from a collision with a jet ski or a boat.

There were concerns expressed among local residents last night about the use of jet skis and boats on this stretch of beach, and renewed calls for their use to be regulated or banned.

This stretch of coast is flagged up as hazardous for bathers.

The police pathologist who conducted the post-mortem said that the cause of death was drowning. She also reported that Ms Johnson, a strong swimmer, had suffered a head injury. However, she said that deterioration of the body meant it was impossible to be sure whether the injury was sustained prior to death, leading to unconsciousness and drowning, or whether Ms Johnson got into trouble in the water and her body was struck after death. She said it was also impossible to be sure what had caused the injury.

Police renewed their appeal for witnesses. If anyone saw Ms Johnson, who walked to the beach in a red coat and swam in a red bikini, from around 5 p.m. on Monday 26 May, please contact the police by calling 101.

It was confirmed that Ms Johnson grew up in the local area and attended the high school in Hamesdon. She worked as an editor for the women's magazine Louise, and a spokesman for the company paid tribute yesterday to a 'talented and much admired colleague'.

A head injury? Tom had never mentioned anything about a head injury. Carmen felt her heart beat faster, but as she read the report again she calmed down. After all, it wasn't really saying anything she didn't know already, just that Zena might have been hit by a jet ski or a boat, that no one could say for sure, and Tom had told her all of that. And of course that would cause a wound. But somehow reading the words on the page – *head injury* – was so graphic. So brutal. Probably that's why Tom hadn't used those words himself.

There was something else that had caught Carmen's eye – the date she died, 26 May. It was almost exactly three years ago, almost to the day. Had Tom realised that? Had he been thinking about Zena this weekend? He'd said nothing about it.

Carmen's mobile rang. It was Jan, her stepmother. Carmen could hear the worry in her voice as she said hello. 'I was just wondering whether you'd heard from Kieran in the last few days.'

Kieran was Carmen's brother – her half-brother, ten years younger. The child Jan had had with Carmen's father the year after he left Carmen and her mother. 'Sorry, Jan, I haven't. Is something wrong?'

'I'm probably being stupid, but I haven't heard from him for more than a fortnight and he's been pretty reliable about calling lately. I just thought he might have been in touch with you.'

They both knew what this might mean. 'Where is he?' said Carmen. 'Is he still at the same place?'

'As far as I know.'

'Do you want me to pop round?'

'Would you? Wouldn't that mess up your day?'

'I don't mind. I'm not busy.'

'I'd really appreciate it.'

Carmen wasn't thrilled about the errand, but she was glad to be given a reason to get out of the house. She showered, picked out fresh jeans and a T-shirt. On her way out she popped her head into the spare room to check she'd turned her computer off, and on the floor beside the desk, almost tucked out of view, she saw the old laptop that she'd pulled out of one of the boxes yesterday. She must have overlooked it when she was repacking them.

She picked it up to shove it out of sight in a drawer, but then she paused and looked at her watch. It wasn't even one yet, she had all afternoon to see Kieran. She sat down at her desk.

The laptop was an old model, thick and heavy. She pressed the power button and waited – would there be any charge left in it? She hadn't noticed a lead in the box, so if not . . . But there was a ping and the operating system started to boot up. The screen came on.

Carmen took a moment to make sense of what she was looking at, and when she did her hand went to her chest, to her heart. The screensaver was a close-up photograph of Tom, side on, in profile, kissing Zena, who was laughing. Their faces filled the screen with happiness, with love.

She looked away, but her eyes were drawn back to the image. Tom was smiling as he kissed her. He was laughing, they both were, he was so happy he couldn't even stop laughing long enough to kiss her. He was younger, thinner, he'd aged in those few years. Zena was beautiful, stunning, and happy too. Carmen could smell the love, she could smell the sex.

She shut the computer down, stowed it in a drawer and went out.

She caught a bus heading north into town. She sat upstairs and let London roll past – well-heeled East Dulwich mums out power-walking with their prams, Rye Lane with its smell of pavements and spices and music blaring out of nail shops, the smog and grime of the Old Kent Road, shoots of street life forcing their way through.

Carmen knew that Tom had loved Zena, of course she did. He had left his family for her: his children, his home, his marriage – everything. But somehow, until she saw that picture, that love had never felt real. It was as though she had never really believed any of it.

What an idiot.

No, that wasn't fair, she wasn't an idiot. She'd just avoided forcing herself to confront an unpleasant truth. That was sensible, wasn't it? Where no purpose would be served?

She got off at the Elephant, walked up the dog-end of the Walworth Road and ducked through a maze of side streets into a block that stood half empty, windows broken, scheduled for demolition. A few determined tenants hung on, a few squatters. The entry system was broken and the lift was long gone. She helped a woman carry a pram to the second floor.

There was an iron outer gate on the flat where Kieran had been living for the last few months, but the lock had been smashed and it hung open. Carmen banged on the door. There was no answer so she banged again and shouted through the letterbox, 'Kieran, it's me, Carmen.' She put her eyes to the letterbox – 'Kieran, answer the door.'

He emerged rubbing his hair and ambled down the hall, skinny in sweatpants and an old T-shirt, grinning at her eyeline. 'Ah, a visitation,' he said as he opened the door.

They hugged awkwardly and she followed him through to the living room. The place was a dump. It wasn't filthy – even as a child Kieran had a habit of cleanliness and it had stayed with him somehow – but it was so depressing. Remnants of woodchip clung on to the walls, there was no carpet on the floor, just stained hardboard, and the only furniture was a decrepit sofa, sagging in the middle. 'Are you living alone here?'

'Yeah.'

'No Psycho?'

Psycho was his friend, good news and bad. 'He comes and goes.'

Carmen sank into the sofa, resisting the urge to brush it down first. 'How are you?' she said.

'All right, I'm all right.' He stood in front of her.

'Are you working?'

'No.'

It wasn't a completely stupid question – there had been a job for a while, helping out a man who owned shops in the area, but it had obviously come to nothing. Once Carmen would have been disappointed, but at some point along this particular road she had stopped waiting for things to come right, for Kieran to sort himself out. There'd been too many turning points, a revolving door. 'How's your health?'

He shrugged side to side – *comme ci, comme ça.*

'Are you taking your medication?'

He nodded.

'Are you smoking?'

He smiled apologetically. Of course he was. 'Don't be cross, Carmen.'

She sank into the sofa. 'Jan's worried about you. You haven't called.'

'I lost my phone.'

'Why don't you go and see her?'

He fidgeted, the first sign of agitation. He hated her pushing him. It never worked anyway, but she got frustrated and it came out. 'What about you,' he said. 'Tell me about you. How are you, Carmen?'

The question took her by surprise. 'I'm OK,' she said, but her voice wobbled. She was like that sometimes, if people showed concern, it moved her. She cleared her throat but Kieran had heard it. 'I'm just feeling emotional. Probably PMT.'

They both smiled – it was an old joke, knob-head men who said things like that.

But he wasn't going to let it go so easily. He sat down next to her on the sofa. 'Tell me though.'

She shook her head.

'Go on.'

'You don't need my problems.'

'Carmen, I'd much rather hear your problems than you ask about mine. Don't you realise that?'

She smiled at him – of course that was true. Sometimes her

frustration with him, with feeling like she had to play nurse-maid endlessly, blanked out the deep affection she felt for her little brother, and that she knew he felt for her. 'Well . . . I guess I'm just finding it hard not working.'

A look flashed across his face – that's a problem? 'I thought you were having a break. Can't you just enjoy that?'

He seemed genuinely curious to know her answer. And she found herself wanting to reply in ways that would seem like a criticism. You can't just do nothing with your life for months on end – it's not good for a person. You have to be productive, busy, involved. It's right to take responsibility for yourself, have some backbone. 'It doesn't suit me being at home all the time,' she said.

'Go out more then. Carmen, you've worked since the day you left school and you don't need to any more. That's a good thing.'

So he had noticed, what she was doing all those years. 'It's not true that I don't have to work, you're wrong about that,' she said. 'Tom earns good money, but things in the City aren't the way they were. I mean, I know it's all relative,' she added, conscious of her surroundings.

Kieran looked sceptical but he didn't say anything to contradict her. 'How're things with you two?'

'Fine,' she said, but her voice wobbled again, and then Kieran was holding her hand, and she was telling him what the boy on St Jude's station had told her and how it had made her think about Zena and start obsessing and feel insecure. She told him she felt overwhelmed by Tom's past sometimes – not just

Zena but Laura and the kids. He listened and nodded along, and when she finished he said, 'God, that makes so much sense.'

'What do you mean?'

'That he killed Zena.'

'He didn't kill her! What are you talking about?'

'Well, he nearly killed that other guy.'

She rolled her eyes. 'For God's sake!'

'Well, he did.'

'That was completely different – can't you ever forget about it? It was years ago.'

Only a couple of years ago in fact. It had happened in the early days, when Carmen and Tom were first together. Tom had been wound up that night – hardly surprising, looking back at all he had been through in the months before, though Carmen didn't see it like that at the time, she wasn't as aware. They'd met for dinner in Brixton. He'd been drinking already, and she was irritated by his mood. It had been their first snappy time. They'd arranged to meet Kieran later on for a quick drink – the big introduction – and Kieran had been very late of course, and annoying when he had shown up, and he and Tom took an immediate dislike to each other and riled each other till Carmen had wanted to scream. She'd taken refuge in the ladies', and on the way back some guy who was a bit pissed had tried to chat her up, which had annoyed Tom more than she'd have expected. Then walking to the train, through the arches, the same guy was behind them and said something to her, a bit suggestive, she didn't even hear it, and Tom had snapped and . . . beaten him up basically. 'He was trying to protect me.'

'Protect you from what? He nearly killed that guy.'

'That's rubbish, it was nothing like that.' But Carmen started crying all the same.

Kieran rubbed her hand. 'Has he ever hit you?'

'Of course not!'

'You can come here, you know. Any time. If you ever need somewhere, you can live here with me.'

She laughed then, through her tears.

'I know it's a shithole . . .' He looked hurt.

'No, it's kind of you, thank you, Kieran, but it's not going to be necessary, everything's fine.'

'Yeah, sounds like it.'

Carmen started to feel annoyed then. 'Can we talk about something else now?'

'Do you know what I think? I think your instinct's telling you something. I think that's why you came here, because you knew I'd tell you the truth.'

'That's ridiculous, I'm here because Jan asked me to come and check on you.'

He shook his head.

'Kieran, you are so annoying! There's not always something deeper going on.'

'Tom's a violent man. And he's a liar – he's been lying to you all along.'

Carmen felt angry now. 'Just shut up, Kieran.'

'You know it deep down, but you don't want to face it, and

that's understandable, you've got a lot to lose. But at some point you're going to have to.'

Carmen wanted to put her hands over her ears. 'Just shut up!' She got up from the sofa and picked up her bag.

'Look at what he does all day.' Kieran followed her into the hall. 'He's a corporate lawyer. Do you think sweet men do that job? I went to school with those guys, I know what they're like.' He put his face close to hers. 'He's a lizard – *sssss*.' He hissed at her.

It was time to go. She said goodbye, shut the door hard and ran down the stairs and out of the block. Bloody Kieran. It was nonsense, all nonsense. He'd always had a grudge against Tom, he just didn't like him. Tom knew it, but laughed it off and said it was because Carmen had been a soft touch and given Kieran money before he came along, and that was true – he was right.

Carmen walked to the bus stop, but it was rush hour now and she had no stomach to queue so she carried on walking. She felt dislodged, agitated – Kieran could have that effect. Why did he have to bring up that night in Brixton? She hadn't forgotten, of course she hadn't, but if you don't talk about something it's almost the same thing. It all came back now, as though it had just happened – they'd just left that guy there, lying on the pavement, she could see him now, not moving. She'd wanted to call an ambulance, she'd thought he was dead, but Tom – Kieran too – they just walked her away, either side of her, shuffled her into a cab.

What a nightmare it had been. She and Tom had taken a taxi

back to her flat and she'd lain awake in bed next to him and told herself she'd never see him again, but in the morning he'd pleaded, said he wasn't himself, that it was the stress of the last few months and all that had happened. It was his damn temper, he'd said, and everything that had happened this last year had made it worse. That was understandable, wasn't it? He promised her he'd never done anything like that before and never would again, it was the stress that had tipped him over. When she'd said she wasn't sure she wanted to carry on, he'd cried, taken the day off work to be with her, pleaded. He'd said he loved her and wanted to spend the rest of his life with her.

He'd said the guy would be all right, that he hadn't hit him hard. They'd looked online to see if there was any mention of the assault – if the guy had died, for God's sake – but there was nothing, and Tom said that showed that he wasn't even hurt. He'd been off his head anyway; he'd probably just sobered up and gone home.

He said he'd just wanted to protect her. And reading between the lines she'd thought, The way you couldn't protect Zena, and felt sorry for him, compassionate. But now Kieran's words came back to her – 'Protect you from what?' – and he was right, that guy hadn't been a threat to her, she hadn't needed protecting. Tom had been jealous, that was all.

Carmen felt sick, thinking back on it, jumbled up inside. She'd never told anyone – not her mother, not her friends. She didn't want them to think badly of Tom. She'd thought she'd left it behind, that it was all forgotten, but of course it wasn't. When that boy had said what he'd said to her on St Jude's station, it was the first thing she'd thought about.

She could close her eyes and see that man now, lying there, blood on his face, not moving.

Maybe Kieran was right, maybe in some strange way her subconscious had taken her to him, the one person who knew. Maybe she'd needed to talk about it, to bring it out into the open. Secrets are never good. They let things get mystified, blown out of proportion.

Tom had never done anything like that since. She had seen him get angry of course – he'd get cross with the kids, the way he had with Mel this weekend, they all knew he had a temper. But there had been nothing directed towards her, and never violence, never again.

But then he'd never had cause around Carmen. If jealousy was his trigger, she never made him jealous. She wasn't someone who flirted with other men, and they didn't exactly flock around her.

But how would he have coped being with someone as beautiful as Zena? She must have had men falling all over her . . .

Carmen saw then how what Tom had said to her last night could be the truth – that she was a better match for him than Zena, that he could be happier with her. It is so easy to see beauty as infinitely desirable, but with Tom's nature it must have been hard to be with a woman that beautiful. Did Zena like to flirt? Carmen remembered what Tom had said – 'She'd wind me up.' Is that what he'd meant?

She walked past King's College Hospital, where she'd been

born, past the Maudsley, where Kieran was taken when things went wrong. He was seventeen, the first time he was sectioned. She'd loved him so much when he was a boy, felt so protective. Everyone felt protective of Kieran; he was such a gentle boy, sensitive, vulnerable somehow. Their father had paid for him to go to private school rather than the comprehensive Carmen went through, and she had seen no injustice in that, she had understood why. But it hadn't been enough. In fact maybe it made things worse. The culture was too competitive, and the other boys had too much money. He was fourteen when he tried skunk for the first time, seventeen when he had his first psychotic episode. He'd been lost to them ever since.

She remembered Jan then and pulled out her mobile phone to call her, to tell her that Kieran was OK, as well as could be expected, and afterwards she felt calmer. It seemed stupid to wait for a bus having got this far, so she carried on walking, through quiet backstreets, across the arterial South Circular and on up the hill to her home.

It was six when she got in, and Tom was back soon after. She was sitting at the kitchen table. He took off his coat, bent down and kissed her. 'Good day?'

'I think I'm going to start looking for a job again,' she said. 'It doesn't suit me, not working.'

He sat down beside her. 'But you'll be pregnant soon.'

'Who knows when that's going to happen. Besides, I need to work.'

'What about freelancing? It would be more flexible.'

'I'm not getting anything though, am I? I think I just need to get a job.'

He thought about it. 'It's nice you being here.' He kissed her, and she found herself thinking, If someone photographed us now, would we look the same way as that picture on the laptop?

Chapter 5

Carmen was in front of the bedroom mirror applying mascara. She could see Tom in reflection lying on the bed reading the sport section from the Saturday paper, positioned carefully so he wouldn't crumple his best suit. They were going to a wedding. 'So Laura and the kids are definitely coming?' Carmen said.

'Hmm.'

'The kids as well?'

Tom didn't answer. He was engrossed in his story. Then many seconds later he said, 'What?' and she repeated the question.

'I think so,' he said looking up. 'Maybe not Mercy, I don't know. Wow, you look lovely.' He put the paper down.

She smiled at him, via the mirror. She had bought a new dress and she knew it suited her, jade green silk with embroidery, cut to her curves. She turned around. 'You like it?'

'Yes, I do. Do you want to take it off again?'

She laughed. 'We can't, we're late already.' But she left the house feeling buoyed.

The day ahead was daunting for her – it was friends of

Tom's who were getting married and all his old group would be there, whom she still didn't know well enough to be really comfortable around, and Laura and the children too.

She enjoyed the journey. They travelled by train, along the south-London suburban loop, into Clapham Junction. They shared out sections of the paper and read companionably, nudging each other from time to time to point something out. Carmen was aware of the looks they were receiving, her tall, dark, handsome husband and herself, dressed up in their expensive clothes. When they passed through a tunnel she checked their reflections in the window opposite – they looked grown up and well heeled, easy and comfortable. Professional. Entitled. Entrenched. It still took her by surprise. She'd never imagined herself like this, with a man like Tom, and it still thrilled and confused her sometimes. She and Nick had been such a different sort of couple, perpetually in jeans and trainers, perpetually on their way, the sorts of people who were wallpaper on a train like this. She hadn't wanted more. If you'd asked in those days, she'd have said that was who she was, who they both were, but the truth was that a person like Tom – the person she had become – had been so far outside her expectations that what she had now would have been beyond imagination.

In the taxi from the station she felt him tense, the air around them cool, as he braced for the event. And then he was squeezing her fingers and they were inside, their bags dropped at the hotel reception, champagne glasses lifted, so that even by the time they had said their first greetings to the groom – an Oxford buddy of Tom's – and moved through to the Victorian conservatory where the ceremony would be held, Carmen felt tiddly. The noise was immense already, a hundred conversations in progress, laughter, opinions, so pleased to be together again. Then Laura was in front of them, Jake beside her in a suit, the first time they'd seen him so grown up. Tom laughed at him, tweaked his tie and he grinned. 'I love your dress,' Laura said, and Carmen smiled and admired Laura's beaded silk shift in return. 'Where's Mel?' said Tom, and the two parents turned almost imperceptibly and were discussing something that had happened.

Carmen was left with Jake, a bit awkward. 'Do you like these dos?' she said.

He shrugged.

'Do you know other kids here?'

'A few.' He shuffled his feet.

'Are you hot?'

He smiled, nodded.

'Take your jacket off.'

But no, he wasn't going to do that. He didn't want to be different to the other men.

His head jerked forward suddenly – he'd been clipped from behind. It was Flora. 'Hello, campers,' she said and kissed them both. Flora, thank God. Flora was Carmen's friend too, a proper friend, of more than a decade's standing, the only person she felt really comfortable with in this room besides Tom.

Flora bantered with Jake, and Carmen relaxed and sipped her drink and watched Tom talking to Laura. They had edged away so she couldn't hear what they were saying against the

70

roar of the room, but she could see Laura was doing most of the talking, and Tom was nodding the way he did when he wanted to get away, and Laura was leaning in and Tom's arms were itching to be folded but his good upbringing was preventing it. Carmen grinned to herself. He was getting a talking-to, she could tell. It was his own fault. He didn't do enough about Mel. At heart Tom was a man who wanted an easy life, wanted problems to disappear.

The room was brought to attention, called together for the ceremony, and in the crush for seats she found herself back with Tom. Laura had melted away. 'Has something happened with Mel?' she asked as they sat down, but the humanist minister was beginning and Tom mouthed 'I'll tell you later'.

The ceremony was moving. They were a long-standing couple with two children; their love was established, their fondness palpable. Tom held Carmen's hand throughout, and when the pair exchanged vows he smiled at her. Their own wedding, nearly two years ago, had been a quiet affair, nothing like this – just her mother and Tom's father and Kieran and a few close friends at the local register office, then a restaurant lunch. They were both happy with that. Tom had admitted he was sheepish of overdoing it second time around, but he was adamant that Carmen must have whatever she wanted. Modest was fine by her.

She had been so in love, intoxicated still. They'd been together less than six months. He'd proposed within weeks – said he knew, they were old enough to know, why wait? Her mother had urged her to take her time – what's the rush? – and Kieran too of course, but Kath had said go for it, and that was what Carmen had wanted to hear.

They were herded to a marquee, for more drinks pre-dinner. 'Tom, you bloody hoodlum,' said a loud voice from behind, and then Tom was half-hugging a giant of a man – Carmen knew him but couldn't remember his name. He remembered hers though – 'Carmen, how are you?' He kissed her. 'You're looking gorgeous as always. What did you think of that then? Almost makes you believe in it all, doesn't it?' He laughed loudly.

'How are you, Grant?' said Tom.

'Not bad, not too bad,' and then they were talking and Carmen was struggling with his wife, who was a humourless lawyer, and Carmen couldn't help thinking about what Zena would have done in her shoes, how she would have handled things, and then she thought that it wouldn't have arisen because Zena would have been talking to a man. Then Flora appeared again and said, 'I'm next to you at dinner' and Carmen thought, Thank God.

'It's hard to say really. I only met her a couple of times.'

Carmen was asking Flora about Zena. They were alone at the table now. The speeches were over, dessert had been cleared, and everyone else was standing around in pairs or groups chatting, or smoking outside, or hanging around the bar. Flora was quite drunk, everyone was, Carmen too though less so. 'Oh, come on, Flora – you must have thought something.'

'Well, I suppose I thought she was a bitch, but Carmen –' Flora leaned in closer – 'do not tell Tom I said that.'

'Of course not, but explain – what was she like?'

'Very charming, very pleasant, but underneath . . .'

'What?'

'Hard as nails.'

'Really?'

'And pleased with herself.'

'Are you sure you don't just think that because of what happened?'

Flora shook her head. 'No. I mean it's just my opinion, I didn't really know her, but . . .'

'That's what you think.'

Flora nodded.

Carmen topped up their glasses. 'Maybe she was putting on a front. It must have been hard for her, meeting you lot.'

'Why?'

'Weren't people judgemental? Because of what had happened?'

'No, everyone was perfectly nice to her.'

Carmen wasn't convinced. En masse, Tom's Oxford friends could be a stressful experience, the clever attractive women, the successful charming men, how tight-knit they were. They didn't even realise it.

'I don't think she'd have cared what we thought anyway. She was oblivious – honestly.'

'Were people shocked?' Carmen said. 'When Tom and Laura split up.'

'Oh my God, yes. It was really shocking at the time. I don't know why really – I suppose because they were the first people it happened to. And they never argued or anything, they seemed so – solid. They had that lovely house and they were so successful and they had all those beautiful children . . .'

Flora stuck a finger down her throat and Carmen laughed. 'Why do you think he did it?'

Flora shrugged. 'Don't ask me. Why don't you ask him?'

Carmen had asked Tom of course, long ago now, and he had said the usual things – that Laura was wrapped up in the children, that sex had dropped off, that temptation had come along. He'd said he knew it was a cliché, that he'd been wrong, stupid, immature.

'The men were full of how pathetic Tom was being, but when Zena was around they all had their tongues out. It was gross really.'

'I bet the wives loved that,' said Carmen.

'Zena certainly did.'

It wasn't an attractive portrait that Flora was painting, and in a way it was exactly what Carmen wanted to hear, and yet she didn't quite believe it. Listening to her friend, she saw how Flora's words reflected back her own ideas about Zena, based on nothing more than the story of Tom's marriage breakdown, a word here and there, and prejudice against a woman that beautiful. Sitting there, listening to her friend, she saw how in her own mind, for these last couple of years, she had cast Zena squarely in the role of villainess – the femme fatale who broke up a marriage. But hearing someone else tell the same tale, she saw it for the cliché that it was. It didn't describe a real person; it was just a convenient narrative that let them all exonerate Tom.

Maybe it was the wine, but she found herself feeling a strange sense of camaraderie towards Zena. Like her, Zena had been an outsider in this formidable group, but unlike her, she hadn't seemed to care what they thought, and Carmen admired her for not giving a shit. 'Maybe she was winding you all up. She must have guessed you would be judgemental.'

'You keep saying that, but I can't see it,' said Flora. 'I don't think she would have thought for a minute we were judging her because I don't think she thought she'd done anything wrong.'

'Well, had she? Wasn't Tom's marriage his responsibility?'

'Carmen, you know what I'm saying. You would have felt self-conscious and so would I. But she had no qualms at all.'

'I suppose she was young still,' said Carmen. 'She probably didn't understand.'

'She was nearly thirty – how old do you need to be?'

Carmen moved on to Laura next, asked Flora whether she liked her.

'She's a good sort, a bit chilly. Very posh.'

'You're all posh!'

'I'm not,' said Flora.

'You are!'

'What are you talking about? My dad's a builder!'

'Flora, I've been to your parents' house. You've got a swimming pool.'

'Well,' said Flora, 'I never knew you had such a chip on your shoulder.'

'I don't, it just sounds funny to me when you describe someone like Laura as posh.'

'Carmen, Laura's family goes back to the Norman conquest. Her parents live in a house with a moat. My dad's a builder from Essex.'

Carmen smiled. It was true – she did have a tendency to see these old friends of Tom's as a pack, when of course things never worked like that in real life. The whole Oxford thing could be overwhelming, but it was just a signifier really, that Tom belonged to one world and she belonged to another. She tried to explain that to Flora, what it felt like to be in all of this when you'd had a comprehensive-school education and not even made it to university. 'You are such a knob,' her friend said. 'It's not like that at all. All of these people think you're great.'

'I just feel different.'

'Well, that's your mother talking. You've got to get over that.'

Carmen asked more about Laura, about when she and Tom first got together. Laura was a few years older than Tom, they met when he got his first law job out of university, she had been his boss. 'He was so young – twenty-two or twenty-three – but they seemed so grown up,' said Flora. 'The rest of us were still messing around in shared houses and travelling and all that, and they just got on with it. They were earning loads of money, he moved out to Norfolk where she lived, they bought that enormous house, they had a baby . . .'

Mel – the first child. Carmen found it hard to think of her as a baby. Tom was twenty-six when she was born, so young, and all his friends still messing around. Perhaps it was no wonder . . .

A friend came up to speak to Flora, and Carmen went looking for Tom. She did a sweep of the marquee, saying hellos as she went, and then walked across the lawn to the main building. She checked the lobby and the bar and the lounge area, but she couldn't find him so she went back outside to the smokers. They'd taken over some benches and they cheered her for joining them, for swelling their ranks. Cigarettes were offered and accepted – she still had the odd one on a night like this – and she was laughing along with the banter when Tom arrived.

He was very drunk, she could tell straight away, and he wasn't pleased at finding her here with all these men, she could tell that too. He put his arm round her and kissed her neck and she bristled. It wasn't affectionate – he was marking his property.

'What's wrong?' he said.

'Nothing.'

He took the cigarette from between her fingers, took a long drag. 'Where were you? I was looking for you.'

'With Flora. Where's Laura? And Jake?'

He shrugged – how should he know?

'Did they go?'

'Ages ago.'

'Is it late?'

He held out his watch. It was gone midnight.

'Jesus,' she said, 'I thought it was about ten.'

She was going to ask him about Mel, what had happened,

77

but she guessed she wouldn't get a sensible answer. His hand traced her spine, her backside. 'Get a room,' said one of the men, and Tom laughed, but Carmen felt uncomfortable. She moved away slightly and his hand disconnected from her body. He moved towards her and she pulled away again.

He raised his eyes at that.

'Why do you have to be like this when you drink?' she said quietly.

He didn't like that. He turned to walk away, and because he was so drunk he misjudged it and barged against her, caught her off balance and almost knocked her over.

He didn't notice, he kept walking, but Carmen felt embarrassed. She righted herself and the others kept talking as though nothing had happened. Pissed idiot. She finished her cigarette, then headed back across the lawn to the marquee. Flora was still in the same seat, talking animatedly to a woman Carmen didn't recognise. Carmen picked up a bottle of wine that was two-thirds full from another table and joined them.

'Ah, you're back,' said Flora. 'Sam, this is Carmen – Tom's wife, you know?'

'Lucky you,' said Sam, and Carmen couldn't tell if she was being serious or sarcastic.

'I introduced them so it's all my fault,' said Flora. 'We go back years, don't we, Carmen? We temped together at some hideous shithole.'

Carmen knocked back half a glass of wine.

'We were talking about the bank crash – how no one saw it coming,' said Flora.

'It all seems so obvious in retrospect, doesn't it? That everyone was borrowing too much,' said Sam.

'It's human nature,' said Carmen. 'People don't ask too many questions when they're getting what they want.'

'Speak for yourself,' said Flora.

Later, when Sam had gone, Flora put her arm around Carmen. She was drunk now, leaning on Carmen's shoulder. 'Are you feeling insecure?' she said.

'No, why?'

Flora shrugged. 'I just wondered, when you were asking about Zena and Laura and so on earlier. I just wanted to say . . . Tom's really happy with you Carmen – you do know that, don't you?'

Carmen didn't answer. Did she? The alcohol was messing with her thinking.

'Are you happy with him?'

She shrugged. Of course.

'Well, if I was you I'd just forget about the past, because he's not going to do it again.'

Carmen put her glass on the table. She felt giddy.

'You do believe that, don't you?'

Did she? She tried to think about it. There were still times when she felt overwhelmed by Tom's life. She remembered the way she used to feel like a speck within it all – something with negligible weight or substance compared to everything else, as though she could just be blown out of the picture at any moment and it would barely be noticed.

But no, that had all changed, she was bedded in. The big question now, she thought, was who is he?

'I need to go to sleep,' she said.

Flora felt the same way. They walked across the lawn arm in arm. Carmen tipped her head back and looked at the stars. 'Tom says he's not sure it would have lasted with Zena,' she said, 'if she hadn't . . . you know . . .'

'Died?'

For some reason they both started giggling at that, at Carmen's awkwardness. How awful.

'I think it's true though,' said Flora.

'Do you?'

Flora nodded. 'She'd have got bored, found someone else.'

At reception they found out that Tom had already picked up the key to his and Carmen's room. She was pleased he'd gone to bed, she wanted to curl up with him now, to forget the unpleasantness from earlier. She parted from Flora at the top of the stairs and found their room at the end of a corridor. She knocked gently but there was no reply. She tried again – nothing. Bugger – he must have picked up the key and then not come up. She looked through the keyhole – no, the key was there. He was in the room.

She knocked again, louder this time. The door next to her opened and a man in underpants appeared. She recognised his face – he was one of the other guests, and annoyed. 'I'm so sorry,' she said. 'My husband – Tom – he's fallen asleep in there. I can't get in.'

The man raised his eyebrows and thumped on the door. 'Tom, you bastard, open the door.' He banged again. Another door along the corridor opened and a woman came out. Carmen was mortified. 'TOM!' the man bellowed.

The door opened. Tom was still in his trousers and shirt, but rumpled and sleepy. He turned and went back into the room without saying anything.

Carmen apologised and said thank you and followed him, gratefully closing the door. 'Well, that was bloody nice for me,' she said. 'Can't you even get undressed?'

But he was half asleep again already.

'Tom, get undressed.' She shoved him and he sat up and pulled off his shirt. She went to the bathroom and when she came out he was snoring.

It took her a long time to get to sleep, partly because of the snoring, partly because the alcohol was jagging on her nerves instead of tripping her into oblivion the way it had done for Tom. Then she was dragged back into consciousness – it can only have been a couple of hours later because the dawn was just showing grey behind the curtain. Her senses gradually registered what had woken her. Tom's hands were on her breasts. He was caressing her from behind, pressed up against her. Jesus, he was still pissed, driven by his impulse, but she was aroused – oh fuck it, she thought, and moved her body with his.

He gripped her tighter from behind, pushed against her. His hand reaching round between her legs. She moved to accommodate his fingers.

'Pretend you don't want it,' he said.

It was something they did sometimes, not exactly PC but . . .

His hand moved to her hair, pulled her head back. Was she in the mood for this? 'No,' she said.

He took that as a green light and pushed her head into the pillow. It wasn't what she'd meant but . . . 'You do what I say,' he said, and then he was inside her, thrusting against her. He came within seconds, then stayed where he was, his weight pinning her down, his fingers reaching for her, until she came too.

He rolled off and when she turned he was grinning at her. 'I am your master,' he said in an affected accent, and then he sensed that she wasn't completely OK and his smile turned to worry. 'Hey – are you all right? I'm sorry, was that . . .'

'It's fine – I'm just . . . exhausted – your bloody fault locking me out, you idiot.'

He didn't remember anything about it and when she told him he laughed, and then she was laughing too. He got up and boiled the kettle and made them both tea and she lay in his arms and they talked about the party and who they had spoken to and what they were like, before they drifted back to sleep and when they woke again it was fully light and she had a headache. It was nearly ten. Tom was still chipper – still pissed, she guessed. They were both ravenous and he rang through to see if they could have breakfast in the room, but no, they would have to go to the dining room, and they would have to get a move on – breakfast finished in twenty minutes.

They dressed quickly and went down. The room was empty-ing and they sat in a corner and ordered coffee and cooked breakfasts and hid behind newspapers – neither of them felt fit to make small talk. But Flora found them and of course they were pleased to see her – Tom had barely spoken to her last night – and she pulled up a chair. 'You didn't cop off then,' Tom said to her.

Flora, who was perennially single, just laughed. Then she and Tom talked about old friends who had been at the wedding and teased each other the way they did, and Carmen half listened and half read the paper and worked her way through her huge breakfast, nauseous but knowing it was for the best. 'You look terrible,' Flora said to her at one point.

'Thanks.'

As they walked back past reception, Flora said she was heading off straight away, and she asked Tom if he'd mind fetching her bag from her room. When he was out of earshot she said to Carmen, 'I forgot to tell you last night – I saw Nick.'

Carmen pretended to be indifferent. 'Oh yes, where?'

'I bumped into him in Covent Garden a couple of weeks ago. He was over from the States. We had a quick coffee.'

'That's nice.'

'It was nice. I'd forgotten how funny he is. Do you ever see him? As a friend?'

Carmen shook her head.

'He did behave like a wanker.'

'Oh, I'm over all of that,' said Carmen. 'He messages me sometimes, but I just think – what's the point?'

'And I suppose Tom being the jealous type . . .'

'It's not that.' Carmen wasn't sure if Tom would mind or

not if she saw Nick, but it didn't matter anyway, that wasn't the reason.

He was coming down the stairs now with Flora's bag. 'It's not heavy at all,' he protested.

Flora gave him a winning smile and a kiss and was gone, and it was only then that Carmen wondered whether sending Tom off like that had been a ruse, to avoid mentioning Nick in front of him. The thought annoyed Carmen. I have to put up with his entire former life in my face every day, she thought – why does he get pandered to like that? And yet somehow she knew Flora had been right to do what she had done, and it bothered her.

Chapter 6

In the morning Tom was in a foul mood and Carmen felt jagged and touchy. Blue Monday – the legacy of the booze. Sitting at the kitchen table, he asked her to pick up his dry-cleaning, which he never normally would and which she took as him making a point for some reason, so she paused before answering. She was about to say, yes of course she would do that, in her best housewifely voice, when he said, 'If you can manage it between TV programmes.'

'What the fuck?! Is that what you think?'

'I was joking. Calm down.'

She had the teapot in her hand. Seething, she banged it down on the table so that tea spilt out in front of him.

'You don't need to get all sarf-London attitude just because I ask you to do one thing.'

'Twat,' she said, and walked out.

He left soon after without saying goodbye and she went back to bed and felt rubbish, not because of what had happened but because she felt so dismal, which she knew was down to alcohol-induced depleted serotonin, but that didn't really help.

Tom texted 'Sorry' from the train. And then 'You're right I am a twat.' And she texted 'I'm sorry too' and felt a bit better, so it probably was because of that.

She tried to sleep but couldn't, so she forced herself to shower and dress and sit in front of her laptop in the spare room. She read the papers online and scanned the journalist vacancies – nothing. Then she moved her computer to one side and fetched Tom's old laptop out of the drawer.

What was she doing? She looked at it and told herself to stop, that it was self-destructive and would only make her feel worse, but she was too far down that trajectory.

She clicked the start-up button. The machine whirred into life and the picture of Tom and Zena came up before her. She told herself she would look at it and look at it until the emotion died away, until she felt cool about it as though she was looking at two strangers, and that whole idea really wasn't working when her mobile rang.

It was her mother. She really wasn't in the mood to talk to Lucia so she turned it to silent, left it on the desk in the spare room and went through to lie down on her bed.

She felt dreadful, her body running with poisons. Why do we do it to ourselves? she thought. The great British disease, binge-drinking. She wasn't a great drunk and she knew it, but then look at Tom. Whenever they both drank too much it ended badly somehow, they just should stop doing it.

But Tom was worse than she was. She never got aggressive.

She closed her eyes and let her mind take her back to that evening in Brixton. She could see him now in his suit and black wool coat, walking towards her across the station, something different about him, his mood heightened by the booze, something hard in his eye. She had been uncomfortable that night from the first moment.

She could see it all again, in Technicolor almost, too bright. They'd drunk quickly, Tom on a roll, and Kieran always drank fast. And she too, trying to paper over the awkwardness and unease.

She remembered walking through the arches, the man calling out behind them. She was frightened, not by the man but by the situation, the tension. The orange light in the tunnel – she had clung to Tom's arm. Why? For comfort? To try to stop him doing something bad? Kieran – where did he go? It was as though he'd vaporised, there was only Tom and she was holding his arm. Why didn't Kieran help her?

People say these things happen in slow motion, but this was the opposite. One instant she was holding Tom's arm and scared and the next she was standing alone and the guy was on the floor and Tom was over him, pummelling his head with his fists.

His body, lying on the pavement, blood all over his face. Not moving.

And then Tom and Kieran were either side of her and they were walking fast. She wanted to stop, to call an ambulance. 'No, Carmen, just walk, just keep walking.'

Carmen sat up. It's one thing to talk about violence, to

tell a story, a guy punching someone else, but it's another to witness something like that. It had been horrible, really disturbing. Kieran had said Tom was a violent man, and it was true, wasn't it?

She needed to stop this. She needed to get out of the house, to see someone, to normalise how she was feeling and thinking. But who, on a Monday morning, now Kath was back at work?

There was someone. She closed down the old computer, put it back in the drawer, and cycled to Penge to see her mother.

She let herself into the flat. She hadn't called ahead – she didn't need to with Lucia. This was still her home. Her mother was sitting at the kitchen table watching a talk-show special on the effects of pornography. 'I was calling you before,' she said as Carmen bent to kiss her head, patted her bun.

'I saw. I thought I'd just come and see you.'

Lucia got up to put some coffee on. 'Have you seen this?' She pointed to a particularly graphic scene on the TV as she scooped ground beans from the tin into an ancient pot.

'It's horrible. Why are you watching?' Carmen looked for the remote to turn it off.

'Men are bloody animals, have you seen what this is like? If we didn't have the law to protect us, God knows what would happen.'

'Not all men are like that.'

Lucia didn't look convinced. 'Men do what they want – don't kid yourself you can control them.' She didn't like men. She had never been able to forgive them as a species for Carmen's father walking out when Carmen was ten.

Her slippers slapped against the lino as she moved round the kitchen, talking all the time. She was in her dressing gown still – not a great sign. She had retired earlier in the year from her admin job at the town hall, and Carmen was concerned she wasn't handling it well, that she was getting depressed.

The two of them sat at the little table. Carmen had eaten thousands of meals here over the years. Lucia poured dark coffee into two cups. 'So how was the wedding?'

'Good. Yes. We had a nice weekend.'

'How's Tom?'

'Fine.'

'And the children? Were they there?'

'Just Jake. Mercy's a bit young and Mel's playing up at the moment.'

'I worry about that girl,' said Lucia. 'I think she's disturbed.'

'She's just a teenager,' said Carmen.

'There's something not right about her. It's not surprising, given what happened, but there you are. The others seem to have come out OK. How's the boy?'

'Jake. He's fine.'

'I thought he was a nice boy. And the little one?'

'Mercy. Fine. Mum, how are you?'

'You've taken on a lot Carmen.'

'Mum, please, can we talk about something else?'

Lucia shrugged as though, yes, we can if you like, but it won't change anything.

'What did you do over the weekend?'

Lucia had been to stay with her friend Sylvia. Carmen had

known Sylvia all her life, had been playmates with her daughter Julia when they were children. Julia had died of cancer a few years ago, and the period since had understandably been very difficult for Sylvia. She had been feeling better, but recently – Lucia now told her – Julia's husband Adrian had remarried, and it seems the new wife had discouraged him from seeing Sylvia, or that's how Sylvia was interpreting things. 'Sylvia hasn't seen Adrian since Christmas.'

'Oh well, I guess it's only natural for him to move on.'

'It's very hard on Sylvia. He used to pop over at weekends. Weekends are hard when you're on your own.'

Carmen acknowledged it, while inside she bristled – Lucia was adept at guilt-mongering. 'It's asking quite a lot though, Mum.'

'What?'

'Well, would you expect Tom to come over every weekend if I died?'

'Thanks for putting that in my head,' she said. But still she thought about it. 'Well, it wouldn't be up to me, would it, but I'd want to see him.'

'Really?'

'Of course, because of the connection to you. Sylvia likes to see Adrian and to see Julia's friends from time to time, and they are considerate and go to see her.'

As Carmen cycled home she thought about Zena's family. She knew nothing about them, Tom had never mentioned them and had no contact with them at all, as far as she knew. It was the same as with Zena's friends – there was nothing, not even at Christmas, and never had been since she'd met him, only months after Zena died.

She thought again, Isn't that strange?

And she thought, Yes, it is.

When Carmen got home she got the old laptop back out, but her mood was different this time. She wasn't fixated on the picture of Tom and Zena, or feeling melancholy now. She was inquisitive. She wanted to know more. She wanted to see what was on there.

It took her some time to find anything at all. She clicked for the Internet but there was no connection set up, so she started digging into the memory of the laptop itself. But where her desktop was a sprawl of random files and rogue downloads and photographs, this one looked empty. Everything of his – she discovered after much searching – was tucked away in a folder within a folder within 'Documents'. How anal he could be.

First she found a folder called 'Work', with cases labelled by some code she didn't understand – a combination of name and date? She opened a couple, but the contents were incomprehensible and tedious. The small print of deals.

Next she looked in a folder marked 'Bank', which was all boring correspondence about mortgage contracts on the Vicarage – Tom had updated their deal annually, remortgaged to borrow more a couple of times.

There was a folder marked 'Children' with separate files labelled 'Mel' and 'Jake' that contained spreadsheets listing their school fees and expenses projected forward. There were also their yearly reports and correspondence. She opened one document – a note to accompany the termly cheque, with Tom expressing 'dismay' about 'the proposal to drop ancient Greek from the curriculum'. Carmen snorted at that. Both children had been pulled out of private school after the separation, when money ran short, transferred to the local state secondary. Carmen guessed Tom didn't send letters like this any more.

She carried on browsing, but it was all business, family, practical matters. There were no love letters to Zena, no cache of secret correspondence, but then of course there wouldn't be, would there? Who still operated like that? Tom's affair would have been conducted by email and text and phone, there was no risk of a paper trail that way. This was just a workaday home computer that had come with him when he moved in with Zena and had its screensaver updated to reflect Tom's new circumstances. There were no secrets here.

The battery was running low and Carmen had still seen no power lead. Maybe this was a fitting end of its natural life, the last time anyone would see that picture of Tom and Zena. She shut the lid without closing it down and buried the machine back in its box.

She went down to the kitchen and made a cup of tea. It was four o'clock, three hours till Tom would be home. She took her tea through to the living room and settled herself in Tom's armchair. It was a battered Chesterton, the only piece of furniture he had brought with him – it had belonged to his grandfather and he liked to sit here in the evenings if he had work to do. On the table beside her was his current laptop, the one he had used since Carmen had met him, the replacement, she assumed, for the one upstairs in the box.

She had never snooped on Tom before, never checked his phone or computer, read his mail, nothing like that until now. She knew she was crossing a line and she didn't feel good about it, but in her present mood it was just too tempting.

She opened it up on her knee. It asked for login details, but Tom used the same password for everything, and she knew it, as he knew hers. They'd made a point of sharing them, of trusting each other. His was 'rusty305', the name of the pet rat he had loved and his mother had tolerated, the number his telephone extension in some previous job.

As the screen flickered into life Carmen's face appeared. She was his screensaver nowadays – just her, not the two of them together, but it was the same sort of close-up as the one on the other laptop. He had taken it their first weekend away together, on the beach. The sun was in her eyes and she was squinting and laughing in a woolly hat, a cold March weekend. She could still feel the bitter wind on her face, the excitement of all that was happening. Tom said it made him happy whenever he saw it.

She did a search under 'Zena', searched his hard drive. Nothing came up.

She logged into his personal email account. She scanned across the front page of emails, all from the last week or so, but didn't open any of them. These weren't what she was interested in, and she was concerned Tom might be able to see somehow. He might even be looking at the same screen at work at this minute.

She did an email search for 'Zena'. There were two hits. Both were marketing for a movie featuring an actress called Zena Washington.

How could there be nothing else? Tom must have emailed Zena when they were together – did he have another account? And then she noticed in the top right-hand corner, where her email backlog numbered thousands, his was in the hundreds. Did he just delete all the old ones? Bloody typical Tom.

And then she saw a folder marked 'Archive'.

She opened it up. There were more than ten thousand emails stored here, they must go back years. She searched under 'Zena' and hundreds of results came up.

Bingo.

She clicked through the pages. They were in date order and the first she came to were emails that mentioned Zena – not emails from Zena, but messages that came after she died. She scanned backwards until she reached correspondence with Zena herself, and suddenly there were pages of it.

Zena, Me (7)

Me, Zena (2)

Zena, Me (8)

On and on it went, page after page after page. She went to the top entry, their very last email exchange. It was dated 23/05 – Zena had died on the twenty-sixth. Carmen could read the final message on the preview page. It said, 'Haven't you got a charger at work?' but there were eight emails in the thread. Did she dare to open it, to read the whole conversation? Would it leave a trace?

She did it.

> Zena: *I'm going to be here late I'll get the train. Can you pick me up at Diss?*
>
> Tom: *I'll wait for you.*
>
> Zena: *No go I don't know when I will finish. May even come up in the morning. Sorry.*
>
> Tom: *I will wait I don't mind.*
>
> Zena: *No go. Get some food in* ☺
>
> Tom: *OK. I'll call you later.*
>
> Zena: *OK but my battery's nearly out.*
>
> Tom: *Haven't you got a charger at work?*

That was it. Tom's last message, sent at 17.47. Three days later Zena was dead. That was the last email she ever sent him, that he ever sent her – what a strange thought.

Carmen scrolled backwards, into their correspondence. She opened a thread at random, from a couple of weeks earlier.

> Tom: *So when/where tonight?*
>
> Zena: *Leicester Square 7.30??*
>
> Tom: *That's fine. Where do you fancy eating?*
>
> Zena: *Tokyo Junction.*
>
> Tom: *Raw fish, my favourite.*

He was being sarcastic, he hated Japanese food. Didn't Zena know that? She hadn't replied. What was the outcome? Carmen would just have said sorry, of course, what do you want? Ended up eating steak or in Chinatown.

She clicked back a few pages, a couple of months, to March.

> Tom: *Laura rang. I've got the children this weekend. What do you want to do? Shall we go to St Jude's?*
> Zena: *Only if the decorators are finished.*
> Tom: *I just called them. They say they can leave the place habitable but it's not finished.*
> Zena: *Then easier to have them in London.*
> Tom: *Heating will be off still too.*
> Zena: *Definitely London. I may come in do some work Saturday anyway.*

Carmen stopped. She felt giddy reading all of this.

She clicked to the end, to the very first message. It was to a different email – Zena's work address. The tagline was: *Hello.*

> Tom: *Dear Zena. If this reaches you, it was great talking to you last night. If you want to discuss vertical stripes in more depth we could have a coffee sometime??? Just in case, this is my number . . . Tom*

Oh, this was too much. Carmen tore up inside – how could he! So he'd started it, he'd bloody started it! He'd never told her that. Carmen had asked him how it happened of course, and he'd said they met in a bar, but nothing more than that. He'd refused to tell her any more, how the affair developed. He'd told her not to ask those questions, said it would poison them, it was best not to know.

He was right. What a shit!

Of course it was him. What had she thought? That a woman who looked like Zena had pursued a married bloke ten years older than her for the hell of it?

Of course it was him. Bastard.

Carmen remembered when she and Tom had met. It had been completely different of course, Tom was single for one thing, and so was she, free agents, they could do what they wanted. Flora had passed on her number and he'd texted her – 'Flora says you're a bit amazing' – and if Carmen was honest she had felt amazing, from that moment on.

Does everyone do that? Kid themselves they're the only one he ever really loved?

She clicked open another email string, subject 'Change of plan'.

Tom: Zena I am so sorry but I can't come tonight. Mercy is ill and Laura has to be somewhere. I have to go up, I have no choice.

[two hours later] Tom: Did you get my email? I'm sorry. You know I wouldn't do this unless it was an emergency.

Zena: Yes, I got your email.

Tom: What will you do now? Can you find someone to go with you?

Zena: I've already found someone.

Tom: Who?

No reply.

[two hours later, at 17:03] *Tom: How about Thursday? Are you free? I'll buy you an expensive dinner . . .*

No reply.

Another string.

Tom: I'm thinking about you instead of working.
Zena: ;-)
Tom: Can you sneak off at lunchtime?
Zena: Only for an hour.
Tom: I'll come to you. I'll book a room.
Zena: Tiger ;-/

Enough. Carmen put the laptop to one side. She felt terrible. It was as though he was saying these things to another woman now, as though he was cheating on her.

But of course he wasn't. He had a history, she had a history. What did she expect?

Once again her nosiness had backfired on her. It was her own fault.

It hadn't been her intention to snoop on Tom and Zena anyway, or at least that was what she told herself. The point had been to see if there was any communication between Tom and Zena's family, Zena's friends.

She scanned forward in time, past the Zena emails, into the emails about Zena that followed her death. There were a couple of pages, correspondence where Zena was mentioned. Carmen flicked through them quickly, only opening anything from a sender she didn't recognise. Most were from Tom's friends, a couple from his father. She opened one from a colleague she didn't know, sending best wishes, another from a business contact. She could see nothing that might be from Zena's family.

Enough. She clicked out of the search and scanned around to see if there was anything that would show what she'd been doing. She knew Tom would be annoyed if he found out she'd been snooping, and fair enough. She looked along the toolbar – file, edit, history – shit. She clicked into history and of course it listed every single email she'd opened. But would Tom ever check the browsing history? Surely not.

Would he?

She scanned the screen, looking for a way to erase these most recent items from the browsing history, but couldn't find anything. Then she had a brainwave. She got back on the Internet and started surfing through newspaper sites and shopping sites and random searches. She went from page to page to page. This way she would make fresh sheets of history on his browser, so that in the unlikely event that when he came in, or tomorrow, he did check, this would be what he saw, the rest would be buried pages down. And this stuff would be easy to explain away. She could say oops, sorry, I couldn't be bothered to fetch my own laptop.

She clicked on a catalogue from a clothing site and it burst into life. A download – damn, another marker, and a visible one too; everyone has to access their downloads from time to time. She went to the downloads folder and there was the catalogue, top of an enormous list, he obviously never cleared this folder out. Her eye scanned down the list – no porn that she could see. Well, that was something.

Luckily the catalogue was easy to get rid of. She pressed delete and it was gone.

She switched off the computer, put it back in its place. It was five thirty, still an hour and a half until Tom would be home. She remembered his dry-cleaning then, but the shop would be shut now. Too bad.

She was tired. She went upstairs and lay on the bed, but when she closed her eyes a paranoid thought bugged her. There was one more thing to do.

She pulled herself out of bed, went through to the spare room and took the old laptop out of the box again. She hadn't shut it down properly, and when she opened the lid it tripped back into life. The battery warning flashed up – only two per cent charge left.

She wanted to check the browsing history here too, to see if there was any trace of her searches on this computer, but of course since it wasn't set up for Wi-Fi there was nothing to worry about. She had just been clicking between files on the hard drive – there was no record of that. She looked across the desktop one more time and then more paranoia made her check the downloads folder too, even though there couldn't be anything there of course, but just in case.

She clicked it open. The cursor whirled, the machine was painfully slow.

The power signal flashed up again – one per cent.

It opened at last. Another huge list, this time ordered alphabetically rather than by date. Her eye scanned through the filenames. They were mostly work documents by the look of them, labelled according to the system she'd seen earlier.

Then something caught her eye. Two files, labelled completely differently to the others, in caps too – 'FORENSIC INSIGHTS' . . .

She double-clicked on them both and the power warning flashed up again: 'Computer will close down shortly. Plug in power lead.'

A page opened, blank at first, then words took shape – Head Trauma. An image started to appear on the page, millimetre by millimetre. Carmen couldn't work out what it was at first. Then she saw it was a photograph of a bloody wound, a skull caved in; she was looking at brain and hair matted purple with dried blood. Another picture started to take shape beneath it – a side view, a distorted face. What was she looking at? For a moment she froze because she thought it was Zena, then she realised no, of course not, but it was a dead woman.

Annotations started to fill in, labels for different parts of the photograph. 'Bone splintered in this fashion suggests . . .'

And then the second page appeared, obscuring the first completely. Carmen clicked to close it, but nothing happened – bloody machine, it was so slow! The cursor spun. Click, click – she tried to move back on to the home page and then a word appeared on the new page: 'Drowning'. An image appeared slowly again, millimetre by painful millimetre, a swollen distended body, a woman again. Then the machine registered Carmen's clicks and took her back to the screensaver page and the list of downloads and she saw the word 'Forensic' again and the date and time – 28 May three years previously – and then the machine blacked out.

What the hell? She needed to write down the words before she could forget. What were they? Forensic analysis? Forensic insights, that was it. She wrote down the date – 28 May – and the time, 05-something. The year was the year Zena died. She drowned on 26 May, Carmen was sure that was right, two days before these documents were downloaded.

She felt completely creeped out. She shoved the dead laptop back into the box and walked through to the bedroom, but then she came back and booted up her own computer. She googled the words 'forensic insights'. It took her to a makeshift site that loaded slowly even on her whizzy new notebook. She recognised the red font as it came up, 'Forensic Insights', and then a picture scrolled into place – a young man's face in profile, a gunshot wound near his ear, fringed in black, then a ring of blue, skin bloodstained, eye frozen in death, staring into what? His killer's face? Oblivion?

She read the homepage.

Welcome. My name is Chev Alstrom and this is a site for anyone who loves true crime, and CSI and those kinds of TV programmes. I worked for 25 years in policing in the USA and as my retirement project want to share the many fascinating insights about forensics and the business of solving crimes that I have learned.

Chev didn't seem to have got very far with his project. There was a short biography signposted from the page, and then a link labelled 'Crime Scenes Analyzed', which led in turn to a list – Drowning, Electrocution, Head Wound, Knife Wound, Shooting, Strangulation, Smothering. Carmen clicked on Drowning and a document downloaded and opened, the same one she had seen on Tom's screen. The woman's body, swollen; the text and annotations. This time she could read the words:

Deliberate drowning is a notoriously difficult crime to prove. Also perpetrators may dump a body in water to dispose of it and this causes great problems for pathologists. Here are some clues:

[arrow to chest area] In a drowning the lungs will fill with water in most cases, although there is a form called dry drowning – where the larynx closes off the lungs – where saturation will be minimal. Composition of water can be checked against where the body is found to see if it has been moved.

[arrow to lacerations on arm] Injuries are common on drowned corpses as the body may crash against hard objects when falling into water or may collide with a boat or propeller or other object in the water, pre- or post-mortem. It is hard for the pathologist to be certain whether the injuries happened pre- or post-mortem. The presence of bleeding may be an indicator, although post-mortem blood may gather during long periods in the water.

[arrow to wounds on face] Corpses may deteriorate quickly as sea life eats the flesh leading to problems of identification.

There was more but Carmen had read enough. It was revolting, gross. She closed the page down. She couldn't face even opening the page on head trauma.

Why had Tom been looking at that stuff? It disturbed her – why would he do that? So soon after Zena's death too . . . The police must have been to tell him that they'd found the body, that Zena had suffered a head wound. And he had done – what? Looked up internet pages on evidence? Graphic pages of forensics? Wasn't that completely ghoulish? When you've just been told your partner is dead?

Was he just beside himself? Googling into the ether? Trying to make sense of what had happened? Carmen did that sometimes, googled looking for answers. Was that what he was doing? She searched under 'drowning' and 'head wounds' now, and flicked through pages of results, but there was nothing from Forensic Insights.

Did he just need to see what had happened to her? Had he been temporarily driven mad by it all? Of course he must have been, she mustn't judge his actions, it was wrong. People do strange things, crazy things under the sort of pressure he was experiencing, the grief. Carmen remembered the time of the download – 05-something, dawn, the worst time for any soul in agony. He'd been awake, pacing, mad, alone in a silent world.

Slowly her distaste turned to compassion. She clicked on the newspaper reports again, read them all, reminded herself of what he had been through. But as she read she felt a chill run through her.

A woman whose body washed up on the beach at St Jude's on
Wednesday was named by police last night as Zena Johnson, 29,
a magazine executive from London.

On Wednesday. On the twenty-eighth. She double-checked online – yes, Wednesday 28 May, there was no mistake. She looked at her scrap of paper – it was on the twenty-eighth that Tom had downloaded those documents, the same day. At 5 a.m. But how could that be? Had the police been already at that hour?

She'd known there was something wrong about the date, about the time. It had niggled at her since she'd first seen it.

She went back to the press cuttings.

According to the police statement, Ms Johnson was staying at her
holiday bungalow in Shell Road with her partner, Tom Cawton,
38, a lawyer. She went for a swim around 5.30 p.m. on bank
holiday Monday and Mr Cawton raised the alarm when she did
not return. Her body was found by dog walkers on the main beach
two days later, at low tide.

Her body was found by dog walkers on the main beach. How could that have happened and the police got to him by 5 a.m.? It didn't add up.

Had he downloaded these documents *before* the police had been? *Before* Zena's body had even been found? It was plaus-ible – after two days of waiting it must have been obvious that Zena had probably drowned, that her body would wash up at some point soon, however much he was hoping and praying.

But then why had he looked up a page on head wounds? How could he guess that was what had happened?

There was only one explanation. He wasn't guessing – he knew. He knew the police were going to find Zena's body. He knew they were going to find a head wound.

Carmen didn't know what to do. She went downstairs, sat on the sofa. The minutes passed. Her mind ticked over.

Maybe I read the time wrong, she thought.

Maybe the download was formatted differently. Maybe it was a twelve-hour clock and somehow what she had read as 5 a.m. was 5 p.m. and the police had already been.

Maybe it was 05-something in some foreign time zone and later here.

Maybe the clock on the computer was set wrong.

There would be an explanation like that, there just would be.

But even so ... who, when they've just found out their girlfriend is dead, chooses to look at that stuff? How grisly. How fucking weird.

Tom was home on time. He walked into the room smiling. Some of what she was feeling must have shown because he was reticent and bent to kiss her gently, almost formally. 'Are you OK? What have you been doing?'

She had thought about asking him to explain, getting this over with, but now it didn't seem possible. 'I went to Mum's.'

'Ah,' he said, as though that explained everything. 'And how is Lucia?'

She nodded. Fine.

He sat down on the carpet, at her feet, even though he was in his suit. 'Christ, I'm knackered.'

He put his head in her lap, and when she didn't respond he lifted her hand so her fingers were in his hair. 'What's for dinner?'

'I haven't made anything. Sorry, I haven't had time.'

'Oh well, I fancy a curry anyway.' He put his hand over hers, caressed it so that her hand caressed his scalp. 'That's nice,' he said. 'God, don't let me drink like I did on Saturday night again.'

'I'm not your mum.'

He laughed, took his hand away. Her fingers interwove with his hair. She had always loved the feel of it, thick and soft, like stroking a dog. 'So I'm forgiven?' he said.

'What for?'

'Being such an arse this morning.'

Carmen had forgotten all about that.

'I thought you were still cross.'

The evening passed. Tom ordered curry and they ate it and went to bed early, lay down beside each other, but Carmen couldn't sleep. The image she had seen on that website kept coming into her mind. A dead woman, naked, her head smashed in – the image she had thought for a moment was Zena herself. It wasn't Zena, but it could have been.

When she finally drifted into sleep the image invaded her dreams, only now it was Zena, and she was alive, her head shattered just the same but she was moving, and she was turning to face Carmen . . .

Carmen woke. Tom was fast asleep. She looked at him. You knew, she thought, you knew. But just formulating those words in her head terrified her and she forced them to change. What did you know?

Tom turned in his sleep and reached out his hand, searching for her body. She edged away so he couldn't find her and after a moment he gave up and settled again.

She got up and took his mobile from his bedside into the bathroom. She locked the door, put on the light and flicked through the directory. She was looking for a name that might be Zena's mother. It suddenly seemed essential that she speak to her. She wanted to know more – how Tom had been with Zena, whether he'd been jealous or angry, what they had been like together. She wanted to know what Zena's mother had thought of him, and why they had no contact. She wanted to know whether, like the people of St Jude's, she too thought that her daughter had been murdered.

Chapter 7

Carmen checked the clock – it was 11 a.m. She'd been busy for more than two hours. She looked down her list of telephone numbers. There were nearly twenty, all with the surname Johnson, handwritten and listed with initials and addresses as well as phone numbers. She'd had to subscribe to a directory enquiries website to get them, had paid twenty-five pounds for a year's access, then copied down every listing under Zena's surname in Hamesdon and the surrounding villages. The news report of Zena's death had said she went to school in Hamesdon, and Carmen's best hope was that her mother still lived around there, that she went by the same name.

There had been nothing on Tom's phone to help her, so she was going to have to do this the hard way. Now it was time for the next step.

She held the phone in her hand and punched in the first number, but she paused so long before pressing dial, the handset cleared it. Was she being ridiculous? How would Tom react if he found out?

She pressed the button. She needed to do this, she would worry about the rest later. She'd made a plan of what to say – she would pretend she was a researcher looking into jet-ski accidents, say she was hoping to talk to Zena's family. Once she was in contact, she would play the rest by ear.

The first call was answered by an elderly man who struggled to even hear her and ended up putting the phone down. The next two went to voicemail – Carmen left a brief message and her mobile number; she didn't want anyone calling the flat. Then she got through to a woman who seemed interested even though she had never heard of Zena – she shouted through to her husband to check with him, and took Carmen's number and said she would ask around. Then there was a dead number, then a mother, trying to understand what Carmen was asking her between screamed demands from her children until she finally got the gist of it and was annoyed at the interruption.

The next call was the most fruitful so far – a man who fished off St Jude's beach, who was interested as soon as she mentioned jet skis and remembered Zena's death. He took her number and said he would think about whether he knew anything that might help her, that she could call again if she wanted to talk any more.

After that it was just more voicemails and dead ends until she got to the bottom of the list.

She went through to the kitchen to make some tea, and of course they were out of milk. Never mind, she needed a break. She walked down to the shops and bought a few bits. It started raining on the way back and she didn't have a coat, but she didn't mind. The drizzle felt pleasant on her arm, brought a quiet to the street.

Her mobile rang. She grabbed it out of her pocket – it was the same code she'd been dialling all morning. 'I'm Cheryl,' said a woman's voice, 'Jez Dwyer's sister.'

For a moment Carmen had no clue whom she was talking to and then she remembered – Jeremy Dwyer, the young guy who'd died in a jet-ski accident a few years before Zena. His death had been mentioned in some of the news reports.

'Mum rang a few minutes ago, said you were writing about the jet skis? She asked me to ring you back for her. She still gets upset when she talks about it so . . .'

Carmen didn't have time to wonder how this had all come about, how the jungle drums worked in a place like St Jude's so that she could ring round looking for one person and end up with another. She was at her front door now and she apologised as she fiddled with her key. 'You said your name was Cheryl?'

'Yes. Jez was two years younger than me.'

'He was about fifteen, right?'

'Eighteen. He'd be twenty-six now. What's this all about?'

'I'm researching a piece for a specialist magazine that looks at accidents and risk. For insurers, people like that.' Carmen pulled a face to herself, it sounded so lame, but Cheryl didn't question it.

'Well, it was a jet ski that killed my brother, so . . . yeah.'

Carmen was struggling to remember the story. Did she even know the details? 'So you're sure it was a jet ski?'

'What do you mean?'

111

'There wasn't any doubt about it? About how he died?'

'Well, his friends saw it happen so . . . no, not really.'

Carmen squirmed inside. She should know all of this. But then it had never occurred to her that she would end up talking to this family. 'Listen, I really am sorry but I don't know the details of your brother's death,' she said. 'I don't know how but it's slipped through my net somehow. Would you mind telling me about what happened?'

Cheryl paused for a moment, then she said, 'Well, he was with a few mates from college, they were having a barbecue on the beach. It was the last day of term. Jez went off for a swim. He loved swimming. He always went in the sea, even in the winter, he was always that bloke.' She paused. 'Anyway, he swam out a bit and then the others heard the jet skis and . . .'

She trailed off.

'That's awful,' said Carmen. 'They actually saw it?'

'Well, as good as. They heard the motors. Then of course he didn't come back. They got the coastguard out, but they didn't find him. His body was washed up the next day.'

'In St Jude's?'

'No. Why St Jude's?'

'I thought that was where it happened?'

'No, we live in St Jude's, but he was away at uni.'

Carmen was confused now. She'd assumed this accident had happened in the same spot as where Zena drowned, on that same stretch of beach. 'I didn't realise,' said Carmen. 'It was in the local paper.'

'Well, we live here, don't we?'

'Of course,' said Carmen. 'Was there an inquest?'

'Yes.'

'And was it made clear that it was a jet ski that killed your brother? Was that the conclusion?'

'There was never any question about that, but what they did do was try to make out it was Jez's fault.'

'How?'

'They said he was drunk, but that was just bollocks.'

Carmen was sitting at the kitchen table now, making notes.

'Supposedly he was outside the safe swimming area,' said Cheryl.

'Was anyone prosecuted?'

'No, accidental death. The same happened with that other girl, didn't it? I can't remember her name . . .'

'Zena,' said Carmen.

'That's it. I remember. It was tough for Mum, when she died, because it all came up again about Jez.' She paused. 'We met her family actually.'

'Whose?'

'The woman who died.'

'Zena?'

'Yes. Her mum, and her husband – the police set it up.'

Not her husband, Carmen wanted to say, they weren't married.

'They had the same support officer as we did – Andy, that was his name – he was a really nice guy. It was weird though in the end, we didn't really know what to say to each other.'

'You've been really helpful. I don't suppose you know how I can contact Zena's mother, do you?' said Carmen.

'No, sorry. She lived somewhere around here though. Listen, I need to go actually, I'm at work. Was that it?'

'Yes, thanks for your time.'

'You know the water-sports place closed down – the one here in St Jude's, that hired out the jet skis? After that woman died?'

Carmen had had no idea. 'Because of what happened?'

'I couldn't say about that, you'd have to ask the guy who ran it. He was a nice bloke actually.' But she couldn't remember his name and didn't know what he was doing now.

Carmen looked up the news reports on Jeremy Dwyer's death and the inquest. She should have read them earlier – she kicked herself now. Unlike with Zena, there had been little doubt in Jeremy's case about the cause of death – his injuries were consistent with a collision with a craft of some sort. But the coroner emphasised the high level of alcohol in Jeremy's blood, and the fact that he was swimming well outside the area designated for bathers, in a lane designated for jet skis and other craft, without any sort of safety gear to make him more visible.

It was a very different situation to Zena's.

Carmen thought about what Cheryl had told her, that she'd met Tom with Zena's mother soon after Zena's death. So there had been some sort of a relationship between Tom and her at that stage. And yet within months – when Carmen first met him – there was no contact, and as far as she knew they had not been in touch since.

Why? What had happened?

Carmen's mobile rang. It was Cheryl again. She wanted to tell Carmen that someone in her office had told her that the guy who used to run the water-sports place in St Jude's now ran a caravan park, just in case Carmen wanted to speak to him. Cheryl still did not know his name, but Carmen went online and soon found it. The contact for the old water-sports company in St Jude's was listed as Kyle, and when she searched under his name and mobile number she found the touring park.

She wrote down the address. It was located an hour south of St Jude's, probably no more than an hour and a half's drive from her flat. She looked at the clock – it was just gone one, she had the whole afternoon ahead of her. She could call him, but why not go and see him? A trip into the country would be nice, might help her get perspective. She picked up her keys and set off.

The site was in woodland. She parked and walked through to the hut that housed reception. 'Can I help?' said the guy behind the counter. He was in his thirties, with surf-dude streaked shoulder-length hair. Every inch a Kyle. She told him so and he laughed.

'I wondered if I could look around,' she said. 'My parents have got a caravan.'

'No problem,' he said, and gave her a map of the site.

She had planned this approach, rather than just launching into questions, to make her interest seem coincidental. He was working on the computer when she came back. 'Nice place,' she said.

'Thanks. We've only been open a couple of years, but it's going well.'

'Do you know, I think I recognise you,' she said. 'Didn't you used to run the water-sports place in St Jude's?'

'That's right.'

She nodded. 'Why the change?'

He shrugged. 'I just grew out of it. It's quite blokey. You mellow as you get older, or at least I did.'

She picked up a leaflet, fiddled with it. 'I remember about that girl who died. Excuse me if I'm being tactless asking, but I've always wondered . . .'

His smile disappeared. 'That was nothing to do with us.'

'Of course, I just—'

'We didn't even hire out a jet ski that day.'

'But it was a bank holiday, wasn't it?'

'Yes, and the weather was appalling. No one wanted to go out on the water – everyone was down the pub.'

'Really? Is that true?'

'Of course it is. Do you think the police wouldn't check that? They knew it was nothing to do with us, but some people just like to have a go.'

'Why? Didn't people like the business?'

'Most people were fine about it, but there's always some, aren't there . . . To be honest I got totally sick of the aggro. I was just trying to run a business that brought people into that village, who spent money and stayed there . . .' He was wound up now.

'I'm sorry,' said Carmen.

116

'I can't believe people are still talking about it!'

'No one's saying anything. I just got it wrong, that's all.'

She returned to her car, but she felt reluctant to drive straight back to London. Having got this far, she had an urge to walk on the beach, to feel the wind in her hair. Should she go to the bungalow? The touring park had been further than she had thought, she was less than an hour from St Jude's here.

The more she thought about it, the more she liked the idea. She could maybe even stay the night, go back to London tomorrow, give herself some time to think. She always kept the key to the bungalow on her key ring and there were clean clothes in the drawers.

She texted Tom straight away, before she changed her mind, said she'd driven up on a whim and had decided to stay over.

She parked the car outside the bungalow and walked to the beach, sat on the pebbles. The gulls were active on the shoreline, swooping and making a racket. It took her a moment to work out what they were doing. The tide was low and they were picking in the sand for shellfish, flying up and dropping their treasures from high up on to the pebbles to crack them open, then diving to gobble the flesh inside before a rival could scavenge it.

Carmen thought about her meeting with Kyle. He'd said it wasn't a jet ski that killed Zena, or certainly not one of his, and she believed him. So what did happen?

This must be about where Zena swam from that day. It all seemed so benign now, but the tide would have been high then, the waves big as they hit the shingle. She imagined Zena stopping about where she was sitting, taking off her coat and leaving it with her shoes, tiptoeing down through the shingle to the water's edge. She imagined she could see her, that she was ahead of her now, plunging into the waves, in her red bikini.

She closed her eyes. *What happened to you Zena? What happened here?* She whispered the question. What happened?

But the only voices to come back to her were the gulls'.

After a while she got up and walked along the shoreline, cut into the village, to the mini-market. She filled a basket with food – milk, cooked chicken, some salad. It was the same guy behind the counter as the last time they were here, the one who had been gossiping about Tom with that woman who was shopping. He didn't pay Carmen any particular attention, just made some remark about the weather as she paid for her groceries. Does he know who I am? she wondered. Am I being quietly observed, commented upon when my back is turned? She wanted to ask him – do you know who I am? Did you know Zena? Can you tell me about her? She paused for a minute, daring herself – but she said nothing.

It had started to drizzle. Carmen walked back along the main street, past the church and the takeaway and the flower shop. She reached the bus stop and stopped underneath the shelter, a moment's respite from the wet. A teenage girl was sitting on the bench, wired up to listen to music, her head bent over her phone so that for a moment Carmen didn't realise that she knew her. It was Mel. What on earth was she doing in St Jude's? And on a school day?

Carmen said her name, but Mel couldn't hear her.

Carmen touched her arm.

Mel looked up and was as startled to see Carmen as Carmen had been to see her. She pulled her earphones out. 'What are you doing here?' she said.

'I've just popped up for the day. What about you? No school?'

'It's a study day. I've been at a friend's.'

'I didn't know you knew anyone in St Jude's?'

'A girl from school. Tamsin.'

Carmen guessed she was lying – Mel had never mentioned a friend in St Jude's before, all the times they had been here, and it was miles from Mel's school – but it wasn't up to her to make accusations. 'How do you get home from here then?' she said.

'Bus into town and then another bus from there.'

'That's a pain.'

'It's not too bad.'

'I'll give you a lift if you like.'

'No, thanks. It's OK.'

On impulse Carmen said, 'I'll wait with you then,' and sat down next to Mel on the bench.

Mel clearly didn't want her to stay and Carmen felt awkward, but she didn't move. She was sure now that Mel was lying, that Laura didn't know she was in St Jude's and that Mel didn't want her mother to see Carmen dropping her off. 'Who's this Tamsin then?' she said.

'Just someone from school.'

'A hell of a long way for her to travel every day.'

But Mel just shrugged.

Carmen back-pedalled. 'I'm glad you've got good friends,' she said. 'I've always thought it must have been hard for you, having to change schools and start again.' For Jake the transition from private to state had been fairly smooth – it had come as he was moving on to secondary anyway. But it had been harder for Mel, who was well established at her high-flying girls' school.

'Is school OK?' Carmen persisted.

'It's fine.'

'You don't come over as being that happy, that's all.'

'It's just school. It's not a big deal.'

Carmen wanted to ask more, but an elderly man joined them under the bus shelter. Carmen stood up so he could sit down. 'I won't say no, your bones are younger than mine,' he said, and nudged Mel with his elbow as he sat – 'but not as young as yours' – and Carmen laughed, and Mel looked as though she wanted to disappear, which made Carmen feel sorry for her, for all her teenage edges and awkwardness. She was about to say she would give her a lift into town, to save her one leg of the journey, when the bus nosed into view.

When she got back to the bungalow she lay on the sofa and thought about Zena again. If her ghost was floating around, presumably she would be here too. She had walked through this house, cooked food here – probably she had lain on this very sofa. She'd spent her last hours on earth in this place.

Carmen fell asleep. Her dreams were vivid and anxious and she woke disorientated. It was gone eight and she was ravenous.

She cooked rice, heated up the chicken and made a salad. At the back of a cupboard she found wasabi and rice vinegar and mixed a dressing. She had brought them up the very first time she had come to the bungalow, as kitchen essentials, but Tom preferred French dressing, more traditional food, and she'd forgotten they were even there. It struck her now that without noticing, in the two years they had been together, her eating habits had changed completely, the very food she ate. The very fabric of her body.

It was starting to get dark. She had never spent a night here on her own before. The bungalow was silent and she felt more alone than she ever did in her own flat, where noises filtered through the walls. That got on her nerves a lot of the time, but now she missed the intimacy, fake or not, of close neighbours. She was often alone at home in the evenings, when Tom was working late, but this was different – she knew there was no one coming back, not at any point, not tonight or tomorrow, and where earlier on she had relished that thought, now she felt spooked by it. Once she imagined someone was watching her through the window, but when she looked out no one was there, no one in the street or the garden.

She rang Tom, but there was no answer at home and his mobile went to voicemail. He was probably on the tube. She turned the TV on, but there was nothing she wanted to watch so she switched it off again. She checked her emails and Facebook on her phone, and found herself on Zena's page again, looking at her profile picture, enlarging it. It was blurred and hard to make out – you couldn't identify her – but

Carmen could see that she was smiling, happy, her black hair in motion, she was swinging her head into a beautiful blur. Where was she? A restaurant? Her shoulders were bare. A club? In bed?

Her thoughts were interrupted by a noise at the back. She went out to look. The garden was depressing in the twilight, weeds growing between the uneven concrete paving slabs, nothing blooming around the edges. They'd talked about doing something with it but never got round to it. They should deck it, she thought, put furniture out here, maybe a few tubs – something that wouldn't dry out. She turned and looked at the rear of the bungalow. Her bedroom window was in front of her, the curtains drawn back; if the window had been open she could almost have touched the bed. There was no lock fitted, none of the windows had locks – Tom said you didn't need them up here, but that seemed to her now to be naive. In London you would have bars on this window, and intruder lights fitted, an alarm. It would be a fearful thing to sleep on the ground floor.

She heard the phone ring inside, the landline not her mobile. They never really used it – it must be Tom. She hurried inside, but the voicemail cut in before she got there. She dialled to pick up the message.

It wasn't Tom. It was a woman's voice, an older woman. 'Tom? Are you there?' She paused and Carmen could sense her uncertainty. 'Are you there?' Another pause. 'Call back as soon as you can, won't you? It's Amy.'

Carmen tried to listen again, but she made a mistake with

the unfamiliar handset and an electronic voice told her the message was deleted. Bloody hell. Who was that? And then the handset rang again, in her hand, making her jump. The number appeared on the screen – it was a local code. She stared at it, not knowing what to do, until it rang out again.

She dialled into voicemail again. It was the same voice. 'Someone's asking about Zena. I need to talk to you.'

Carmen dialled 1471 and wrote down the number it gave her. She checked it against her list. It was one of the first numbers she'd written, one of the first of the Johnsons. She'd left a message this morning.

She called the number straight back, before she had time to think or stop herself. 'You don't know me, I'm Tom's wife, Carmen,' she said. 'You left a message for him just now, but he's not here, just me. I thought I'd call you back in case it was important.'

There was a pause. 'Tom's wife?'

'Yes. Didn't you know about me? I'm sorry.'

The woman seemed confused rather than upset. 'What's your name, did you say?'

'Carmen. Are you Zena's mother?'

'Yes. I wanted to talk to Tom. Is he there?'

'No, he's in London.'

'Oh.'

If Carmen had had time to think about where the conversation should go next, she would not have dared say what she did, but she didn't leave time for silence, she just ploughed ahead. 'Listen, can I come and see you?'

'You want to see me?' Zena's mother sounded confused.

'Yes.'

There was a pause. 'When?'

'How about tomorrow morning?'

Chapter 8

Zena's mother lived in Oxton Leigh, a traditional Norfolk village a few miles outside Hamesdon. It took Carmen a while to find the house. It was at the end of the high street, beyond the pretty cottages, on a pre-war council development, four sides of terraced houses built around a square patch of grass where children were riding bikes.

She was early – she wasn't due till ten – so she parked and looked up at the house, number 7, a two-up two-down sandwiched in the middle of the row. Was this where Zena grew up? It wasn't what she'd imagined, nothing like it. She'd assumed Zena was privileged like Tom, that she came from that world.

As she waited, she found herself thinking that Tom must have been here, that he and Zena would have come together to visit Zena's mother, for Sunday lunch or Saturday tea.

She rested her chin on the steering wheel. She could hear the children on the green, playing. Had he come here when they were having an affair? Had he sat here and kissed Zena while Laura and the children were at home suspecting nothing? Had he come in the days after he'd left all that devastation behind him, and sat here and been happy?

It wasn't a pleasant thought, but it was probably true.

She rubbed her forehead against the leather of the steering wheel. Was this the root of the problem – the root of her mistrust? The reason she had become suspicious when she'd heard those rumours instead of just brushing them off as nonsense? The man who had come here with Zena wasn't the Tom that she knew, it was another man. Her Tom was lovely, dependable, a man she could trust. The Tom who had sat here was selfish, disloyal. A liar.

She got out of the car and snapped the lock. Two children appeared beside her, hanging off their bikes and staring. She stared back and they rode away. She walked up to number 7 and rang the bell. There was no reply so she rang again. 'Wait,' a voice called from inside, and there was a lot of fiddling with a chain before the door opened.

Carmen pulled back from the woman on the other side, though she couldn't have said why. Her connection to Zena was obvious in her tall sinewy body, in her long black hair, braided into a plait that fell over her shoulder. But where Zena had radiated strength and vitality in her skin and her dewy eyes, this woman just looked unhappy.

She led Carmen through to the sitting room and asked if she wanted coffee. Carmen said no, thank you. They sat down. 'Mrs Johnson . . .'

'Amy.'

Carmen smiled.

'So you're married to Tom?' said Amy.

'Yes.'

'How long's that been then?'

'Nearly two years.'

'Did you know him before?'

'Before? Before Zena? I met him the year after she died. Why? Did you think . . .'

What? That Carmen and Tom had been having an affair when Zena and Tom were together? Is that what she thought?

'They weren't together long,' said Amy.

'No, I'm so sorry.'

Carmen struggled to think of something to say. She felt dragged into the strange ennui of the room and of the woman. The blinds at the windows were drawn down and the light was muted. 'Have you lived here long?'

She nodded. 'We moved here after Zena's father left.'

'I didn't realise . . . When was that?'

'Oh, twenty years ago, longer maybe.'

'So Zena was a child still.'

'She was about ten.'

'Does Zena's dad live nearby?'

Amy shrugged. 'I've never seen him since the day he left.'

'Didn't he keep in touch with Zena?'

'A bit, when she was younger. He's South African. I think he maybe went back there.'

'Didn't he come to her funeral?'

'I wouldn't have known where to find him – he's probably dead.' She paused. 'We had a lovely house before, detached, five bedrooms, but it was mortgaged to the hilt, I found that out when he left. I couldn't even sell it because of the negative equity. It was repossessed.'

'How awful.'

'The council gave us this.'

Carmen looked around the room. It seemed too bare to be someone's home, where a person had lived for twenty years. There was furniture, but no pictures on the walls, no photos on the shelves, no books or ornaments. No photos of Zena. Carmen thought of her mother's flat, the clutter every-where, layers of it, like some archaeological trove that you could dig through for evidence of every stage of Carmen's childhood.

Carmen's father had left when she was ten, a strange parallel. Had Zena's mother been angry and depressed as Lucia had been? Had Zena lived a reduced life as a teenager too? 'How long did Zena live here?' she said. 'When did she leave home?'

'When she was fifteen.'

'That's young, isn't it? Wasn't she still at school?'

Amy shrugged – I know, but what can you do? 'She was headstrong, like her father. You couldn't tell Zena what to do.'

'But where did she go?'

Amy shrugged. 'Off with her friends, or some man. There were always boys, from when she was twelve or thirteen, always someone sniffing round.'

'She was very beautiful.'

'She liked men, she liked sex.' Amy looked at Carmen. 'You're shocked that I'd say that, aren't you?'

Carmen was shocked, but she didn't say so.

'I don't see any point in lying about your children. She could never stick with one boy – she was always off with a new one. That's just how she was.'

Carmen felt a need to take a break, to leave this room. 'Can I say yes to that coffee after all?' she said. 'I'll make it. Don't get up.'

'Help yourself.'

The kitchen was as neutral and depressing as the living room, with cheap grey lacquered units and a marbled plastic worktop. Again there was no decoration, no fridge magnets or pictures or cards, no cookery books. When Carmen picked up a cup from the drainer there was a thin sheen of grease on it. She washed it and dried it against her jeans and found instant coffee above the kettle in a cupboard. There was no milk in the fridge.

Carmen thought about how Zena's father had left at the same point in her childhood as her own father did, such a strange coincidence, though it must have been harder for Zena. Carmen's father had continued to be a constant presence in her life – she had spent every other weekend with him and Jan, and Kieran after he was born, and sometimes stayed a night during the week as well. Their home had always been her home too – to some extent at least. It sounded as though it hadn't been like that for Zena.

Carmen had known girls whose dads had exited their lives, or who had never really been around, and it had affected their perception of men, their relationships later on, one way or another. Not that the rest of them had exactly got it right . . .

There was another parallel too. Zena was an only child, which meant she was left alone to deal with the fallout of her father leaving her mother, the way Carmen had to. Carmen knew how hard that could be and still was, when there's only you. How strange that Zena had experienced that as well – Carmen had had no idea. She would like to have been able to talk to her about it, what it had been like, what it continued to be like. There were so few people who understood.

She and Zena shared the same profession too.

A thought flashed across Carmen's mind: is it just coincidence that we have these things in common?

The kettle boiled. Carmen poured hot water on to the coffee granules, stirred them in. She was reluctant to go back through to Amy – how flat she seemed, and the house was the same. There was heaviness in the air – a greyness and lifelessness. Had that come after Zena died? With Amy's grief? Or did her unhappiness stretch back much further?

Lucia had not always been easy to live with when Carmen was a teenager, but she was alive, there was never any doubting that. Lucia was made of colour and strong emotion and their home had been warm, a dynamo in Carmen's young life as well as a drain.

What would it have been like to grow up here? For a powerful, energetic girl, emerging into life? Almost unbearable, she thought.

She carried her drink back through. 'Will you tell me more about Zena?' she said.

Amy looked unsure. When had someone last asked her about her daughter?

'What did she like doing?' said Carmen. 'When she was at school – what was she good at?'

'Oh, she wasn't clever or anything,' said Amy. 'She was good at sport. She ran for the school, and swam and all of that. She got that from her dad – he was sporty. She got her brains from me.'

Carmen smiled, thinking Amy was joking, but Amy didn't smile.

'She wasn't stupid,' said Amy. 'She hated not being the best, that was the thing. I think that was why she gave up running in the end, because she wasn't winning any more.'

'Why not?'

'Just her age, I think. Her body changed, but she wasn't interested in competing for the fun of it. She had to win, always.'

'Was she good at writing? I'm thinking about her working on the magazines.'

'Oh, she loved magazines, always went out to buy one with her pocket money. Pop stars and all that. And clothes. Just wait a minute.'

She went out into the hall. Carmen sipped her coffee and grimaced. It was disgusting.

Amy came back with a shoebox. 'I kept this – silly really.' She put it on Carmen's lap. Carmen opened the lid. There was a bundle wrapped in tissue paper. 'Go on,' said Amy.

Carmen pulled the fragile paper aside. Inside was a cardboard cut-out figure of a girl with long black hair, hand-drawn and coloured in with felt-tip, and a selection of clothes made from card with tabs that you could attach to the body. Carmen smiled at Amy. She remembered these. The doll was clearly meant to be Zena herself – she had Zena's long black hair, a sign she was confident about her looks. Carmen remembered wanting to be blonde when she was younger, like the girls on TV, then when she was a teenager wanting to have dark skin like so many of the girls around her at school.

'She loved clothes,' said Amy. 'She always dressed well.'

Carmen looked through outfits, each one carefully drawn and detailed. There was something touching about the earnest efforts of a young girl. 'They're very sweet,' said Carmen, as she wrapped them back up. 'Amy, how did you feel when she got together with Tom? I mean, he was married and—'

Amy reached over for the shoebox. 'I didn't know anything about that at the time.'

'Didn't she tell you?'

Amy shook her head. 'She wouldn't confide in me, and anyway she'd know what I would say. But that was Zena all over – she wouldn't worry about someone being married, not if she'd set her sights on them. That was her father in her.'

'A bit . . . selfish?'

'Single-minded. If she wanted something, she wouldn't think about the obstacles in the way, she'd just have to have it.'

Carmen nodded.

132

'Zena wasn't cruel,' said Amy. 'She was never nasty like some of the girls were to their mums when they were teenagers. Never vindictive – she didn't hold grudges, nothing like that. She just . . . had to have what she wanted. She did exactly what she wanted – you couldn't control her.'

'Did you like Tom?'

Amy nodded – of course. 'He was steady, Zena needed that.'

'Were they . . . happy?'

Amy shrugged. 'Zena was never happy with anything for long, it wasn't in her nature. Listen, you should tell Tom there's been a journalist asking questions. She left a message on my machine. Will you tell him?'

'Yes, but—'

'I haven't called back and I won't, tell him that.'

'I will, but why wouldn't you call her back?'

Amy shook her head. 'I don't want to make trouble.'

'Why would it make trouble?'

'For Tom. He went through enough when Zena died.'

He went through enough? What about Amy, what she must have gone through? Carmen put her cup on the floor and leaned towards the older woman. 'Amy, it must have been terrible for you. I'm so sorry.'

Amy didn't answer at first, but then she shifted in her seat and said, 'There were times when Zena was younger when I used to sit here and wait for the police to knock on my door and tell me she'd been raped or murdered.'

She was silent for a moment.

'I knew,' she continued. 'I saw the police car pull up and

133

these two officers walking towards my door and I knew then. They told me she was missing, but I knew that she was dead straight away.'

'What do you think happened?' said Carmen gently.

'She drowned. Don't you know that?'

'But I thought she was a good swimmer.'

'She was, but she was reckless. Headstrong, like her father. She wouldn't listen.'

'Is that what happened? Did she not listen?'

'I don't know,' said Amy.

They were silent again, and then Amy said, 'You know, it was worse for Tom than for me.'

'Why do you say that? It must have been awful for you.'

'But no one accused me of killing her, did they?'

Carmen's heart beat faster. 'Sorry?'

'Hasn't he told you about that? The police suspected him. It was dreadful.'

'The police?'

'After they found her. They took him in. Didn't he tell you? I can see why he wouldn't – it's not something a new wife would want to hear, is it?'

Carmen felt sick.

'They came here and asked me lots of questions. Whether he hit her, whether he was good to her, was he sleeping around . . . that sort of thing. Whether Zena was sleeping around.'

Carmen didn't know what to say.

'They questioned him for hours. Hasn't he told you any of this? I told him, the boyfriend is always the first suspect. I told him he had to put up with it, just keep telling the truth and it would be OK in the end.'

'And they believed him? In the end?'

'Well, they left him alone anyway.'

Carmen was reeling. 'What did you think? Did you think he was involved in her death?'

'Of course not.'

'What do you think happened?'

'They said it could have been lots of things. One of the men said that it could have been that a wave tipped her off balance and she bumped her head on the sea floor. My doctor said he thought that was the most likely. The waves are strong there.'

'Your doctor?'

She nodded, and Carmen understood that Amy must have been to see her doctor afterwards and talked to him about it and he had given her that salve, the belief that her daughter died naturally, just lost consciousness in the arms of the sea.

'She loved swimming,' Amy said. 'When she was little she would nag me to take her to the beach every day in the summer. She didn't know what it meant to be scared. She'd throw herself in those waves when she was this high.' She indicated with her hand, no higher than the sofa arm. 'I would be terrified, shouting after her, but she always popped up smiling.' The corners of her mouth twitched at the memory. 'She was completely fearless. She didn't think anything could hurt her. She just didn't understand.'

She put her hand to her mouth and Carmen thought she was going to cry, but she breathed deeply a couple of times and composed herself. Carmen was moved by her grief. She reached over, touched her arm. 'When did you last hear from Tom?' she said.

'I don't know, quite a while. I don't blame him though. It's bad memories, isn't it?'

And he wouldn't want you talking to me either, thought Carmen. There's too much he hasn't told me.

She left soon after, got in the car and drove off straight away, but outside the village she pulled into a lay-by. She felt stunned by what Amy had told her. Tom had been a suspect in Zena's death, he'd been questioned by the police for hours. It had all happened just months before Carmen had met him and he'd never said a word to her about it.

How could he do that? How could he have made love to her, and taken her to dinner, and taken her on holiday, and asked her to marry him as though none of it had happened? How could he have lied to her, so brazenly and for so long? The thought of it made her feel sick.

It was only now that she realised she had gone to Amy's expecting to find proof of Tom's innocence, not the opposite. That she had set out on this whole quest looking for evidence that everything in her marriage was the way it seemed to be and that she had nothing to worry about, not the reverse. She had never really believed that her world was about to be turned upside down and inside out. She'd just wanted to know for sure that this man she'd married so quickly, and perhaps without asking enough questions, was everything he said he was, that there was nothing suspicious in Zena's death, so that she could clear the skeleton out of the wardrobe and close the door on any doubt and get on with their life together.

How could she do that now? At the very least he'd lied to her, lied through his teeth.

But even as she faced it, she started to question what she saw.

OK, the police had suspected him, but they'd believed him in the end.

And was it really lying, what he'd done? Did he ever actually tell her an untruth? *Men lie by omission* – that was one of Lucia's maxims – men lie by omission. Women feel a need to reveal everything, to clean the slate, but men are different. If there is something a man doesn't want you to know, he won't tell you.

Amy seemed to think it was natural that he'd not told her. And Amy had no doubts about his innocence – and she was Zena's mother for God's sake.

Carmen started to see a light. Could it still be OK? Could they just go back to normal?

She switched her phone on. There was a text from Tom – 'What are you doing?' – just connecting with her. She looked at the picture beside the message, the shot they used on the company website, Tom in a suit and tie, smiling his professional smile – *You can trust me* – the one he put on to make her laugh. She touched the picture. She loved that face, it was the face of the man she loved, but even in that picture he was lying, wasn't he? Pretending to be something he wasn't. Manipulating. She'd grown up in a world where people were straightforward, where they said what they thought, often too bluntly, but Tom had grown up in another.

Could it still be all right?

She touched his face again. She needed to explain to him that truth is crucial in a relationship, however hard it may be. That if he was lying to her or not telling her the whole truth, she would always sense it, her subconscious would know and ring alarm bells. It was just the way Kieran had said, though he had called it instinct.

She drove south and was home by two. The flat was silent and tidier than she'd left it. She picked up the post from the doormat and switched on the kettle. She made tea and took it to the table, sat down and opened the post. It was mostly junk mail. A subscription renewal. A credit-card bill.

For a moment she couldn't make sense of the last letter. It was on headed paper, a company she didn't know, and the greeting was 'Tom', not 'Dear Tom', she realised afterwards, just Tom. The envelope was handwritten – she'd mistaken the scrawled *Mr* for *Mrs* and opened it by mistake. 'Tom, it was good to talk to you at the weekend, just complete these forms. Sorry things aren't so great but I think you're doing the right thing here. Top up as and when.' It was signed with a large, overconfident 'Bill'.

Carmen knew Bill. He was one of Tom's old friends. She didn't like him; he travelled a lot for business and Tom had told her he slept with prostitutes when he was away, cheated on his wife. She didn't know exactly what he did for a job, but it was something to do with finance.

She turned to the form, several printed pages, an application form for an offshore investment. Tom's details had been filled in – his name, address and the sum to be invested: £500,000.

Five hundred thousand pounds. Half a million pounds.

She looked at the next page. There were reams of impenetrable jargon about tax liability, risk, disclosure, and lines marked with a pencilled star where Tom was supposed to sign. She had no idea what all these words meant, but she knew straight away what the meaning of it was. Tom, who had told her he hadn't had a decent bonus for years, that they couldn't afford a house yet, nor a fancy holiday – none of which was an issue for Carmen, she was not greedy, she had never asked for more, she was happy with things the way they were – but all the time he had half a million pounds, and without telling her he was sending it abroad. Out of reach.

Chapter 9

Carmen sat at the desk in the spare room staring at the window. It was raining, she watched the drops form on the glass and run down, merging together. She felt empty, as though there should be much more to feel but there was only numbness. The feeling took her straight back to the dying days of her and Nick, her depression then, her inertia. She had thought she would never feel that way again, but here she was.

The idea that her marriage might end was terrifying to her. She couldn't look at it squarely, but aspects crept into her mind, practical matters mostly, and it took all her strength to keep batting them back. How the hell will I pay the mortgage? *You'll have to get a lodger.* But how depressing to go back to that. *Well, thank heaven you have the flat, otherwise you'd never be able to buy a place now.* I don't even have a bloody job, how will I cope? *You'll have to find a job. Anything.*

Oh God, could it really all be going to end? It was unbelievable, unbearable. But predictable too ... The barrage in her head kept on ... What was I thinking, that I could have all of this? *Stop it, stop it – why not you?* But then why does this keep happening to me? Why do my relationships keep going wrong?

I will never have a baby now. If I meet someone else it will be too late.

And it was at that point she started to cry.

Tom called her from downstairs. He was cooking lunch, she could smell garlic. She had been in here for more than two hours, pretending to work. He called again, his voice bright, and she knew that soon he would come up. He knew something was wrong, had known since she'd come back from St Jude's two days ago. It was obvious, she was barely speaking to him. She couldn't pretend any more that everything was all right. But nor had she been able to confront him. She was too scared to hear what he might tell her, to face what the consequences might be. She'd just shut down to him.

The door opened behind her. She didn't look round. She sensed him standing there, watching her, unsure how to proceed. 'I've made lunch,' he said. 'It's ready.'

'OK.'

He walked over and stood beside her. 'Are you busy? I can keep it warm.'

'No, just give me a couple of minutes.'

He stepped back then, away from her, towards the door, awkward, and she felt a flash of compassion for him. She had to do something, say something. They couldn't carry on like this, it was unbearable for them both.

Downstairs the table was set with cutlery and glasses, a bowl of steaming pasta and a salad ready to serve. She sat down opposite him. 'I hope you're hungry,' he said, spooning pasta on to her plate.

'Yes,' she lied. 'This looks good.'

'I haven't cooked it for years. It's just asparagus and parmesan.'

She picked up a piece of pasta with her fingers, ate it. 'It's nice,' she said. 'Thank you.'

'I love cooking for you. I just wish I had more time.'

She had the letter about the money in her pocket. It had been there for two days, a weight. She took it out and put it on the table. 'I opened this by mistake.'

He looked at it sitting there, unsure, aware like her that some crucial moment had come. 'What is it?'

She pushed it towards him. He picked it up, unfolded it, took the paper out of the envelope and read. 'Ah,' he said, and she could feel his relief. What had he feared? 'Is this why you've been upset?'

'I haven't been upset.'

'I was going to tell you about this. I talked to Bill at the wedding – it's some scheme of his, I don't know. I forgot all about it to be honest.'

Had Bill been at the wedding? Carmen hadn't seen him. 'I thought you thought Bill was a tosser.'

'Well, he's not my favourite person, but he's good at this sort of thing.'

'What sort of thing?'

'Investments.'

'Tom, it says half a million pounds here!'

'Well, I wouldn't put that much in . . .'

'Where the hell did that come from? I thought we were hard up!'

'Did you?' he said. 'Why?'

And then she started to think – why? Was it possible she'd just got it wrong? 'But you're always saying we can't afford things.'

'I'm not.'

'Yes, you are.'

'What, like when I said don't worry about finding another job until you're ready?'

That was true – he'd been brilliant about that. And of course it meant they weren't hard up.

A window opened in her heart, just a little one, a glimmer. Was it possible . . .?

'I never comment on what you buy,' he said.

That was true too. They had a joint account, for household expenses, which she now paid nothing into, and which since her redundancy she had used for all her spending – not just food and so on. But then she hardly bought anything.

Could she just have got this so wrong? 'What about last year's holiday? When we went to Cornwall?'

'I thought you loved Cornwall.'

'I do, but you said . . .'

'I try to keep a tab on things, that's all, to make sure we don't waste money. It doesn't mean we're hard up. If I let you just spend, spend, spend, we'll never be able to afford a nice house.'

'That's so unfair, Tom! I never ask for anything.'

He reached across the table, took her hand. 'I know you don't.'

'And you're missing the point anyway. Tom, half a million pounds for fuck's sake – I had no idea you had that sort of money.'

'I haven't. I was pissed when I spoke to him.'

'Well, how much have you got?'

'I don't know – a couple of hundred thousand maybe.'

She opened her mouth. 'What, in your bank account?'

'It's not that much, Carmen.'

'You are joking.'

'Well, it's not enough to buy the home I want for you and me, is it? But if I invest it like this, then in a couple of years it might be.'

She looked at him.

'I want a nice house for us. I want things to be perfect for us.'

She looked at his body. He was leaning in towards her, not defensive at all; he seemed to be quite genuine. Was that it then? When Tom implied there wasn't a lot of spare money, did it just mean something entirely different to what it meant to Carmen?

She picked up her fork. Her body felt lighter. Was it really all going to be OK? Had she perhaps just got the wrong end of the stick? She looked at him. He was waiting to see how she was taking it, and she immediately felt suspicious again. If it was all so innocent and above board, why hadn't he said anything?

'I suppose this is some sort of tax dodge,' she said. 'Is that why you didn't tell me?'

144

'I didn't not tell you! I was going to tell you.'

'So is it? A tax dodge?'

'Well, it's tax efficient – that's part of the idea of an offshore investment.'

'You know how I feel about that.'

'OK, but Carmen, do you want a nice house or do you want to just hand over thousands of pounds in addition to all the tax I already pay?'

'I believe in paying taxes, you know that.'

'And so do I, and I've already paid nearly half of what I have earned in income tax, and what is left is mine – ours. We can do what we want with it. This isn't illegal, Carmen. It is perfectly legitimate.'

'Is it?'

'Carmen, you have got no idea what some people get up to. I am one of the good guys, OK?'

He was talking passionately, he meant what he was saying, she was sure. And of course there was part of her that was pleased to hear he was looking out for them, providing for them. 'You should have told me.'

He took her hand. 'Listen, I'm sorry, Carmen. If I could go back now to last weekend and just tell you, of course I would, but I was pissed, as were you, and I forgot. And I do have to say that if I'd seen this letter before you opened it, it would have reminded me and I'd have told you.'

They ate. And when they were finished he said, 'What do you want to do this afternoon then?'

'I don't mind. What about you?'

He flicked a glance at her and she could tell that what he wanted was sex, and normally he would just have said 'Let's go to bed', but he didn't know whether things were sufficiently smoothed over for that to be OK, and he was right, they weren't. In fact Carmen was feeling terrible again, all the same feelings were flooding back, and almost more intense for the brief respite. The urge for things to be OK between them was so powerful, but they weren't, and she couldn't pretend. This wasn't just about the money, of course it wasn't. 'Tom, we need to talk things through,' she said. 'Properly.'

He sighed, put his fork down. 'I don't know what else to say, Carmen, I really don't.'

'Not about the money, about Zena.'

'Zena?'

'Yes, Zena. That stuff that boy said, about . . . how she died . . .'

'Not that again!'

'Tom, I need to talk to you about this.'

His eyes widened and he put his hand on his forehead as though she was being neurotic and she snapped. 'Don't do that! Don't ever do that!'

'What?'

'Make out I'm being mad! I'm not being mad, I need to know what bloody happened.'

'OK, but I've told you everything. I haven't kept anything from you.'

'No, you have not. You have not told me everything.' She

could hear the pitch of her voice rising. 'You have not told me anything!'

He was shocked by her anger, and wary again. Of her? Of what she was going to say? 'What do you mean?'

'You didn't tell me that the police suspected you, did you?'

He was stony-faced. 'What?'

'You never told me that you were a suspect. Why didn't you tell me that?'

He paused, just for a moment. 'Didn't I?'

'No!'

He didn't ask her how she knew this, how she'd found out. 'Didn't I tell you when we met? I'm sure I did.'

'No, Tom, you didn't tell me. Like you didn't tell me about this money.'

'That's completely different.'

'Why?'

He rested his head on his hands. 'I could have sworn that I told you.'

'You didn't.'

'Well, if I didn't, it was only because it was so awful – can't you understand that?'

'Of course I can.'

He was surprised by that, placated. He stopped, rubbed his forehead.

'But I need to know. Can't you see that? I need to know what happened. Or else I am suspicious – can't you see?'

He jumped on that. 'Suspicious?'

'Yes. Yes, frankly. And it makes me do weird things.'

'Like what?'

She paused. How could she tell him? About going to see Amy? 'I went through your old computer,' she said. 'I found it in one of those boxes in the spare room.'

He looked at her. That blank look again. Was he angry? She should tell him all now that she had started – about reading his emails, about searching through his files, about tracking down Zena's mother – but she was frightened she'd gone too far.

'What did you find?' he said.

'Well, that screensaver of you and her for a start.'

Even as she said it she regretted it. Why start with that when there was so much else? She'd found those downloads – why didn't she tell him about those? Where was her courage?

'I'd forgotten about that picture,' Tom said. 'I haven't used that computer for years. But you silly girl for looking and upsetting yourself.'

'It's your fault, you didn't tell me anything. What did you expect me to do? After what that boy said, I read the newspaper reports, all that stuff about a head wound – I didn't know any of that, you didn't tell me. I thought she'd drowned! You didn't tell me anything about a head wound. Why didn't you tell me, Tom?' He was looking at her now, straight into her eyes. 'What the fuck happened to her?'

He got up and came round to her, crouched beside her, took her hand. 'Carmen, look at me,' he said.

She was avoiding his eye, pulling away, worked up. She had started this and now she was scared.

'Look at me,' he said.

148

She did.

He held her hand tighter. 'Carmen, I didn't kill her, I swear to you.'

She looked away.

'You don't believe me, do you? God, Carmen, you have to believe me. Whatever else you hear, you have to believe that I did not kill her, I did not hurt her. I swear to you.'

She looked at him. She saw panic in his eyes as it sank in that he was on the cusp of losing her. He pulled on her hand. 'God, Carmen, I swear to you, I swear it. You have to believe me.'

She looked at him. His fear now was palpable, panic that she wouldn't believe him, and with it his veneer was gone, she was looking at him in the raw, and suddenly her instinct said this is true, he's telling me the truth, and the relief was overwhelming.

Did he sense it? 'It's my fault, Carmen, I know that,' he said. 'I should have taken time with us, told you everything, but I so wanted to get on with life and I so wanted you. I didn't want to frighten you off. It all seemed so . . . massive. I couldn't see how it wouldn't frighten you off.'

'I need to know everything,' she said. 'I need to just know so there are no secrets.'

'I don't know where to start.'

'Just sit down now and tell me. Everything. From the beginning.'

He clambered back to his feet and sat in the chair beside her – an obedient dog. 'I just . . .' He sighed, as though it was sheer physical effort to drag himself back into that time, shook his head.

Carmen helped him. 'You were at the bungalow and it was the bank holiday Monday?'

He nodded.

'And Zena went for a swim.'

'Yes.'

Carmen waited for him to pick up the story, but he didn't seem to know what to say. 'When? What time was that?'

'Late afternoon, I guess. About four, five.'

'And then?'

'Well, she didn't come back.'

Carmen waited again, but he didn't continue. 'When did you start getting worried?'

'Later. I called the police about midnight, I think, I don't know. They came round later, I remember that, about two in the morning.'

Carmen reached over and took his hand. 'Tom, it must have been so awful.'

He looked at the table. 'I wasn't that worried at first,' he said. 'I thought she'd just gone off to the pub or something. She knew some people around there. She grew up there, you know. I thought she must have bumped into someone.'

'But wouldn't she have texted you or something?'

'She'd left her phone at home.'

Of course – she was swimming.

'So what were the police like when they came round?'

He shrugged. 'You never know what the police are thinking,

do you? They just filled in their forms. At first I thought they didn't believe me – you know, weren't taking it that seriously. I guess they get lots of calls like that and then the person turns up. That's what they said – that in almost all cases the person just turned up the next morning. And I thought she might too.'

'Really? Stay out all night without saying anything?'

He shrugged.

Carmen thought how different their relationship must have been. She would never do that to him.

'Then they found her shoes,' he said.

'Her shoes?'

'When she went swimming she used to leave her clothes with her towel on the beach, but they must have been washed away because I walked down to the beach, to the place where she swam from.' He rubbed his eyes. 'That's right, I'd forgotten I did that.'

'You went down to the beach?'

'To look for her.'

'When?'

'I can't remember. When she didn't come back. But I couldn't see her. And her clothes weren't there – that's why I thought she must have got dressed and gone off somewhere.'

'So that was reassuring?'

'Yes.'

'But then they found her shoes.'

He nodded.

'When was that?'

He thought about it. 'The next day, I think.'

'The Tuesday?'

'I suppose so.'

'Where were they?'

'On the beach in St Jude's, washed up with the tide. Someone found them. The police came to show me them, to see if they were hers.'

Carmen thought about it. 'So you must have known then,' she said. 'That she'd drowned.'

'I don't know. It was all quite confusing.'

Carmen thought about it, about what he had been through. She had known the basics before but she had deflected it somehow, not allowed it to be real, not allowed herself to think about all he had endured so recently before they met. She reached across and put her hands over his again. 'Were you on your own all this time?'

He nodded. 'There was a police guy there for a while. Support – there for me, you know. He came and went. I can't remember.'

'Didn't you call anyone?'

'Who?'

'I don't know – your dad?'

Tom shook his head as though it was obvious that he wouldn't have wanted him around. Tom wasn't close to his father. His parents had separated when he was a child and he'd lived with his mother. And then she'd died when he was a teenager.

'What about your friends? Didn't anyone come to be with you?'

'I don't think I told them.'

'Why not?'

'I don't know. Maybe I did, I'm not sure.'

'But no one came?'

'Look, I can't remember Carmen. Is it important?' Tom was staring at the table, his hands together now in front of him – he was clearly hating this. 'I don't think I wanted anyone there – can't you understand that?'

But Carmen couldn't imagine going through what he had on her own. She would have called friends, family, Kath, Lucia. She would have wanted someone at the end of a phone line at least – she'd have wanted them there.

Are men just so different?

Tom drummed his fingers on the table. 'I wasn't alone anyway. Like I said, that police guy was in and out, and there was Amy – Zena's mum, she came at some point. And it wasn't just nothing, just sitting there, the police were back and forth filling in their bloody forms, and the coastguard came.' He looked at her. 'You know what? I would actually rather never think about any of this again.'

Carmen didn't say anything.

'Go on, ask what you want to ask,' said Tom.

'I'm not sure what I want to ask. I just want to know what happened, that's all, so there are no more surprises.'

He rubbed his finger against a mark on the table and then leaned over and wrapped his arms around her and hugged her. He buried his head in her shoulder, kissed her neck. 'This is what is important, Carmen,' he said, squeezing her. 'Me and you, our future, I wish you could see that.'

She kissed his cheek.

He smiled, relieved. 'And, Carmen, I'm sorry I didn't tell you before. It wasn't deliberate. It's just—'

'I get it.'

He nodded. 'Go on then.'

'Well, what happened after that?'

'They found her body.'

'When was that?'

'The next day.'

'Wednesday.' The twenty-eighth. The day of the downloads.

'I mean, Carmen, you asked about why I didn't call anyone, but it all happened so quickly. It was all . . . a blur.'

'Tom, I get it.'

He looked at his hands.

'Just tell me what happened,' she said.

He sighed. This was clearly hard work for him. 'They came and said they had found a body and they thought it was . . .' He broke off.

'Do you want to stop for a bit?' said Carmen.

'No. Let's do it now. Go on.'

'When did they come? What time?'

'I don't know, midday.'

'Not early morning?'

'No.'

'And it was the Wednesday, definitely.'

'God, I don't know, I'm getting confused. Does it matter?'

Carmen shook her head. He'd said it was Wednesday and she knew that anyway, from the newspaper reports. She must have been mistaken about the time of that download, that was all. 'Did they want you to identify her?'

'They said I didn't have to, but they thought I might want to see her anyway.'

'Did you?'

He nodded.

'Did you go straight away?'

He shook his head. 'Later.'

'That day?'

'The next day, I think.'

'That must have been awful.'

He didn't reply.

Carmen didn't know what to say. She told him so. He cleared his throat and said, 'You wanted to know about the police.'

'Yes.'

'After they found her, their attitude changed, I could sense it,' said Tom.

'In what way?'

'I don't know. I mean it's always hard to know what the police are thinking – I just sensed something had changed.'

'How? Were they suspicious with you?'

'Not suspicious, just – different. Less sympathetic.'

'Really? When they told you they'd found her body?'

'I can't remember exactly, maybe not then, but I sensed a change.'

'They suspected you?'

'I guess so.'

'Why?'

'Because she had that head injury. When they found her. You said about that before, you know about that.'

'You told me she drowned.'

'She did, that's what the inquest said, that the cause of death was drowning, but the police didn't know that then, not till after the post-mortem. There was just this . . . injury when they found her. So of course they thought . . .'

He stopped.

She couldn't say the words either.

After a few moments Tom sighed again. 'I don't know what they thought exactly, but I think they thought that maybe I'd – hit her over the head or something and dumped her body in the sea. I mean, it was crazy, I don't know.'

He looked really sad. She felt sorry for him.

'Did they say that?'

He shook his head. 'They just asked me whether we'd argued.'

'Argued? What, the day she went missing?'

He nodded.

'What did you say?'

'I said no.'

'And had you argued?'

'No.'

But he had paused that time, just for moment.

'Tom?' said Carmen.

He looked at her, looked away. 'It wasn't an argument.'

'Jesus,' said Carmen.

'It wasn't an argument!' said Tom again.

'What was it then?'

156

He put his head in his hands.

'Tom, why don't you just tell me what happened?'

He didn't answer.

'Tom, you're freaking me out.'

'We didn't argue,' he said again.

'So why did the police think you did?'

'Someone told them that they'd heard shouting. From the house.'

'Who?'

'I don't know. Some nosy fucking parker walking by.'

'And were they right?'

Tom paused, and then he said, 'It was the kids.'

'The *kids*?'

'Jake and Mel.'

'Jake and Mel?' said Carmen. 'They were there?'

'Yes. They were just fighting – just being kids. And maybe I shouted at them, I don't know. I told the police, that must be what whoever it was heard.'

'I didn't know they were there,' said Carmen. 'You've never told me that.'

'Didn't I?'

'No!'

'Does it matter?'

Carmen thought about it, what it meant. 'Were they there the whole weekend?'

'I can't remember. Maybe just overnight, I think, from the Sunday.'

'So they were there when Zena went off swimming?'

'Yes – no, I think they'd gone by then.'

'Where?'

'Home.'

'You drove them?'

'Laura picked them up.'

'Laura picked them up?'

'Yes.'

'She never picks them up.'

'She did more in those days.'

'Why?'

'I don't know, they were younger. You're asking all these questions – does it matter?'

Carmen shook her head. It didn't really, did it? 'What else did the police ask?'

'Oh, I don't know.' He looked around the room. 'Horrible stuff. Was Zena seeing someone else? I remember that. Was I seeing someone else? Did we argue a lot? Had I ever hit her? Had she said she wanted to leave me? Had I been drinking?'

'Had you?'

'God, I can't remember! No – I had the kids, didn't I? I mean, maybe one beer or something.'

'Did they caution you?'

'No, it wasn't like that, although—' He stopped.

'What?'

'Well, at one stage I think they did ask me to "attend an interview under caution, at the police station".' He said it sarcastically.

'Jesus, Tom. How long did all this go on?'

158

He shook his head. 'I can't remember.'

'Days? Weeks?'

'No, a few days.'

'What happened at the interview?'

'They cancelled it.'

'Why?'

He shrugged. 'Presumably they found out something that made them realise I didn't kill her after all.' There was bitterness in his voice. 'Probably the post-mortem.'

'No wonder everyone in St Jude's thinks you did it,' said Carmen.

'Thanks.'

'But, God, Tom, how awful!'

He shrugged. 'Do you know what? Everything that was happening was so . . . unbelievably awful . . . so bloody unreal, that I honestly didn't give a shit. I didn't care what the police thought and – do you know what? – even if they had charged me and locked me up, I wouldn't have cared at that point.'

She put her hand over his. 'But they left you alone after that?'

'Yes.'

They sat in silence for a moment. 'I'm glad I know,' she said, 'but you should have—'

'Told you before, I know,' he said. 'But you can see . . .'

'Of course.'

She felt drained. He must feel awful. She got up and put the kettle on, made tea for them both.

'I'm sorry about looking at your computer,' she said.

'It's OK, I understand, but don't do it, Carmen, it's not good for us. And you're just going to wind yourself up.'

She was stung by the chide. 'You should have been honest with me.'

'I know that. But can you just not do it again? Can you just stop all of this?'

The tea was comforting, necessary. She felt as though she had been through an ordeal and she knew he must too. But there was such relief for her too, and it went deep because it fitted, what he'd said, with what she knew. Even the details she hadn't mentioned – those downloads – if the police had started questioning him about Zena having a head injury, it made sense that he had done some research. A bit grisly perhaps, but – he was a lawyer. There must have been something wrong with the timing on the computer, that was all.

'So what did happen to her?' she said. 'What do you think?'

He shrugged. 'I don't know. She drowned, one way or another.'

Later on they had sex and it was sweet and loving. Tom held her and was gentle and moved by the experience, and Carmen was relieved to lie in his arms and feel close to him again. She told herself that this had been their first big challenge, and they'd come through it.

'You look serene,' said Tom, and kissed her forehead.

'Maybe this is the start of our real marriage,' Carmen said. 'The end of the honeymoon.'

She fell asleep in his arms, but her dreams weren't peaceful. They were full of Zena – Zena banging on her door, forcing her awake, in bed with her and Tom. Over and over again, refusing to leave her in peace.

Chapter 10

On Wednesday Carmen decided to try working at the British Library. She'd heard from an old colleague that it was a refuge for freelancers, and she hoped that the change of scene and the atmosphere and books and periodicals would inspire her and give her ideas. Maybe she'd even make some contacts.

She was stepping out of the tube at King's Cross when the voice message alert went off on her mobile. It was Kieran. 'Where the hell are you? I'm with this girl who knew Zena – you've got to get over here. We're in this pub in Borough – what's this place called, mate?' Carmen heard him asking someone, who asked someone else, and eventually he told her the name. 'It's near the tube. Come over as soon as you can.'

Carmen rang his mobile but it was turned off. Bloody hell, she thought, and she set off for the library, but then she turned around and went back down the steps to the underground.

Absolutely typical – the pub was nowhere to be found around Borough tube station, and after ten minutes of wandering and asking she discovered it was near Southwark station instead, which meant another twenty minutes' walk. By the time she found it – and Kieran, already quite drunk and almost sitting on top of a scrawny girl – Carmen had lost patience. 'This place is nowhere near Borough tube. What were you talking about?'

'Hey, Carmen, good to see you. You seem in need of libation. What do you want to drink?'

'Just a Coke.'

'I'd offer to pay, but I'm a bit broke, I'm afraid. This is Hope, by the way.'

And so Carmen found herself paying for a pint for Kieran and a vodka and lime for Hope, as well as her own Coke and a bag of crisps. She gave Kieran a tenner, but he said that it wouldn't be enough, so she gave him another.

He went to the bar and left Carmen with Hope. Carmen sized her up. She was tall and so thin that her head seemed too big for her body, dressed in a T-shirt and microshorts. Carmen swallowed her irritation before she spoke – none of this was the girl's fault after all. 'So how do you know Kieran?'

'I don't really, I just met him a few days ago. A friend said something about Zena and I knew her so we met up.'

'Carmen doesn't like wasting time,' said Kieran, back with a tray. 'Busy, busy, time is money.'

Carmen ignored him. She opened the crisps and put them in the middle of the table. 'Here, help yourself,' she said to the girl.

'You two don't look alike, do you?' said Hope.

'Well, she is my sister, I promise you,' said Kieran.

'Half-sister,' said Carmen, still pissed off.

Kieran pulled a sourpuss face.

'How did you know Zena?' Carmen said.

'From the magazine,' said Hope. 'I worked there three years ago – well, it was, like, work experience really, just a few months. I'm a model, but I want to be a stylist. I mean, I didn't know her well – she was pretty high up and I was just doing work experience, you know?'

In other words she never spoke to you, thought Carmen. Oh, this is such a waste of time . . .

'Everyone was so upset when she died,' said Hope.

'You were there then?'

Hope nodded, and so did Kieran, an inane half-grin on his face. 'Tell her what people said,' he said.

'What do you mean?' said Hope.

'About her boyfriend killing her.'

'Oh, that was just a joke. You know, the way people do, trying to feel better about it, I think.'

'Black humour,' said Carmen.

'That's right. It was just one of the blokes on the picture desk – he said something, but he was just joking. She drowned, didn't she? But she was a good swimmer. He said that, that she was a good swimmer and he bet her boyfriend had her knocked off.' She looked at Carmen. 'He's your husband now, isn't he?'

'Yes.'

'It was only messing around,' Hope said. 'It was just this one guy and he was only joking.'

Carmen looked at Kieran as if to say, See? But he was grinning still, numb to nuance.

'He was married before as well, wasn't he?' the girl said. 'When he first met Zena? They said that too, in the office, that when she was first seeing him people kept telling her he'd never leave his wife, but then he did.'

'People knew about it? She didn't keep it secret?'

Hope shrugged. 'I wasn't there then, but it sounded like people did know.'

Carmen thought about how it must have been, Zena talking about her married boyfriend at work, them egging her on or warning her off, it all sounding like a game.

'This girl who told me, she said she knew he would,' said Hope.

'What?'

'Leave his wife,' said Hope. 'I think Zena just was that sort of person, who got what she wanted, you know the way some people do? I don't mean anything horrible, just – lucky, I guess.'

That was one word for it. Carmen thought about how Amy described Zena, that when she set her sights on something she had to have it. 'What was she like?' said Carmen.

'Looks-wise?'

'Every way.'

Hope thought about it. 'Well, she was gorgeous, you know, really good-looking and she had beautiful clothes, lovely clothes. But she was nice on the inside as well.'

It sounded like clichés. 'Do you really mean that? Are you just saying it?'

165

Hope looked surprised, adamant. 'Oh no, she was a lovely person.'

'In what way?'

'Well, she was just, like, nice. I remember she was really kind to that little girl . . . her stepdaughter.'

'Mel?' said Carmen, surprised.

'That's it. Zena brought her into the office for a few days once. She spent an afternoon with me in the fashion department sorting out clothes.'

'But she can only have been about . . . twelve?'

'That's right, yes. She adored Zena, just like hero-worshipped her. You can see that, can't you, a little country girl that age, she would have just worshipped her. I would have done.'

Carmen had had no idea that Zena and Mel were close. Another thing Tom had failed to mention . . .

'She was kind to me too. I remember once she sat down with me and asked me all about myself and what I wanted to do, and she told me to never give up on that and that it would be a struggle but that I had talent and that I had to have faith in myself and carry on.'

'Zena said that to you?'

Hope nodded. 'I've never forgotten it. I got the feeling she really understood, that it hadn't all been easy for her either.'

Carmen felt chastened by that. In her irritation she'd dismissed Hope as a bit of a drip, but Zena had been kind to her. It wasn't much, a few words of encouragement to a vulnerable girl, but most people wouldn't have bothered. Hope had been the workie, around for a few weeks, the bottom of the heap, but Zena had taken the time to find out about her, to talk kindly to her and encourage her.

It was the first time, she realised, that she'd heard anything really positive about Zena. She had spoken to Flora and Tom and to Zena's mother even without any sense that they thought Zena was a nice person. Hope was the first one who seemed to have really liked her.

Kieran went off to the toilet. Hope's eyes followed him, and Carmen thought she was going to say something about him, maybe ask Carmen about him, but in fact she said, 'A lot of the men fancied her.'

'Zena?'

Hope nodded, looked at her, and Carmen sensed that she was hinting at something more specific. 'Anyone in particular?'

'Well, I remember I went for a walk one lunchtime and I saw her coming out of this nice restaurant with this man in a suit. I only found out later who he was, but he was, like, head of the company or something really high up.' She fiddled with her glass. 'This girl I worked with told me who he was, and she didn't seem surprised he was with Zena.'

Carmen picked at the crumbs of the crisps. 'Probably it was just work.'

'Of course.'

They sat in silence.

'One girl did say some bitchy stuff,' Hope said.

'What?'

'Well, like that Zena was sleeping her way up. About that guy.'

'So people were talking about it?'

Hope nodded. 'I mean, I don't know really, I guess so.'

'There were rumours?'

'Yes, though people were careful what they said because his wife worked there too and she was a bit of a cow.'

'His wife worked there?'

Hope nodded. 'She was important like him. Quite a scary woman. Or that's what people said, I never spoke to either of them.'

Carmen sipped on her Coke. It was finished – she just got residue from the ice. Had something been going on? Zena liked older men, powerful men – Tom had been ten years older than she was. And older men liked her, that was obvious too.

If there was any truth in the rumours, it was shocking. Tom and Zena had only been together properly for six months when she died. Even counting the time they were seeing each other in secret, their relationship had lasted less than a year. Was she already bored? Already looking for someone new?

Kieran came back and Hope said she needed the loo as well and went off. 'So what do you think? Good stuff, eh?' said Kieran.

'Kieran, how did you meet Hope? What's going on?'

He adopted a puzzled look.

'Oh, come on, it wasn't a coincidence, was it? How did you find her?'

'I just met her.'

'A week after I told you that stuff? She said a friend said something.'

He had his indignant look on now – another part of his

fibbing repertoire, which he always forgot Carmen had been witness to since he was a toddler and could see straight through. 'Just tell me the truth, Kieran.'

He started fidgeting. 'I was just trying to help.'

'Kieran . . .'

'I just . . . was talking to a friend.'

'Who?'

'No one you know.'

'About what?'

'Just what you said.'

Carmen rolled her eyes. She knew what this meant – that he'd told everyone he'd spoken to since the day she went to his flat that Tom had killed Zena. That the bloke his sister had married was a murderer. 'Kieran!'

'What? I just mentioned something, and this guy recognised the story and said he knew a girl who worked at the magazine, that's all.'

'How did you even know where Zena worked?'

'You told me.'

Was that true? Had she mentioned the magazine to him sometime in the past and he'd remembered? Or had he looked it up? And as she thought this Carmen's temper started to evaporate. It was bloody annoying, but it was touching too, that he'd done this for her. 'Look, Kieran, I know you meant well, but please don't talk to anyone else about this, OK? Please can you just leave it?'

He held up his hands.

'Please?'

'OK, but she told you about that man Zena was fucking around with, right? Tom wouldn't have liked that much, would he? Look what he did to that bloke who just spoke to you!'

Carmen rubbed her eyes. She wished so much now that she'd never talked to Kieran about any of this. 'I'm not thinking that way any more,' she said. 'I was just wound up.'

'So that's why you came all the way over here.'

Bloody smart arse. 'I'm serious, Kieran, it was just stupid thinking. Tom didn't kill Zena, he just didn't, the police checked it all out and there is no question of that, OK? You have to stop this.'

Kieran looked sceptical.

'But thanks, I do appreciate you looking out for me.'

They waited in silence for Hope to come back. They were both looking across the pub as the door to the toilets opened. Hope stumbled as she passed through and nearly fell – it was almost as though she was so thin she couldn't stay upright. She waved to them that she was going out the back for a cigarette. 'Is she OK?' said Carmen. 'She's so skinny – is she a junkie?' She kicked herself even as she said it – 'Sorry . . .'

But Kieran had already taken offence. 'I'm not the only one who's fucked up.'

'Kieran, I . . .'

'Look at the shitty men you go out with!'

'I've told you, it's not like—'

'It's not just Tom, though he is a cunt frankly – you let Nick fuck you around for years.'

'What do you mean?'

'If you don't know, you really are stupid.'

Carmen stood up. 'Say goodbye to Hope for me,' she said, and walked off in such a fury she went in the wrong direction and ended up by the river, on the South Bank. She kicked a pebble hard and a group of tourists stared. Bloody Kieran.

She stopped and leaned on a railing, looked out over the Thames. She watched the gulls, the river bus pulling into the dock on the other side. A couple of boys had managed to get down on to the riverbank, urchins searching among the detritus.

She got her phone out and dialled Jan's number. Her stepmother's voice was calm and instantly soothing. 'I've just seen Kieran,' Carmen said. 'I thought I'd let you know.'

'Thanks. How is he?'

A complete twat. 'He's OK.'

'You went to his flat?'

'We met in a pub.'

'I'm seeing him on Sunday.'

Carmen didn't say anything and Jan said, 'Is everything OK?'

'Jan, do you think I'm fucked up?'

'Of course not.'

Carmen was silent.

'Why are you asking this?'

'Do you think I make bad decisions about men?'

'No, of course not. Carmen, is something wrong? With you and Tom?'

Carmen didn't answer.

'Do you want to come over?'

'No, it's all right, it's just something Kieran said. About Nick really, not Tom.'

'What about Nick?'

'That I let him . . . treat me badly.'

'Really? How?'

'Women – you know.'

'Well, how would Kieran know? Listen, Nick loved you. He was just a bit . . . immature.'

'But I stayed with him, didn't I?'

'No, you left him.'

'After fifteen years! That's how long it took me to see.'

'Life's not like that, Carmen, it doesn't work like that. You two grew up together, you were kids when you started going out. Things changed so much in that time – both of you changed. You two were happy for a long time.'

Carmen was silent for a moment.

'Are you OK?' said Jan.

'I'm fine,' said Carmen. 'Thanks, Jan. I'd better go.'

When she rang off she saw a text had come through. It was from Kieran: 'I'm sorry what I said but I'm right about Tom. Cognitive dissonance. Look it up.'

Carmen googled the words as she stood there. 'Where there is a conflict between different beliefs held by a person, leading to denial and feelings of discomfort.' Uh? She read another definition. 'Cognitive dissonance occurs when a person denies what is obviously true in order to uphold a pre-existing belief

172

system. The subsequent conflict is internalised and can lead to agitation, anxiety or depression.'

Bloody Kieran, he'd been in too much group therapy.

He was wrong about this.

Carmen had lost heart in her trip to the British Library and headed home. She made a sandwich and took it up to the spare room. She thought about what Hope had told her – she should just forget about it, it was probably all nonsense anyway, and even giving it more thought was beneath her dignity. But some sort of compulsion was urging her on, and in the end she gave in to it. She pushed her plate to one side and looked up the website of the publishing company that produced the magazine. She clicked on to the page of board members, and from the information Hope had given her about this man being married to a powerful woman in the company, she soon found him. Ross, publishing director, pictured alongside the chief executive of the company, his wife Stephanie.

He looked completely different to what she had expected. Carmen had imagined a corporate-director type, stitched up in a suit and pleased with himself, but Ross looked more like a well-heeled hippy. He was handsome, well into his forties or even early fifties, but with a relaxed tanned face, rugged rather than worn, and sun-kissed ruffled hair. Carmen clicked on his biog.

Ross joined the company in 1989 working as an account manager with the advertising sales team, but soon graduated to become a publisher. After working across many of our titles, in 2001 he was appointed group publishing director. In 1998 Ross brought his passions together when he married Stephanie, a rising star in the firm and now our chief executive. Ross is a keen yachtsman and a regular at Cowes week.

Carmen would never have put him and Stephanie together as a couple. She looked ten years older for a start – her hair was unflatteringly grey, she wore glasses and there was nothing stylish about these or the generic business clothes she was wearing. Where Ross breathed physicality and openness, Stephanie was the opposite. They didn't look anything like husband and wife, but perhaps that was just about the photographs. Stephanie was chief executive of a well-established publishing company and so obviously a woman to be reckoned with. If he was publishing director, that also made her his boss. Had he fallen for her brains? Her power? What she could do for him? What sort of man was he?

Carmen went on to Facebook and searched under his name. There he was – a different picture, in sailing clothes, out on the water – but the same easy smile. Ross had 376 friends on Facebook. Carmen searched for Zena and yes, there she was, that strange, blurred profile pic. Carmen clicked on her name but she got the same result as always – a home page with no details.

So they were Facebook friends, but what did that prove? They were colleagues, had lunch together – of course they were Facebook friends. In fact maybe if anything it showed innocence – would clandestine lovers be friends on Facebook for everyone to see?

Carmen clicked on Ross's picture, enlarged it and stared

at it. He wasn't Carmen's type. She could see he was good-looking, but she would instinctively have mistrusted him, he was too smooth, you could just tell by looking at him. But Ross and Zena – well, maybe. It was ridiculous to try to judge by a photograph, but if Carmen had to guess she would say they were cut from the same cloth – there was that same vitality, the same confidence, the same freedom somehow. Ross looked like the sort of person who would do exactly as he liked, same as Zena.

Carmen found herself wanting to meet him, to see for herself what he was like. She found herself wanting to talk to him about Zena. Not only because she wanted to know what their relationship had been, but because she wanted to hear more about her.

His contact details were on the biog. She drafted an email giving a brief résumé of her journalism, saying she wanted to talk to him about some ideas, about what she could do for the company, could he give her fifteen minutes of his time? She attached her CV.

She deleted it. What was she thinking? It was madness.

She wrote the email out again, attached her CV again, pressed send.

After two hours there had been no reply – of course he would ignore her, and part of her felt relieved about that. And then an email came in: 'How about tomorrow, 10 a.m.? Come to our office.'

She typed back, 'Thanks, that's great, see you then.'

She stared at the screen, her mouth wide open. What the

hell had she done? How was she going to handle this? And yet now it was actually happening, she felt excited as well as nervous, thrilled even, and somewhere down inside, she knew she'd manage, whatever came up.

Tom was in a great mood that evening. Carmen cooked pork chops and mashed potatoes, traditional food that he liked, and after they had eaten they sat together at the table, chatting and catching up.

She didn't tell him about meeting Kieran, none of that. She had considered telling him everything – about Hope, and the rumours around Zena and Ross – but in the end she'd dismissed the whole idea. How would she explain it for a start – Kieran finding this girl? And what point was there in telling Tom such cruel gossip? Besides, she certainly wasn't about to tell him her plans for the following morning.

That night she dreamed about Zena again. She was wearing the dress Carmen had seen in the photograph taken at the awards ceremony, the silver sheath, and she was smiling at Carmen, watching her. Then Carmen realised that she was at the same event, only she was the one on stage and Zena was in the audience, watching her and smiling, and then her face started to melt.

Chapter 11

Tom left for work well before Carmen needed to get going, so she had plenty of time to shower and put on her best professional clothes – a black jersey dress that she rarely got to wear these days, a vintage Pucci scarf that Nick had brought her back from a shoot in Italy, brown boots. She tossed her hair out and clipped it in a topknot, put on lipstick. It felt good to get dressed up like this, to put on the armour, to walk out of the door and down to the station like a working person again. Who knows, maybe this Ross would offer her a real job – what the hell would she do then? But the thought made her happy.

He kept her waiting of course, but not for too long, and his secretary brought her a decent cup of coffee and some fizzy water. The company's publications were laid out on a stand in the lobby – they were mainly niche journals and hobby magazines, with a couple of bigger-name titles, including the one Zena had written for. She flicked through a copy as she waited. It hadn't changed much since Zena's day, still the same mix of fashion, beauty and lifestyle features. It wasn't bad, it was good even; it just wasn't really Carmen's thing.

'Carmen?' He smiled and came to meet her, held out his hand. He was wearing chinos with a white shirt worn loose, not a suit, and somehow that was annoying, the self-assurance – I don't need to do these things that other people do, work to these codes. Yet there was a warmth about him that she hadn't expected.

He led her through to a big office. Was that Tracey Emin on the wall an original? 'I was intrigued by your email,' he said. He spoke with a faint accent, too slight to place, north European. 'You said you had ideas for us.'

'Well –' she sat down – 'I thought maybe the kind of interviews I do would be good for your women's mags, a bit of a different perspective from just fashion.'

'Our women's magazines are not just about fashion.'

'Of course not, but ... sorry, it's just my work, what I do, it's a bit different. It's that bit more serious, I suppose. Did you look at my work?'

'Of course. I read the story where you interviewed single mothers.'

'Did you like it?'

'It was very interesting, but I am not sure how it would work in our magazines. It was a newspaper piece. So I am wondering what you were thinking for us?'

'Well, I've done much more than just that, and new things.'

He indicated she should tell him.

'Like, right now, I'm working on a piece about trafficking, girls who are . . .'

He was shaking his head. 'No, that is not for us. Our magazines are for women looking to escape the unpleasantness of the world, to unwind. Our readers are not unintelligent or uninterested, but they do not want to be confronted with these things while they are relaxing.'

Of course. Oh well, she had been making it up anyway. She had thought about writing a piece like that, that was all.

She didn't know what to say after that. He helped her out. 'Are you looking for a job?'

'Yes, do you have anything?'

'Not at the moment, but you obviously have talent, I can see that. You have to think about whether you want to adapt that to the work we do here.'

'I could, I'm sure. I mean, what's important to me – it's not so much who I'm talking to that matters, it's telling the truth about their lives. Not just some two-dimensional picture – do you know what I mean? People aren't like that, are they? And their lives aren't like that. And I think people know when they read things that are truthful. I think that's when they connect.'

She found herself blushing. What she was saying was exactly what she thought and felt about her work, but she hadn't put it into words before, not like that, and it felt emotional to do so, intimate. Ross held her eye as she spoke, nodded. He was really listening, being open, encouraging. She hadn't expected that.

'So why don't you tell me something about yourself?' he said. 'Something true, as you say.'

She paused, felt her blush deepen. And then she took a risk. 'My husband's ex used to work here,' she said.

'Your husband's ex?' He pulled a wry, questioning face.

'She worked for *Louise*.' Her heart was beating faster.

'What was her name?'

'Zena. Zena Johnson.'

'Zena was your husband's ex?'

'Yes, they were together when she died. You knew her?'

He shrugged. 'Of course. She was one of our stars.'

Nothing seemed to have changed. He didn't seem to be more guarded.

'It must have been very hard for your husband.'

'Yes, it was, yes.'

Ross stood up. He wanted her to go. She stayed in her seat.

'Did you know her well?' she said.

He shrugged. 'We are all colleagues here.'

'What was she like?'

There was a sharpening now, in the way Ross looked at her. He saw that as an inappropriate question, and of course it was, but why, in his eyes? Because it was weird, her coming here and asking about his dead colleague? Or because he had something to hide?

Carmen held his glance, refused to look away, to back down. Could she bluff this one through?

He laughed in the end. 'You are good at your job, I can tell that. You are not scared to ask questions,' he said. 'Zena? She was . . .' He looked around the room, seeking the right words. 'She was . . . talented, and she was ambitious.'

'She wanted to get on?'

'I don't just mean at work. She was ambitious in life. She wanted a lot from life. She wanted . . .' He paused, looking for the right word but couldn't find it.

'She was demanding?' said Carmen.

He shrugged. 'Of life, yes.' He looked at Carmen, whose face must have been registering the discomfort she was feeling, because he laughed. 'You shouldn't ask questions about your predecessor like this if you don't have the stomach.'

Carmen half smiled. 'Did you like her?'

'Yes, I liked her. She was –' he looked back at her – 'bold. Not unlike you in fact. That is very appealing in a woman. It is very attractive when a woman demands a lot from life. You want to give her the world.' He half smiled at her and she felt slightly uncomfortable. Was he flirting with her?

He saw her out to reception, having agreed that she would send him more ideas and that he would bear her in mind if anything suitable came up. As he said goodbye and shook her hand, a woman came out of an adjoining office whom Carmen recognised to be his wife, Stephanie. She was more attractive in the flesh, she had presence, carried herself with a confidence that didn't come across in her photograph. She glanced over at them and her look was cool, hard to read.

Carmen wasn't ready to go home so she walked through Soho and stopped off at a tiny Italian coffee bar. She sat up at the counter and sipped a cappuccino, checked her phone. Tom had texted – 'Clive's 40th 16 July, are we free?' – which irritated her. What was she? His PA now? And there was a

Facebook notification from Kath – a reminder about Lily's naming ceremony, which was coming up.

While she was on Facebook Carmen looked up Ross's profile again, his smiling face, but it didn't look quite so smug to her now. She'd liked him more than she'd expected. OK, she wouldn't want to be his wife – he was a flirt, that was very clear – but he had a nice way about him, the sort of man women like, and she thought his offer of help to her had been genuine. She should make use of that, get herself out there. On impulse she clicked the button on Facebook, sent him a friend request. It couldn't do any harm, to have Ross in her contacts. And she knew there was no danger there – he wasn't her type, not sexually.

Had he been Zena's?

Ross liked Zena for the person she was, and there is nothing more attractive than that. Did Tom like her in that way? Had he understood who Zena was when he got together with her? When he left Laura? Or had he been in love with a fantasy, the woman he wanted her to be?

Ross was a different species to Tom. Tom might look suave with his suit and his city smile, but at heart Carmen still believed he was a dog who wanted a good home, a domesticated creature, a man who wanted an easy life, an ordered world. A domesticated life would soon bore Ross, Carmen was sure of it – and it would have bored Zena too.

Tom had left his whole life for Zena: Laura, the children, his home. How would he have reacted if just months later . . .

And so Carmen's mind was off again, thinking, mulling it

all over. Was it possible? Was it possible that Zena drove Tom so crazy that he lost it completely?

When she got home Carmen found herself back in the spare room standing on a chair, opening the top box in the pile and reaching for Tom's old laptop. The battery had run flat the last time she had looked at it, when she had seen that awful download, but she decided to give it a go, however unlikely. But now as she reached in to take it out of the box she found there was a charger packed in alongside it – she must have just missed it before. What a dunce.

She plugged the laptop in and as it booted up the picture of Tom and Zena came into view again, but it barely affected her now, not in that emotional, possessive way. She looked at Zena's face, smiling, happy, totally in the moment.

Ross's words came back to her. He'd said Zena was bold. *Not unlike you in fact.* How weird that he'd seen them that way – as having something in common, as similar even. Carmen had never even contemplated that; she had seen Zena as a different species. Now, as she looked at the smiling face, questions formed in her mind as though she was communicating with the dead girl. What if things had been different and we'd met at work? Would you have made me laugh? Would I have made you laugh? Would we have been friends?

Slowly the ancient hard drive did its work and the folders popped into view. Carmen wanted to look at that downloads folder again, to check the time and date when Tom accessed those awful forensic documents. To confirm – was it before the police came or after? And if before, could she see any way an error might have occurred? How this could have happened? That detail had been bugging her since she had first seen it and she wanted to know for sure.

The downloads folder appeared at last and she clicked. It opened slowly.

There was nothing inside. It was empty.

She clicked again. Nothing.

She switched the computer off and back on, went through that whole rigmarole again, then again clicked on 'Downloads'.

There was nothing there, no files at all.

Perhaps she was looking in the wrong place. She remembered the labyrinthine way the documents had been filed on his hard drive and she tried to navigate back to them. There had been a folder called 'Documents', she was sure, with all the others inside it, but she couldn't find it now.

This was crazy. She remembered some of the things she'd looked at here. Letters to the school for example. She searched under Mel's name – she'd had her own folder she was sure, and Jake too. She searched but there was nothing.

She looked in the computer's trash can. It was empty. She looked for the date last emptied – Sunday, just four days ago.

And then she realised – Tom had done this. She hadn't touched this laptop since last week. He must have found the lead and powered up the computer and deleted everything on it – all his files, all his downloads, everything. They'd had their big talk on Saturday, when she'd told him that she had looked at this computer – he must have done this on Sunday. But when? They were together all day, all weekend. Except when she went to the shop on Sunday morning – that was the only time they'd been apart. But Jesus, she'd only been gone for half an hour, he would have had to work fast. He must have been determined, planned it in advance. And he'd said nothing to her. She remembered coming back; he was lying on the bed watching TV as though he hadn't moved.

She felt a chill run through her, that he could do that, that he had done that.

What was he trying to hide? Those downloads she'd found? But then why delete everything? It didn't make sense. Was he just trying to stop her nosing? More angry than he had shown? But it was such an extreme response.

Her blood ran cold. What else would she have found on here if she'd been able to take her time?

Chapter 12

Carmen was sitting on the beach below the bungalow. She'd driven up early. She had avoided Tom the night before – he'd been out late at some work event and she'd texted to ask if he'd mind sleeping in the spare room. He was happy to do that when he came in after midnight, so he didn't wake her – considerate Tom. Though in fact she'd been wide awake, lying in the dark, listening for him.

This morning she'd pretended to be asleep when he came in to their room to dress. He kissed her cheek as he left for work, whispered that he'd see her later in St Jude's. They were spending the weekend there with the children. She was going ahead to buy food, air the place, it was all arranged.

The tide was high today, coming in fast, bowling against the pebbles and dragging them back screeching with each return. Watching them, Carmen thought it could almost be true what Amy's doctor had said to her – that maybe the waves pushed Zena over, threw her against the seafloor and knocked her out, dragged her body back into the depths. It really could be true, there was enough power in the waves today. I wouldn't walk out into that sea, thought Carmen.

But it wasn't true, was it?

She thought about Amy sitting where she was sitting and watching Zena as a child plunging into these waves; of Amy catching her breath and shouting after her to stop, and Zena emerging through the crashing water grinning and triumphant.

'Hello.'

A voice cut into her thoughts. Carmen turned to look. Behind her stood a small woman, loaded down with carrier bags. She looked vaguely familiar.

'I hope you don't mind me saying hello,' said the woman. 'It's just . . . you live behind us. I'm Paula.'

'Of course,' said Carmen. She'd seen her in her garden, hanging out washing. She stood up and introduced herself.

'I saw you sitting there and I just thought I'd say hello. I've wanted to before, but it's a bit awkward over the fence.'

They both smiled. The woman projected an uncomplicated friendliness. 'Are you on your way home?' said Carmen.

'Yes.'

'I'll help you with your shopping if you like.'

'Oh, don't worry, it's my own fault. I got off the bus at the other end of the village because I like the walk down the beach, but it was a bit stupid with all these bags.'

'It's fine, I need to get back anyway.' Carmen took three of the carriers and they set off through the shingle.

'You live in London, don't you?' said Paula.

187

Carmen said yes and felt self-conscious that Paula must see her as a rich Londoner, a privileged second-homer. She felt an urge to say, Look, this isn't really me, I'm like you, just ordinary. 'My husband bought it before we were together, to make it easier to see his children,' she said.

'I've seen them. Where do they live then?'

'Near Diss with their mum. He was with someone else for a while, before me; that's when he bought the bungalow.'

'I know, the woman who died,' said Paula, and paused. 'In fact I was one of the people who found her body. Me and this other man.'

Carmen was astonished. 'Really?'

'Maybe I shouldn't say that . . .'

'Did you really?'

Paula nodded. 'I was just out walking the dog. I didn't even know who she was then. I didn't find out till afterwards.'

'That must have been – awful.'

'It was really. I had Cheyenne with me, my daughter, she was only little, only about five. Listen, am I being tactless, saying this to you?'

'No, not at all. What happened?'

'Well, it was a horrible day, raining, so there weren't many people about. I saw it . . . her, I mean, her body, on the beach, and so did this other man, and we called the police and they came but we had to wait ages.'

'Was she just lying there?'

'Yes, in her bikini, just lying on the pebbles like you or me but not, because . . . well, obviously she didn't look . . . you know.'

'What time was it?' said Carmen.

'What time?'

'You know – was it morning? Afternoon?'

'About lunchtime, I think. About this time.'

They were at the end of Paula's road. She reached for her bags but Carmen offered to take them to her door and they carried on. 'My husband Shaun, he knew her years ago.'

'Really?'

'She grew up round here, didn't she? They were about the same age.'

'Did you know her?'

Paula shook her head. 'I didn't remember her at all to be honest, but Shaun recognised her straight away. We saw her in the village. She didn't recognise him though. I mean, they didn't know each other well.'

Paula stopped walking – they were outside her home. Of course Carmen was dying to continue the conversation, but she didn't know what questions to ask, and she felt awkward, as though she needed to be careful. In a little place like this, whatever she said might become public knowledge. 'I bet there was a lot of gossip,' she said.

'Well, I don't listen to that. I'd better get in – the dog's waiting.'

There was a springer spaniel in the window, looking out at them. 'Would you like to have a coffee sometime?' Carmen said, impulsively.

Paula looked a bit surprised but said, 'I don't mind, yes.'

'When are you free?'

'Oh, just pop round sometime.'

When Carmen got home she sat on the sofa and thought about what Paula had told her, about finding Zena's body. She thought about Tom sitting where she was sitting now, alone, waiting, as Paula walked down the beach through the rain, as Zena lay dead on the shingle, as the police were called. She worked it out – it would have been more than forty hours since Tom had last seen Zena. What was he thinking? Was he in a silent torment? Was he still hoping and praying? Or was he scared of what the tide might bring in?

He hadn't wanted anyone with him. He'd wanted to be alone. That had bothered her since he'd told her, it just wasn't right. Why didn't he call a friend? Tom had old friends, good friends. Who would choose to be alone at a time like that? Unless you were lying and it was easier not to have to put on an act. If you were lying, it would be easier to deal with it alone.

The police had come here later that day, to tell Tom they'd found Zena's body, to question him. They were suspicious by then. They knew there had been an argument – Tom had told her that – and they were suspicious that he'd attacked her, killed her, somehow dumped her body in the sea. They'd questioned him that afternoon and again later on, but at some point they'd stopped questioning him, left him alone. Was that because the evidence had shown them they were wrong? Had the autopsy exonerated him?

Or was it just that there was no clear evidence either way?

Did the police think Tom was innocent? Or did they think that he had got away with murder?

If only I could know that, thought Carmen – if only I could see it in black and white, that they knew it wasn't him, that in the end they believed it was an accident. If only I could hear a police officer say, 'It wasn't him, of course not, just ignore what you hear, it's gossip, nothing more.'

Or the other way . . .

There was an officer who'd stayed with Tom. Tom had told her that – a nice man who'd given him support. Would he be able to tell her anything? But how could she find him?

Someone else had mentioned the same man – Cheryl, the sister of the boy who had died. Cheryl had met Tom and Amy after Zena had died and it was that same officer who had brought the families together. A nice guy, Cheryl had said. Had she said his name?

Carmen often made notes without thinking when she talked on the phone – a journalist's habit. She emptied her handbag, looked through – yes, there it was, written in her little note-book:

Cheryl

Jeremy

Jet ski

Uni

Drinking

Andy

That was his name. Andy.

She googled the number for the local police station.

Chapter 13

Carmen waited in a small room lined with hard chairs. The only other person there was a young woman who looked completely out of it and stared at a fixed point on the floor. Carmen was nervous, although everything had gone OK so far. She had thought it would be difficult to persuade the police to speak to her, but when she had called the station and asked for Andy in victim support, she had got straight through, and he'd said come in and we'll see what we can do. Although obviously she hadn't told him the whole truth.

She'd been waiting twenty minutes already, but they had warned her he was busy. An officer came to fetch the other woman. Carmen checked her phone for the tenth time and there was an email saying Ross had accepted her friend request on Facebook. He'd sent her a smiley.

Bingo. Now she might have access to Zena's home page.

She logged on and ... yes, there it was, Zena's profile, a list of posts, the first one showing Zena in a red bikini top, a head-and-shoulders shot, on the beach, a selfie. 'Our weekend place – sun is out!' She checked the date. It was two weeks before Zena died.

Carmen scrolled down the page. It was a catalogue of Zena selfies. Zena in a low-cut party dress with a couple of other women – 'Great night at Bar 7 with the work crew'. Zena with her hair in a towel – 'Dyeing tonight'. Zena with the prime minister's wife – this one was from the awards night that Carmen had seen on the magazine website, she could see the top of Zena's silver sheath dress though this was a close-up. Both women were smiling, and it was captioned: 'Still high from this extraordinary experience'.

And so it went on. Zena sitting on a bus. Zena in a hat. Zena with a famous fashion designer – 'Get me, front row'. It was strange, so different to the sort of Facebook page Carmen was used to. Her friends posted snapshots with their kids, or jokey shots, or news reports and petitions to sign. This was more like a teenager's page, or that was how it seemed to Carmen. Self-absorbed. Happy.

Carmen clicked on Zena's friends. There were 183, several working at the same company, quite a few men. Apart from Ross there was no one whose name Carmen recognised, and no one who listed St Jude's or anywhere nearby as a location.

The door opened. 'Carmen? I'm Andy.' He smiled and held out his hand to shake hers, and she smiled back and the smile stayed on her face. He had the sort of face that had that effect: friendly eyes that looked straight into hers, brown hair with a wave that made him look boyish. An open, warm face.

'Come through, where we can talk,' he said, and she put her phone in her bag as he led her out and along a corridor. 'Did you come far today?'

'Just from St Jude's.'

'That road can be a nightmare.'

'It wasn't too bad.'

He invited her into a small room with a table, offered her a seat, then sat down opposite. 'So what can I do for you?'

She had told him on the phone that she wanted to talk about Zena's case, said she hadn't been around when the death had happened, implied she was a relative. Now she looked at his kind face sitting across the desk from her, and she took a chance. 'Can I be honest with you?'

If he was surprised he didn't show it. 'It's usually best.'

'When I said I was a relative – actually I'm married to Tom Cawton. I met him a year after Zena died.' She looked at him, looked away. 'I guess the reason I'm here . . . I need to know what happened.'

He moved his hand slightly and his fingers touched the file that was on the desk in front of him. Carmen sensed a change in his attitude, a closing-up, and regretted speaking out. She should have stuck to her story.

'I see,' he said.

He said nothing more for many seconds that felt like many minutes, and Carmen found herself fighting a great pressure from within to gabble on. She knew the pressure came from his silence, and her own sense of guilt because she hadn't told him the truth, but it was hard to resist. I have done nothing wrong, she told herself. Why shouldn't I come here and ask?

'The conclusion of the inquest was that she drowned,' he said finally.

'I know that, but it doesn't tell me what happened, does it? I have to know – can't you see that?'

'Wouldn't it be more appropriate to talk to your husband?'

'No. I mean, I have done, but . . . I know he was a suspect. I know he was questioned.'

His hand still rested on the file. 'He was never charged with anything.'

'Yes, but . . .' She looked at him. He looked at the file. 'I know you were with him, during that time.'

He knew what she was asking.

He tapped his fingers on the table. 'Your husband's a lawyer. What happens during an investigation is confidential. I can't just talk to you about it.'

Carmen studied him, tried to work out what he was thinking, but the shutters were down. Maybe he wanted to tell her more, maybe he did, but he wasn't going to. Besides, his silence was telling her plenty, wasn't it?

'I'm sorry, I shouldn't have come here,' Carmen said, and stood up.

The officer stood up too and they walked towards the door. He reached past her to open it. 'I wish I could have helped you more,' he said, and she felt a moment of panic. She turned to him then, touched his sleeve.

195

'Please,' she said, 'I need to know if I'm married to a violent man.'

His hand was on the handle but he didn't turn it. He paused and they stood almost touching.

'Please. I won't ever repeat anything you tell me.'

They stood there like that. 'Please.'

When he spoke he spoke quietly. 'OK. But this is off the record and if you ever refer to anything I say now, I'll deny it. I'll say that our conversation ended thirty seconds ago.'

'It won't happen, I promise.'

'The answer is that we don't know what happened to Zena. Her death was probably an accident, but we don't know for sure and we probably never will.'

'So it is possible she was killed.'

'It's possible.'

'So Tom . . .'

'He was a person of interest from the time we first realised there was a serious chance that Zena was dead.'

'Because he was her boyfriend? I've heard the partner is always the first suspect.'

'No, because he lied to us.'

'He lied to you?'

'He told us he had not been to the beach at all that day, but he was seen there that evening.'

'He went looking for her,' said Carmen. 'He told me.'

'He told us that too, but only once we told him he'd been seen. If people lie to us, it makes us suspicious.'

Carmen blushed.

'Plus we had reports of an argument at their house shortly before Zena went missing.'

'Who told you that? A neighbour?'

'I think it was more than one person. People come forward in a small community.'

Carmen thought for a moment. 'Tom told me you got suspicious when you found her body, because there was a head wound.'

'Of course, but like I say, there were already concerns.'

'Because he lied?'

'Because he lied, and because there were frictions in their relationship. And because it was raining.'

'Why did that matter?'

'Would you choose to go swimming in the rain?'

No, she wouldn't, of course not.

Kyle, the guy who ran the water-sports operation, had told her the weather was bad that day, but she hadn't thought about it like that.

'So why did he stop being a suspect?'

'Because the autopsy showed that she died from drowning and not from the head injury, and that pointed towards an accident.'

'So the injury happened in the water?'

'It wasn't that clear-cut. From what I remember, they couldn't say where the injury happened or even whether it happened before she died or after. But what was said for sure was that the cause of death was drowning, not the head wound, and that immediately made the whole situation less suspicious. The most probable explanation became that she got in trouble in the water, or there was an accident of some sort, and that she drowned as a result. Accidental drowning is very common.'

'So in other words he didn't hit her over the head and dump her in the sea?'

'Well, if he did, she was still alive when she went into the water.'

Carmen looked up. 'Is that what you think happened?'

'I didn't say that. I'm just telling you about the evidence. With drowning, everything is hard to prove. Including innocence.'

'But it doesn't make sense. How could he carry a body to the sea in broad daylight and not be seen?'

'He didn't report her missing until late at night.'

Of course, of course. But still . . . 'I read it might have been a jet ski.'

He shook his head.

'Why? How can you know?'

'Her injuries weren't consistent with a jet-ski collision. Plus, like I said, it was raining – there were no jet-skiers on the water.'

It was the way Kyle had said. 'How did Tom react when you started to suspect him?'

Andy shrugged. 'Your husband's a lawyer. He's cool under pressure.'

'What about when he was told about the head wound? How did he react to that?'

'That came later. I wasn't there.'

Carmen was confused, and he saw it.

198

'They didn't tell him straight away, when they found her body.'

'Why not?'

'To see how he'd react, what he'd say. They left it a day or so. It's how we work sometimes.'

Carmen realised her hands were clasped as though she was praying.

'Are we done?' said Andy.

She looked at him. There was a wall all around him. She thought about her instinctive liking of this man, before he knew who she was. And yet he'd stuck his neck out to help her. 'You spent time with him, didn't you?' she said. 'Do you think he was lying?'

He paused for a few moments, and then he shook his head and said, 'I can't help you any more.'

There was nothing else to say. Carmen left and drove around for a while. When she got back to St Jude's she didn't go to the bungalow but parked in the centre of the village and walked to one of the seafront cafes. She sat at the back, at a little window table looking out over the shingle garden, her hands cradling a mug of tea.

Less than a week ago she had sat at her kitchen table with Tom as he had begged her to believe that he had never hurt Zena, and she had believed him. She had been certain in that moment, and after the terrible doubt and anxiety it had felt like falling in love all over again. Clear blue skies, relief, hallelujah!

But only a few days on and it had all crumbled away, all that certainty, her belief in him. First meeting Hope and discovering about Ross, that Tom was possibly being driven half mad with jealousy. Then the way Tom had cleared the computer. Now this.

It wasn't just that support officer's obvious uncertainty about Tom's innocence, it was those downloads again. Andy had told her that the police didn't disclose Zena's head injury to Tom when they first told him she was dead. So how could there be an innocent explanation for his downloading those documents, whatever time he did it? Even if the 5 a.m. she remembered was wrong – even if they had been downloaded at 5 p.m. – Tom should still not have known that Zena had a head injury.

And yet he had known.

She had realised as soon as Andy had told her, the implications, but she had said nothing to him. She could have asked him more, asked him why, or when, but she hadn't wanted to draw attention to this point.

She was protecting Tom. Why?

Sitting there sipping her tea, Carmen faced head-on the fact that she didn't believe Tom any more. She didn't believe in his innocence. How could she, after the way he'd acted?

She had known when she went to the police station today. She had known before that officer had even opened his mouth, even if she had not yet admitted it to herself.

She nursed the warm mug. None of it felt like a mystery any more. She could see how it had happened, and it all made sense. Zena and Ross. Whether she was flirting with him, sleeping with him or about to leave Tom – that was irrelevant. The point was that a new man was in the picture, she'd met someone else, as had been certain to happen at some stage because everything Carmen had heard or knew about Zena said that that was true. And Tom, if he'd found out, of course he wouldn't have been able to handle it, because that was the sort of man he was. And so soon after leaving Laura and the children to be with Zena – what would he have done?

Well, she knew, didn't she? She had seen for herself the way Tom responded when he was jealous, that night in the arches in Brixton.

Carmen sipped her tea and thought these thoughts and wondered at how calm she felt, how clear her head was. You spend so long in the fog, worrying about what-ifs that will probably never happen, barricading yourself psychically against them with this thought and that, this worry and that distraction. And yet here it was. The worst had happened and all was calm and all was clear.

She felt that she understood, and she sympathised. She understood who Zena was and who Tom was and what had happened between them and what had happened next. She could see it all, like a story written out on a page, a tragedy that had the roots of its conclusion written into the very first line.

And the strangest thing of all was that even though she now felt sure that Tom was guilty, it was somehow all right. She didn't want her marriage to end, and she didn't feel it needed to. They could go on. She was not afraid; she didn't believe Tom was a danger to her. I can live with what I know and what I don't know, she thought. This does not need to be the end.

Her phone beeped. There was a text – it was from Nick, her ex, just saying hello, how are you? He was in London for a few days if she fancied a coffee. He contacted her like this from time to time so it wasn't a total surprise, but her response to it was. Her calm of a moment before was completely punctured and she experienced a tsunami of emotion. Tears streamed down her cheeks and she had to bend her head so no one would notice. She felt an overwhelming desire for things to be the way they used to, for things to be simple. You're wrong, Kieran, she thought. I knew Nick, I really knew him and I trusted him, and the remembrance of how that felt flooded her with loneliness and with grief.

Chapter 14

It was after nine when Tom and the children arrived. Mel and Jake were the first to the door, and pushed past Carmen in the rush for the TV remote control. 'Is there anything to eat?' said Jake.

'I've made a curry.'

'What sort?'

'Thai green chicken.'

'Sick.'

Carmen heard the TV click into life. Mercy was waiting in front of her, her finger pulling her lip down to show a gap in her teeth. Carmen crouched down. 'Look at that!' she said. 'Did the tooth fairy come?'

Mercy nodded. 'She gave me a pound.'

'Unfair, I used to get 20p,' called Jake from the living room.

'That's inflation, Jake,' said Tom.

He was standing in the doorway, a holdall in each hand. Carmen looked up at him.

'What, four hundred per cent?' said Jake.

Tom put the bags down and reached out to take her hand. She let herself be pulled to her feet. Her stomach was tight with emotion.

He reached for her, pulled her to him. 'Yeuch,' shouted Jake from the sofa, and normally Tom would have laughed and let go of her, but he pushed the door shut and took her in his arms again.

It's as though he knows, she thought.

He touched her cheek. 'I love you,' he said.

It's as though he knows.

Saturday dawned hot and bright, with clear blue skies and white sun. They spent the day on the beach, Carmen in a camping chair by the water, reading the paper, playing with Mercy on the sand flats that appeared below the pebbles at low tide. Everything was normal, as it should be, and yet nothing was. She and Tom talked about this and that, his week in the office, stories in the news – everyday things that only heightened the sense of unreality. Carmen felt detached, as though she was looking down on them all sitting there, watching a scene play out on TV.

She told Tom about meeting Paula on the beach here the day before, and what Paula had told her about Zena, that she had been one of the people who had found her body. Tom said how strange that was, that he never knew it before, never even thought about who found her.

The waves lapped around Carmen's chair, her feet. 'Do you think about her, when you sit here?' Carmen said.

'Not now.'

'Is this where she swam from that day?'

He shrugged. 'I don't know. Somewhere near here.'

'Why didn't she swim further along, where it was safer?'

'She didn't like the walk. And it was quieter here.'

A little later Carmen said, 'Did you think about selling the bungalow? After it happened?'

He had returned to the paper. He looked up. 'No,' he said.

'Wasn't it hard though, coming back?'

'At first. But then I was with you and it was all different.'

He'd had the bungalow decorated when they got married, painted over the uniform white. She'd chosen the paints, a different colour for each room. She'd seen it as symbolic, him marking a break with the past.

Carmen shivered. She moved her chair out of the water, up on to the pebbles.

'Do you think it's weird that I didn't sell the place?' said Tom.

'I was just thinking it must have been strange for you, that's all.'

'You have to remember I'd only just bought it when Zena died. We'd only been a few times. And remember I know St Jude's from years ago, from my grandparents – there are lots of memories for me here, quite apart from all of that.'

'Of course, I was forgetting.'

Tom's grandparents had lived in St Jude's, and he'd spent a lot of time there as a child, including being shipped up from London for holidays while his mother worked. And of course Zena had grown up nearby. It must have felt like a great coincidence when they discovered this link between their child-hoods, that they had been spent, at least partly, on the same soil. They would have seen it as fate, Carmen thought. And of course as well as needing somewhere to bring the children, Zena's mother still lived nearby. No wonder they bought the bungalow so quickly.

'Tell me about your grandparents,' she said.

He'd loved them, loved those parts of his childhood – he'd told Carmen all about it in the early days of their relation-ship, as they shared their stories over lazy hours and weeks in restaurants and in bed. They were both long dead, buried alongside Tom's mother, their daughter. She'd died in a car accident when Tom was a teenager.

'I've told you.'

'Tell me again. I want to hear about them.'

He put his paper down. 'Well, they were just very nice people. Grandfather was a doctor, though he was already retired when I was a child, but he did lots of voluntary work, and Grand-mother was one of those pillars of the community, on the parish council and all that sort of thing, always making jam and looking after people. It was just – their house was a lovely place to be, for a child. I loved to be there.'

'Making jam with your gran?'

'Or fishing with Grandfather. He used to bring me here fishing like those guys over there. Or going to see neighbours, or working on things.'

'What things?'

'I don't know – in the garden, big bonfires, doing something

206

at the church. I just remember everyone smiling all the time, everyone cheerful.'

'It sounds lovely.'

'They were always busy but they included me. They always had time for me.'

'Unlike your dad.'

Tom raised his eyebrows.

'Even when he and your mum were still together? Was he not more involved with you then?'

'He was away most of the time.'

'But your mum was around for you.'

He shrugged. 'She was working a lot, and when she wasn't . . .' He didn't finish.

'What?'

'Looking back now, I'm not sure that she really wanted kids. Maybe she was just too young, I don't know, I just felt like . . . a nuisance to be honest. I mean she was nice but . . . she wanted me to be no trouble.' He paused. 'She liked to show me off, she liked it when I was successful, and popular, but if I had a problem . . .' He shook his head. Then he smiled at her. 'Poor me, eh?'

'So you didn't tell her your problems?'

He shook his head. 'Everything had to be fine. I mean, it wasn't that big a deal, people make too much of these things.'

Carmen would usually tease him for that, his way of telling her something and then pulling back, making out it was nothing, but she didn't today. 'Lucia may not be perfect, but she was always on my side,' she said.

Carmen had never heard Tom criticise his mother before. She should have realised – he'd always talked about her with admiration but no real warmth. She had been quite something, a real beauty, and when her marriage to Tom's father broke up she'd moved into design and made a name for herself. Carmen had just assumed they were close enough. She'd refused to send him to boarding school like many of his friends, he'd told Carmen that, which had seemed to say a lot.

'I don't think my mother was a very happy person,' he said.

'You've never talked about her like this before.'

'Haven't I?'

'No.'

'Maybe they're new thoughts. Your influence.' He leaned over, touched her knee. 'Making me think more.'

'Have you been thinking about the past?'

'Not particularly. Why?'

She shrugged. 'I don't know. History repeats itself, doesn't it?'

'Does it?'

'Well, at an obvious level, your dad was an absent parent, wasn't he?'

'Thanks for pointing that out, Carmen. Actually I am nothing like my dad.'

She smiled. 'Sorry.'

'What else are you saying? That Laura was like my mum?'

Carmen hadn't thought about that at all, but Tom obviously had. 'Well, was she?'

'Not really, no.'

'But a bit?'

'Well, she's quite a cool person, not very emotional.'

'So would you describe me as warm then?'

He laughed. 'Just a bit.'

'Was Zena warm?'

He looked away. 'I thought she was, at first.'

'But she wasn't?'

He shook his head. 'No.'

He picked up his paper then, and Carmen didn't ask any more. She felt she knew what had been left unsaid: Zena was hard not soft, sexual but not warm.

Tom looked up. 'So with your therapist's hat on, what else can you tell me?'

'Well . . . this is probably really obvious, but do you think your mum dying had anything to do with you getting married so young?'

'You think I was looking for a surrogate mother?'

'Well, maybe, or another family – I know it sounds a bit obvious . . .'

'It has been said before.'

Carmen leaned forward in her chair. 'Tom, why didn't you and Laura get back together? After Zena died?'

'We've talked about this. It was too late.'

'Did you try?'

He shook his head. 'It wouldn't have worked. Everything had changed.'

Carmen was about to ask him more when he said, 'So according to your theories, what was I looking for with Zena?'

She shrugged. 'I don't know. You tell me.'

He brushed his foot against the water. And then he looked at her and there was real sadness in his eyes, an intensity. She thought he was going to tell her something, something important, but then she felt the moment pass.

When he spoke again his voice was lighter. 'At least I know what I'm looking for in you.'

'What?'

'Someone to spend the rest of my life with.'

Carmen felt irritated, patronised. She knew he had been about to tell her something that was true and maybe hard. 'What were you going to say about Zena?'

He sat back in his chair. 'I don't know. Theories, they sound good, but . . . you can't explain everything.'

Later on, he and Jake drove over to the supermarket and bought meat, bread and salad, carried it down to the beach with the barbecue gear. Even on a scorching day like this the section of the shore by the bungalow was not crowded. Most people clustered near the car parks on the main beach, which was sandier with a gentler slope into the sea, but the few who had made it this far evaporated as the warmth went out of the sun until they were alone. Tom set the barbecue up beside one of the timber groynes that punctuated the beach and they sat together in its lee, looking out across the sea towards Europe.

The charcoal turned white and Tom started the meat. Jake told them about his end-of-term school play – *Mulan*, which was bad enough since it was based on a Disney film and they were in Year 9, but it got worse because he had been cast as one of the leading warriors, which sounds like a great role but he had to disguise himself as a woman to infiltrate the enemy, and one of his classmates, the leader of the opposing army, had to try to get off with him … They all laughed of course, and Mercy said 'What, a boy has to try and kiss you?' and Mel looked up from her phone and said, 'You are so gay, Jake,' and Jake kicked her and she said it again and he slapped her and she laughed at him and said, 'But you are, everyone knows that.'

Jake kicked her again, harder, and Carmen nudged Tom, who said, 'Mel!'

'Well, he is,' said Mel, and Jake kicked her really hard.

'Mel. Stop that,' said Tom.

'What do you mean, me? It was him who kicked me.' She kicked Jake back.

'Mel!' said Tom.

'You always side with him.' Then she swore and leaped out of her chair and marched off up the beach.

Mercy looked upset and Tom pulled her on to his knee. 'It's OK,' he said. 'She's just being rude.'

'For a change,' said Jake.

'What's gay?' sniffed Mercy.

Carmen left Tom to explain and walked after Mel up the shingle to the top of the beach, but she was nowhere to be seen, disappeared already. She looked back down the slope – Jake was laughing, she could see. He walked up to meet her. 'Dad's trying to tell Mercy what gay means,' he said.

'You shouldn't let Mel wind you up like that,' she said.

He shrugged.

'Is she like that at home?'

'Sometimes. She's OK.'

He didn't want to talk about it.

The four of them sat together and ate more food and Jake entertained them with stories from school, opening up in the space left by Mel. And that made Carmen feel sorry for Mel, for being the toxic one, because everyone would think the same way, and that made her think of Kieran and feel sad for him too.

Every now and then she glanced up the beach to see if Mel was on her way back. 'Should we go and look for her?' she said to Tom after a while.

'She's fifteen. She can look after herself.'

'She knows people here,' said Jake.

'From school?' said Tom.

He shrugged.

'Do people go to your school from St Jude's then?' said Carmen. 'It's miles away.'

Jake shrugged again.

Carmen had never told Tom about the time she bumped into Mel in the village on a school day. She had forgotten about it in the midst of everything else. Maybe she would have told him now, at this moment, but then Mel appeared.

'Where have you been?' said Tom.

'Nowhere.'

'Where?'

'Just about.'

'Have you been with your friend?' said Carmen.

'Jake said you've got friends here,' said Tom.

'I've just been walking about. Can we talk about something else, please?'

'I'm just asking about your friends,' said Tom. 'Who do you know here?'

'Just someone from school.'

'Well, you should invite her over when we're up here.'

'She could come for lunch,' said Carmen.

'Is there any Coke left?'

'Here's some, Mel,' said Mercy, and carried the bottle over to her.

'Thanks.'

'*Eeeeeeaaaaaaaa.*' A shriek came from further along the beach, so sudden and distressing that they all stood up.

'What is it?' said Mercy, hugging into Mel's side.

The noise came again – they could see movement now too, something moving, further along but before the next groyne. They ran over, no one thinking to protect Mercy from whatever was there.

It was a seagull, tangled in fishing line, floundering on the pebbles, the nylon wrapped around its wings and throat, caught around its foot so it couldn't stand. It was struggling to get free, the line cutting into its feathers, into its flesh.

'God, help it!' said Carmen, and looked to Tom. 'Can't you help it?'

He stepped towards it, unsure what to do. Mercy started to scream. 'Daddy, get it out.'

But as he approached the tortured creature panicked and flapped its useless wings and screamed again. Tom stepped back.

'Help it, Daddy! Help it!'

'Get her away,' said Tom to Mel.

'Daddy!'

'Get her away!' ordered Tom, and Mel turned with her and led her up the beach.

Still the poor bird struggled and screamed.

'I don't know what to do,' said Tom. 'If I go near it, it makes it worse.'

'We should call the RSPCA,' said Carmen.

Then Jake moved forward, so quickly they didn't really know what was happening. He walked right up to the bird and lifted his foot and stamped on its head.

Carmen put her hand to her mouth. She thought she must have screamed, but nothing came out.

Then Mercy was screaming, standing at the top of the beach screaming, with Mel trying to turn her around.

Jake lifted his foot, stamped again and the dreadful noise from the bird stopped, but Mercy was still screaming, 'No!'

Carmen ran up the beach to where Mercy was standing with Mel, Mel trying to shield her, to turn her away. 'Come on, we're going home,' Carmen said, and took Mercy's hand, and she and Mel pulled her, hysterical now, across the pebbles. Gradually her screams turned to sobs. When they were out of sight they stopped, and first Mel and then Carmen hugged her, and then Carmen realised that Mel was crying too and she hugged her as well.

'Why did he do that?' hiccupped Mercy.

'He stopped it hurting,' said Carmen. 'The bird couldn't be saved. It was going to die. It was better it died quickly.'

They took her back to the bungalow and Carmen made hot chocolate and sat both girls in front of the TV and they were all calm again when Tom and Jake arrived back half an hour later, laden down with all the bags and chairs and detritus of the day.

'Are you OK?' Carmen said to Jake, and he nodded and went to join the others in front of the TV.

'Is Jake OK?' Carmen asked Tom, later in bed.

'Yes.'

'What happened on the beach, after we left?'

'We just packed up and came home.'

'Did you talk about it?'

'Not really. He was good, wasn't he? I didn't know what to do.'

'But it was so brutal.'

Tom reached out and held her. 'You're such a city girl, Carmen. Jake's grown up in the country – killing animals is part of life for him.'

'Well, Mercy didn't seem so happy with it. Or Mel come to that – she was crying.'

He kissed her face. 'Were you upset?'

'Yes.'

'Carmen, imagine if he hadn't done it. It would have been worse, wouldn't it? If the seagull had taken hours to die and we had done nothing.'

It was true of course, but still. 'Weren't you a bit upset? To see that?'

'Well, it was horrible, but I am proud of him for doing it.'

He was right, of course. Jake had taken responsibility when no one else would, but still.

She shivered.

'He's grown up with Laura – she's a countrywoman, she can stamp on a mouse if she has to. We're very soft about these things.'

'You feel the same as me then?'

'Yes, but I'm not proud of it.'

Tom wasn't a country boy. Tom was a Londoner like her, only a different kind, west not south; Georgian terrace not housing-association flat; £7,000-a-term school not inner-city comprehensive. They connected and they disconnected all the time.

He pulled her to him, kissed her on the mouth, gently coaxed her lips apart. She pulled away. 'Not in the mood?' he said.

She shook her head.

'Is it the bird?'

She half nodded.

He rolled on to his back. She rolled on to hers so they were lying side by side. 'Why did Jake see a counsellor?' she said. 'After you and Laura split up.'

'Did I tell you about that?' he said. 'I'd almost forgotten. Oh, I don't know, there was some incident – something and nothing.'

'What happened?'

Tom thought for a moment. 'He cut himself, made some marks on his arm.'

'My God!' said Carmen.

'It was something and nothing, just being a drama queen.'

'Tom!'

'Well . . .'

'Was he upset about the break-up?'

'I suppose that's the obvious explanation.'

He hadn't told her about that either, another thing . . .

Carmen reached over, put her hand on his chest. He put his hand over hers.

'Tom, tomorrow – do you mind if I don't come back with you? I want to stay here for a couple of days – get some work done. It's quiet here.'

If he was surprised he didn't say so, but he moved his hand. 'OK, if that's what you want.'

Tom woke her in the night. He was having a nightmare, thrashing about like a small boy except he was a huge man. She shook him and he opened his eyes and he didn't recognise her, just stared at her.

'Tom!' she said, frightened.

And then he woke properly and his face relaxed and he put his arms around her and pulled her tight to him. 'I'm so scared of it going wrong,' he said. But the next breath he was snoring and she never knew whether he was talking about them or something else entirely.

Chapter 15

Tom and the children left at teatime on Sunday. At midday on Monday Carmen was at the station in St Jude's waiting to meet Nick, her ex-boyfriend, off the train.

She felt sick with anticipation, and fearful that she would be caught out somehow, because she hadn't told Tom that Nick was coming.

What the hell am I doing?

She kept asking herself and she didn't have a good answer. If Kath or another of her friends had appeared and asked her, 'What are you up to Carmen?' she would have said something like, I don't know but I'm in this crazy situation, the foundation of my world has turned out to be a lie, and I'm probably going to go with it, but right now I need to go back to this old world, just for a bit. Just for a moment I need to go back to the person I was before all of this started, to find my strength.

It would be the first time she had seen Nick since they split up three years ago. He got in touch every few months, just a chatty text to say hello, how are you, and catch up on gossip.

His tone was friendly and light and she replied in the same vein, but she had never responded to his invitations to meet up.

But his last text, as she sat in the cafe in St Jude's, had caught her at a weak moment. She'd replied, said she wasn't in London, she was at their place on the coast, and he'd texted straight back: 'I can come there, I fancy a bit of sea air.'

His face flashed past as the train came in – he was in the front carriage, but she could see that he was grinning with his whole face the way he did, and when he stepped out on to the platform she was grinning too – she could not have held her muscles still even if she had tried. He rushed towards her – all she could see was his smile, and when he reached her neither of them knew what to do because the obvious thing was to hug but they couldn't do that. He reached forward spontaneously and gripped her arm and squeezed it before letting it go. 'You look exactly the same.'

'It's only been three years. I'd hope so.'

A woman was watching them. 'Come on,' he said. 'Let's get out of here.'

Inside her pocket she felt for the switch on her phone and turned it off.

They walked along the main street and he chattered away to cover up his nervousness though it was still completely obvious, which was something she had always liked about him and forgotten all about, the way he tried to be cool but it was always so clear how he felt. He told her about the woman who had sat opposite him on the journey and the painstaking way she had extracted and eaten one item of food after another out of the trolley bag she had sitting beside her so that her lunch lasted the whole journey. He acted out the way she had eaten each item and Carmen giggled along. They could have been seventeen again, walking home from school, or twenty-two, walking back from Soho on a Saturday night, or thirty, walking back to her flat. So much so that it would have seemed the most natural thing in the world to put her arm through his and she had to stop herself doing so.

'Where are we going anyway?' he said.

'I don't know. Are you hungry?'

'After watching that woman eat all the way here? Yes.'

'Well, we can go to the pub or I can put some food together and we can go to the beach?'

He said he'd prefer the beach, so they stopped off at the bungalow and suddenly they were alone together and the laughter stopped. Nick tried to keep it going – he darted from room to room, showing himself around and calling out comments – but Carmen felt self-conscious and he quickly picked up her mood.

He came and stood in the doorway of the kitchen, watching her.

'It's so weird,' he said.

'What? Seeing me?'

'Yes, that. Seeing you in this life.'

'What do you mean?'

'I don't know, this.' He held his arms out. 'This.'

'We don't live here, you know that. I still live in my old flat in London.'

'It's not that.'

'You mean the second-home thing?'

'No, I don't know, it's like you've grown up.'

'Well, I am thirty-five.'

'That's not what I mean.'

'What do you mean?'

'I don't know – you've changed, I guess.'

'Of course I have. So have you.'

He shook his head. 'I haven't changed at all.'

'Yeah, right.'

He was shaking his head still. 'No, I haven't, Carmen, not at all, I promise you.'

Carmen, slicing cucumber, felt herself become more brisk. 'Is chicken and salad and bread all right?' she said.

Perfect, he indicated.

'I was going to make sandwiches but I thought you might have gone all LA and stopped eating bread?'

He laughed, delighted to be teased about his success.

They carried a blanket down to the beach and she set the chiller bag between them. She'd put together some leftovers – bread, chicken, tomatoes, mayonnaise, and a bottle of wine. Even before she set the food out on the blanket she poured herself a glass and drank half of it straight down and felt better.

He laughed at her. 'I've missed you, Carmen,' he said. 'Can I have some of that?'

She poured him a glass.

'I don't mean that in a heavy way, about missing you, just that ... we're old friends, aren't we? I mean ...' He stopped himself.

She didn't reply, just smiled vaguely. But she thought about it and she thought, no, that's completely untrue, we're not old friends, we've never been friends, always girlfriend and boyfriend or 'taking a break', never friends. But she didn't say anything because she knew what he meant. That feeling of being with someone you have known for so long, spent so much of your life with. Someone from before.

A couple with a dog walked close by them and stared and it wasn't the first time that day it had happened. When they had passed by Carmen said, 'What is wrong with these people. God, it's so different to London, like going back thirty years. Do you think they've never seen a black man with a white woman?'

'I don't think it's that,' said Nick.

'What then?'

'I think they recognise me.'

'No! Do you think that's what it is? How weird.' She looked after them. The woman turned back once, caught her eye and turned away. 'God, do you really think that's it?'

He shrugged, as though to say, Comes with the territory.

'Are you sure? I mean I know you're doing well, but – would they really recognise you?'

'It happens a lot now.'

'Wow, that must be so strange.'

'I've got used to it,' he said. 'I mean often they don't know who I am, they just sort of recognise me. They say hello because they think they know me.'

'What do you do?'

'I say hello back.'

She smiled. He would as well, that's exactly what he'd do. 'Tell me about your life,' she said.

'What do you mean?'

'I don't even know where you live.'

'I've rented a place in LA, but I'm travelling a lot. I spent a lot of last winter in Thailand filming a big drama – it's out in the States next year. It's not a massive part, but it's interesting.'

'That's great. And you're working all the time?'

'A lot of the time, at the moment. It probably won't last.'

She could tell he was just saying that, that he thought this was it now. 'It's amazing,' she said.

'It's mental really.'

'And is it all very celeby?'

'What do you mean?'

'I don't know, parties, premieres.'

'Well, yeah, a bit.' He grinned again. 'You get used to all that pretty quickly.'

'I bet you love it,' she said, and he grinned again. He couldn't contain it and why should he? His dream had come true, hadn't it? Who'd ever have imagined it?

She poured more wine and lay back on the blanket. It was a relief to slip into a lobotomised neutral, to let the alcohol take her to that gilded place where everything seems like it's just fine. Everything. Lying here with Nick who was famous, married to a man who might have killed someone – all just fine.

There were some great clouds in the sky, white with dark undersides, well shaped. Maybe it would rain later. It was colder

223

again, when the sun was covered over she felt herself shiver. 'It's weird how you got successful after we split up.'

Nick was sorting through the picnic bag, looking at the food. 'The two things weren't related.'

'I know, but it's still weird.'

'You've done well too. I've been reading your stuff.'

Had he? That was nice. 'Yeah well, I haven't even got a job any more.'

'Who needs a job? Just find some work – you're really good.'

She pulled a sceptical face.

'What's that?' he said.

'I don't know, it's tough out there at the moment.'

'Well, keep going. You're talented.'

'So are lots of other people.'

'Hey, what's happened to your confidence? You never used to talk like this,' he said. 'Remember how you were when you started out? The odds really were against you then. You need to believe in yourself a bit more. I've realised that these last couple of years, the only difference between us and the people who went to the smart schools, it's just confidence, they're no better than we are, they just expect more. I've seen that so clearly working with them. Are you hungry yet?'

'You go ahead,' she said, but as he snapped open containers she thought that maybe she should eat something now too, because she really was feeling quite woozy and they had the whole afternoon ahead of them, so she pulled herself upright and reached for a plate. She sat up and took a piece of chicken in her fingers, bit the flesh from the bone. She could hear her jaw inside her head as she chewed. That was the wine, ramping up her senses.

'How's Lucia?' said Nick.

She raised her eyebrows and he laughed. 'The same,' she said. 'Worse – she's retired so she's got nothing to do.'

'What about Kieran?'

She pulled a face. 'The same again really, nothing's changed. He's living in some squat. He did have a job for a bit, but it didn't come to anything.'

'Is he still . . .?' He whistled, tapped two fingers on the inside of his forearm.

'What do you mean?'

'You know – is he still . . .?' He repeated the action.

She put down the drumstick. 'He's smoking a bit.'

'God you were always in denial about Kieran,' he said.

'That's not true!'

He pulled a face, as though to say, It is so obvious.

'What? You mean the drugs?'

'Yes, the heroin. Not weed, Carmen, heroin. And speed and crack and any other shit he can get his hands on.'

She was jolted by his words. But it was true, there had been a time when they found out he was using heroin and other stuff, she had forgotten about it. 'That was ages ago. When did you last see Kieran?'

He held up his hands. 'I haven't seen him, I'm sorry, I shouldn't have said anything.'

'No, go on.'

He shook his head.

'You've got something to say, say it.'

He sighed a bit dramatically. 'It just used to get on my nerves, that's all, that you always saw him as this victim, and he's not a victim, he's a selfish . . . spoilt . . . smackhead. Your dad and Jan – it was all about Kieran, he always came first. They spoiled him and they didn't spoil you.' He bit into a piece of French bread. 'It can't have been good for your self-esteem, can it?'

And I suppose you shagging around was great for my self-esteem, Carmen thought. She poured herself more wine. She felt agitated now, of course she did, surprisingly angry. 'Kieran says the same about you anyway.'

'What?'

'That I was lying to myself about you.'

'About what?'

'That you were sleeping around all along.'

He pulled another of his faces, this time pained, aggrieved, outraged. 'I was not sleeping around!'

'What, apart from when you were?'

There were two times that she'd found out about – a fling with an actress when he was working away for three months, and just as they were recovering from that, a one-night thing at a party. The first time she'd forgiven him, the second time she'd ended it.

'You know everything that happened,' he said, 'and if I could change it, I would.'

'Let's not talk about it,' she said. 'It's not important any more anyway.' And she thought, Maybe that's true. Time had passed. It had been so painful when it happened, when she'd found out – gut-wrenching torture that she would not have wished on her worst enemy, truly. And afterwards there had been a time when she'd thought, If I had a gun I would kill you now, just to kill this pain. But she didn't feel that way any more.

She lay back on the rug and stared at the sky. The alcohol had left her feeling strangely remote, as though she could stand outside herself and look down. She let her mind drift back to that time when she was first at the paper, the vigour of those days, how she had made all of that happen, changed the course of her life. Everything had felt possible then.

It felt like a different universe, like a different person. These last years had been hard – splitting up with Nick, finding Tom but also all the doubts and baggage that came with him, losing her job. It made her feel sad, thinking back to the bold girl she had been, it made her feel wounded. And it made her feel angry too, determined to find her again.

Nick's infidelity had hurt her and after the break-up she'd carried the rejection with her, and yet she'd been the one who'd finished the relationship – Nick hadn't wanted it to end. She was the one who'd said no, enough.

'Are you OK?' Nick said.

She looked at him, dragged back to the present. You think I'm thinking about you, she thought, about you being unfaithful – it's always about you. She remembered how irritating she had found that when they were together, how self-centred he could be. She didn't want him to be here any longer. She wanted him to leave.

She closed her eyes. Maybe she dozed off for a moment or

two, maybe her mind just wandered. When she opened them again she could see him, on the other side of the rug, sitting but it seemed from this angle like he was towering above her. He was checking his phone, tapping in a response to someone or other. He must regret coming, she thought, as much as I regret asking him. 'I think I'm a bit pissed,' she said.

He looked across at her and smiled. 'Why don't we just go back to yours and watch telly?' he said, and that made her laugh, and suddenly the sun came out and they were OK again.

They did exactly that. They packed up the picnic and the rug and left the beach and walked back to the bungalow. Already, by the time they'd got there, Carmen's head was aching from the wine – she had drunk most of the bottle. What an idiot, she thought, but she couldn't really bring herself to care, and somehow with Nick it didn't matter anyway.

They sat at either end of the sofa, picking at leftovers from the picnic, watching TV, laughing and chatting about things that didn't matter. Carmen dozed off again and when she woke she had a headache. Nick was tapping into his phone. 'Have I been asleep long?'

He looked at the clock. 'About half an hour.'

'I'm surprised you didn't go.'

'I did think about it,' he said, and she could tell that even though he was pretending it was a joke, he was annoyed.

She wished he had gone. She felt jaded and wanted to be alone. 'We can walk to the station now if you want,' she said.

'I thought I'd buy you dinner.'

'Don't you need to get back?'

'Nah.'

She still wanted him to leave, or most of her did, but she felt responsible for dragging him up here, and it was only one day, who knew if they would ever do this again? 'OK,' she said. 'Thanks.'

He smiled and went back to checking his messages, apologised that he needed to clear some. She excused herself and went to the loo. Sitting there, she switched on her mobile – there was nothing from Tom and she felt guilty about what she was doing. She tapped out a text – 'missing you xxx' – and sent it.

They went to the village pub. Nick ordered a bottle of wine, and even though Carmen knew it was a bad idea to drink more, she was grateful for it. The ease that had come and gone between them all day came back with it. They slipped into talking about people they both knew from the past, working through the list until the names became obscure and the conversation thinner. They drank steadily and ordered steak and chips, and she kept a close eye on the clock, then at nine she told him they must go – the last train left at nine thirty.

She walked with him to the station. She was quite drunk again and felt a glow of warmth that they had come together and relief that it was almost over. But when they got to the station there was a barrier across the entrance and a handwritten notice: The 21.30 is cancelled due to driver illness. The next train will be at 05.45.

'You'll have to get a taxi into Diss,' she said immediately. 'There are trains later from there.'

He didn't argue. They walked back into the village, to the taxi office, where the guy said the first available car would be at eleven thirty, and he wouldn't budge on that. 'Let's go back to yours and wait,' Nick said.

Carmen was edgy because her plan had been to ring Tom when she got home and she didn't want to do it with Nick in the house, but what could she do? So they went back to the bungalow, and when they got there Nick said, 'Listen, isn't this a bit stupid? Why don't I just stop over?'

'But I need to work tomorrow.'

'I'll go first thing.'

Carmen sank down on the sofa. It was the last thing she wanted.

'What's the matter? Is it because of Tom? Why don't you just call him and explain?'

Yeah, right, she thought. God, what an idiot she was. What had she been thinking?

Her brain was heavy. She didn't feel drunk – they had been drinking too long for that. She felt leaden and depressed and she wanted to be alone, for this blinding mistake to be over.

'He doesn't know I'm here, does he?' said Nick.

She didn't answer.

He didn't say anything. He didn't ask her why. She felt defeated suddenly and sat down beside him in the half-light. She knew she should get up and turn the light on, but she didn't. She felt him take her hand in his and they sat there like that, in silence.

He moved closer towards her. 'Carmen,' he said, 'is this what

230

you want?' He shifted again so their bodies were touching. 'Is this what you want?'

No, she wanted to say, but she didn't say it. She knew what was happening, but she didn't say anything. She still found him attractive – of course she did. She felt his hand touch her body, move across the front of her shirt. She sat upright, not moving. His other arm reached round her, supporting her back, as he rubbed his hand over her stomach and her breasts. She didn't move at all but she felt sick, giddy. He was holding her close now, his lips brushing against her cheek, across her lips, pressing gently. He slipped his hand inside her shirt, reached inside her bra. He sighed, leaning against her, and she could feel his erection pressing on her thigh. She felt dizzy, unable to move.

And then they heard a key in the door and she leaped off the sofa and tucked her shirt into her jeans and ran into the hallway and slammed the living-room door, all within seconds, as two people stumbled through the door. Carmen turned on the light in the hall. It was Mel, with a man.

'Argh!' Mel screamed, pulled back, struggled to focus on Carmen. 'Fuck, what are you doing here?'

'What are you doing here, more to the point?'

Carmen was taking it all in, in those seconds. Mel had been drinking, she wasn't steady, her speech was slurred. The guy who was with her had stepped backwards instinctively so he was standing on the doorstep now. He was a man, not a teenager like Mel, in his twenties. He was holding a bottle of vodka. 'I better go,' he said.

'No, you stay here,' said Carmen.

But he was turning already, walking down the drive. 'What's going on, Mel? Who is he?'

Mel fell then, first against the door and then forward on to Carmen, heavily, and Carmen banged her shoulder hard, painfully, against the wall. Mel fell on the floor and Carmen realised she was really drunk, not just a bit tipsy. She lifted her, half carried her into the living room. Nick was standing half concealed behind the door, the other side of Carmen to Mel. Carmen indicated to him to get out, and he slipped away. She was almost certain Mel hadn't seen him, thank goodness.

Carmen dumped her in the armchair. 'I'm gonna be sick,' said Mel.

Carmen ran through to the kitchen and fetched the washing-up bowl, thrust it on to Mel's lap. She was only just in time, Mel was gagging already. She leaned over the bowl and retched and then she vomited. Carmen grimaced. Her own stomach was not at its strongest, and she half turned her body away while she kept one hand on the bowl to steady it.

Eventually Mel quietened down. 'Done?' said Carmen.

Mel didn't answer. Her head was resting on her arm, her hair trailing in the sick. Carmen braced herself and took the bowl through to the toilet and flushed the vomit away, and then flushed again and swilled out the bowl. Nick was standing in the doorway of her bedroom. He grinned at her. 'Nice.'

She raised her eyebrows in agreement.

'Who is she?'

232

'Tom's daughter.'

'Can I do anything?'

'Just stay out the way – I'm sorry,' she said.

'It's fine.' He closed the door.

Carmen turned the light on in the living room. Mel was slumped forward. 'Do you want to lie down?' said Carmen.

Mel shook her head.

'Was that your boyfriend?' said Carmen.

Mel didn't answer.

'How come you've got a key? Is it the spare?' said Carmen. They kept one in the kitchen drawer.

Silence.

'Have you done this before? Come here when we're not here?'

'I need to lie down.' Mel made a move to climb out of the chair, but fell forward. Carmen helped her across to the sofa and Mel collapsed on to it. She put her arm over her eyes. 'Turn the light off, can you?'

Carmen did as she asked. They were not in darkness. The curtains weren't drawn and the orange from the street light threw shadows across the room. A branch from a rosebush in the front garden was giant in relief on the bare wall and moved slowly, back and forth. 'I hate this place,' said Mel.

'Do you?'

Mel said nothing.

'Don't you like coming here?'

'It's fucking freaky.'

'Why?'

Silence.

233

Carmen sat down in the armchair. 'Is it because of coming with me?' she said.

'Don't be stupid.'

'Is it because of what happened with Zena?'

Mel shook her head, but not a no, more an I don't want to talk about it.

Carmen sat forward in her chair. 'I didn't realise until recently that you and Zena were close.'

Mel lay still, her arm over her eyes. Carmen thought she wasn't going to answer, but then she said, 'That's not true.'

'Isn't it?'

Mel didn't reply. Her breathing became more shallow and Carmen guessed she had fallen asleep, but she so wanted to know more that she went over and tapped her on the shoulder, and when that got no response she tugged at her. Mel stirred then and opened her eyes, but she was dazed and clearly had no idea what was happening.

'You mustn't go to sleep on your back, you might choke,' said Carmen, and with some effort helped her to roll on to her side. Mel's eyes were still open, she stared blankly ahead of her.

'I thought you and Zena got on well,' persisted Carmen. 'I thought you went into the magazine with her.'

'I didn't know what she was like then, did I?'

'What do you mean?'

Mel didn't answer.

'What do you mean, Mel?'

'She was a bitch.' Mel looked hazily at Carmen.

'Why do you say that?' said Carmen.

234

'She made Mum and Dad split up, didn't she?'

Of course, thought Carmen, Mel would have been too young to grasp what had happened at first, that Tom and Zena had had an affair while Tom was still with Laura, that there had been betrayal. She would have been told the party line, that Mummy and Daddy weren't getting on and here was this new lady.

But then at some point she must have realised.

'You're all right, you know,' said Mel. 'I used to think you were a bit of a loser, but you're not.' She put her arm over her eyes again. 'Can you get me some water?'

Carmen fetched her some, and then eased a cushion under her head. Mel closed her eyes again and Carmen was about to get up and leave her when Mel said, 'Didn't Dad tell you about it?'

'What?'

'Him and Mum splitting up, how it happened?'

'Well yes, but—'

'Did he tell you Zena used his credit card so Mum would find out what they'd been up to?'

Carmen was confused. 'What?'

Mel didn't reply.

'Mel, I don't understand, what do you mean?'

Mel roused herself. 'She used his credit card so Mum would see the receipt and know they'd been fucking in some hotel room.'

'His credit card?'

'She told me all about it, as though she'd been really clever.'

235

'She told you?'

'She *wanted* Mum to kick him out, fucking bitch, and she succeeded, didn't she?'

Carmen knew nothing of any of this. Tom had never said anything about a credit card or that Laura had thrown him out. Carmen had always believed that he'd been the one to end the marriage, that he'd left Laura to be with Zena.

But no, he didn't choose her, he was given no choice.

He'd said there'd been a row. He'd said that he and Laura had had a massive argument and it had all come out, so not lying exactly but not telling the truth – the same old story. Slippery Tom. But why not tell her this? Why protect Zena? 'Is this true?' said Carmen, but Mel didn't answer, she was asleep.

She had to ring Tom, tell him what had happened, get him to call Laura and let her know that Mel was safe. But then how could she, with Nick here? What if he wanted to drive up?

So she rang Laura instead. She did it on impulse – she had Laura's number on her phone and she called her and woke her and told her what had happened, just the bare bones, that Mel was OK but that she had turned up drunk and was asleep on the sofa. She didn't mention the man, but still Laura was very shocked. She told Carmen that Mel had told her she was staying over with a friend, a girl Laura knew well. 'Do you think she knows about this?' she said.

'Maybe,' said Carmen. 'They cover for each other, don't they?'

Laura thought for a moment. 'I'll come and get her.'

'Now?'

'Yes.'

'Are you sure? She's flat out. She can stay, it's no problem.'

'I want to come. And she's got school in the morning.'

Carmen knew there was no way Mel would be fit for school, but she didn't say anything, she didn't want to alarm Laura further. 'What about Jake and Mercy?'

'It's OK, there's a friend here. I'll come now.'

A friend? A boyfriend? Carmen didn't have time to speculate. She hadn't expected Laura to come straight over. She needed to get Nick out of the house. When she rang off she went straight through to the bedroom where he was hiding and found him asleep on top of the bed. Where the fuck was that taxi? She was about to wake him when she looked at the clock and realised it was past midnight – he'd missed the last train now anyway. She had to accept that he was here for the night. She thanked God once again that Tom wasn't coming, that she hadn't called him, but Laura was on her way and she needed to warn Nick to stay in this room while she was around – not to come out at all or make a sound.

She tapped him on the shoulder and hissed in his ear, 'Nick, just stay in here, OK? Mel's mum's coming and you need to stay in here. She mustn't know you're here – have you got that?'

He grunted and nodded and she knew he'd taken it in and she knew she could rely on him.

Chapter 16

Laura stood over her daughter, just looking at her. It was nearly 3 a.m. – she hadn't arrived till gone two. 'I don't know what to do,' she said almost to herself, and Carmen wasn't sure whether she meant about the whole thing or whether to continue to try to find a way to get Mel into the car. They'd attempted to wake her already, but she was unrousable, unconscious. 'Maybe it would be better to leave her, if you really don't mind.'

'That's fine.' Carmen had suggested that Laura let Mel sleep it off and come back in the morning, but Laura seemed unable to make that decision.

'I don't know.'

Carmen touched Laura's arm. 'Listen, why don't we have a cup of tea and see how she is in a few minutes. Then if we still can't wake her, you can leave her.'

Laura seemed relieved to have some sort of plan and they went through to the kitchen. Carmen put the kettle on, warmed the pot and brought mugs and milk to the table.

'I'm sorry for being so indecisive, it's not like me,' said Laura.

'Oh, don't worry, it's hardly normal circumstances.' Carmen wanted to touch her, to squeeze her arm or do something comforting, but it felt wrong somehow.

'I just don't understand what happened. You say she just let herself in?'

Carmen nodded. 'She didn't know I was here.'

'I didn't know she had a key.'

'Neither did I.' Carmen poured tea into the mugs. 'Milk?'

'But where had she been?'

Carmen hesitated. She didn't know how much she should tell her. 'She wasn't on her own when she came here. There was a man with her – a boy.'

Laura looked bewildered. 'Who?'

'I don't know.'

'You said a man. Was he older?'

'A bit.'

'How old?'

'About . . . twenty-five, I guess.'

'Twenty-five?!'

'I'm not sure. When I came to the door he – went away.'

It sounded bad, Carmen knew it, but she had to tell Laura.

'I just don't know what to do,' Laura said.

'I wouldn't worry too much.' Carmen reached towards her; again her instinct was to take her hand and comfort her but again she stopped short, as though Laura had a force field around her. 'Teenage girls are a nightmare. I think a lot of them go through this.'

'Do they? Her friends aren't behaving like this.'

'How do you know? You wouldn't know.'

'I didn't behave like this.'

'I did,' said Carmen.

'Did you?' Laura looked at her.

'Well, not exactly like this, but I did lie to my mum about where I was so I could go out. And I was drinking.'

'At Mel's age?'

'Younger.'

'Did you?' said Laura. 'I was at boarding school – there was nothing like this.'

'Really?'

'Well – yes actually, there were girls who got in trouble. Yes, in fact, when I think about it, with drugs and so on. Unsuitable men.'

'Unsuitable men?'

'I remember one girl had to be fetched back from New York.'

Carmen laughed and Laura smiled and for a moment she seemed ready to see the funny side, but then her smile disappeared. 'I just don't want her to ruin her life. She's so young . . .'

'She won't ruin her life, it won't be like that.'

'How do you know?'

Carmen didn't have an answer for that because of course Laura was right, how did she know? It might not turn out all right, it might get worse. Look at Kieran – they'd spent years waiting for things to turn out right with him and there was no sign they ever would.

'She's not as tough as she looks.'

'None of us are,' said Carmen.

Laura put her hands around the mug, sipped her tea. 'Maybe I'm not the right person to deal with all of this.'

'Of course you are,' said Carmen. 'I mean, I don't really know you, but you strike me as a tower of strength and that's exactly what she needs.'

Laura half smiled, grateful. 'I suppose I should be having this conversation with Tom really. What does he say?'

'I haven't told him yet.'

Laura was surprised by that, interested, Carmen could see, and she immediately wished she hadn't opened her mouth. She felt under pressure to provide some kind of explanation. 'He's away,' she said, and then regretted that as well – what a stupid lie, Laura and Tom were bound to talk about all of this tomorrow, it would come out . . . 'Actually that's not correct, he's not away, but – it was just so late and he's working so hard at the moment, I thought it would wait till the morning. Maybe that was the wrong thing . . .'

Laura didn't comment. Did she sense something? Was she being discreet?

The two women sat in silence, a strange intimacy. Carmen felt a growing urge to ask questions that she knew she shouldn't. But there was so much Laura could tell her. She knew Tom better than probably anyone alive. They had been together for nearly fifteen years for God's sake, Carmen had known Tom for less than three. She would love to be able to ask Laura about him, about what had happened, what had gone wrong, what she'd known and what she hadn't known, how she saw things now. About who he was.

241

'Is something the matter?' said Laura.

Carmen had been staring at her without realising it. She looked away quickly. 'Sorry, it's just strange, sitting here with you really. Nice. I mean not nice because of . . .'

Laura smiled. 'I understand, and I'm pleased to meet you properly too. It's just unfortunate about the circumstances.' Her confidence was coming back, her polish. 'After all, there's no reason for there to be any awkwardness between us, is there? It's not as though Tom and I were together when you met. And of course we've got him in common, haven't we? Wives of Tom – we could start a club.'

Carmen smiled, even though she was indeed feeling awkward. 'It is a bit strange though,' she said.

'Probably more for you than me because it's all in the past for me. It feels like another life now.'

'Does it?'

'Yes.'

Her openness emboldened Carmen to ask more. 'Were you and Tom happy? Before—' She broke off. 'Sorry I shouldn't—'

'No, it's fine. We were happy, for a long time.' She looked at Carmen. 'Are you and he . . .?'

'Yes, of course,' Carmen said.

'I'm glad. You seem like a nice person and Tom is at heart.'

'You still think so?'

'Of course. I mean obviously he's not completely to be trusted, but then which of them are? And he can be a bit spineless, do you find? He used to drive me . . . insane, the way he won't take responsibility for things. He always sort of

242

managed to turn it round so it was never his fault, do you find that?'

Carmen smiled, acknowledged it.

'Do you think he was happy with Zena?' said Carmen.

'Well, I'm not really the person to ask.'

Carmen was pushing it and she knew it. 'Sorry.'

'It's all right, I can see that you would want to know, but my opinion wouldn't count for much. She is – was – not exactly my favourite person.'

After a moment though, Laura spoke again. 'But if you want to know what I think, then no, I don't think they would have been happy together long term and I think that was starting to show already. He wasn't relaxed with her.'

They both felt a bit awkward after that and the conversation ran out of steam. They went back through to the living room and had another go at waking Mel, but it was pointless, she was dead to the world. Laura accepted now that it would be best to leave her to sleep it off. 'I'll come and fetch her straight after the school run.'

'Oh, don't worry, I'll drive her over when she wakes up,' said Carmen.

'Are you sure?'

'It's no problem.'

She fetched Laura's bag and coat from the kitchen and they stood in the hall as Laura put her coat on.

'There is something I should probably tell you,' Carmen said. 'Mel was talking earlier about Zena – about what happened – and she seemed really quite upset. I was surprised because

243

she's never talked to me about it at all. I mean, maybe you know . . .'

'What did she say?' said Laura.

'Nothing really, it's just . . .' Carmen was unsure now, this was a potential minefield. 'I never realised before, that Mel disliked Zena so much.'

'She said that?' Laura seemed surprised.

'Yes. I never knew that. In fact I thought it was the opposite. I really hope you don't mind me saying this . . .'

'No, go on, please.'

'It's just, for some reason I thought they were quite friendly. To be honest it made me feel a bit bad, because I get on fine with Mel and of course I try, but we're not close.'

Carmen was being a bit manipulative here, she knew, aligning herself with Laura, but Laura seemed quite cool about what Carmen was suggesting, to just be considering it. 'Mel did have her head turned by Zena, I'd forgotten,' she said.

'That must have been hard for you, wasn't it? I'd have found it hard.'

'To be honest that year was so . . . hideous I'm not sure it made much difference.'

She smiled tiredly, and Carmen smiled with her. 'You're very mature.'

'I'm not, believe me. I suppose in a way I was just pleased Mel seemed to be all right about it all, it was just one thing less to worry about.' She paused. 'Mel shouldn't have had to go through all of that. None of them should. Jake too – he had a rough time.'

'Tom said. He saw a counsellor, didn't he?'

'That's right. He's always had a temper, like his dad.'

'Did Mel get any help?'

Laura shook her head.

'Maybe it would be a good idea.'

'Maybe,' said Laura. 'Maybe we need to do that.'

Laura left and Carmen undressed and went straight to bed, on the bottom bunk in the children's room, but sleep didn't come. She was exhausted but her body was jagged from the alcohol and she started to worry about how she was going to work things in the morning – how she would avoid Mel seeing Nick, and once that anxiety was in her mind it became a loop she couldn't escape. She became so concerned about oversleeping and the two of them finding each other that each time she drifted off she jolted awake again.

At the first signs of daylight, before 6 a.m., she made tea and took a cup through to Nick, who was sleeping soundly, fully dressed, still on top of the covers. She sat on the bed beside him, watched his body rise and fall. How did she feel about him now? Different for sure, something had shifted with seeing him, a spell had been broken and she'd come back down to earth. She remembered now how frustrated she used to get with him, how annoying he could be. She remembered how she'd wanted to move on. She felt stronger.

She shook him and told him that he had to leave as soon as possible, that there was a train at quarter to seven from St Jude's that would connect him with the main line and the fast commuter trains. He pulled a face, but she said, 'Please Nick – Mel's still here,' and he complied.

On the doorstep he put his arms around her and kissed her cheek, his lips pressed hard against her skin. She closed her eyes and breathed in the warmth of his familiarity, his affection, felt it strengthen her. 'Last night before that girl came . . .'

'Can we just forget that,' Carmen said, and pulled away slightly.

'Of course,' he said, after a pause.

They stood together in the cool morning until he had to go. 'I'm glad you came,' Carmen said. 'I'm sorry it was a bit . . .'

He kissed her cheek again. 'Take care, eh?' he said. 'You're very important to me.'

She shut the door quietly after him and went through to the kitchen and made coffee. Then she woke Mel, who was disorientated and pale. Carmen coaxed her to sit up and drink the hot coffee while she went through to the bathroom and showered. As she towelled herself dry she heard Mel throwing up in the toilet next door.

She dressed and went back through to the living room. Mel was curled up fetally on the sofa. 'Come on,' said Carmen.

'I can't, I feel awful,' said Mel, but Carmen told her she had to take her home now, and helped her into her coat and led her out to the car. If they didn't leave soon they would get stuck in the rush-hour traffic.

Mel sat with her eyes closed, a carrier bag open on her lap in case she vomited again.

'I want to talk to you about last night,' Carmen said.

Mel didn't respond, but Carmen sensed she wasn't asleep.

'Who was that man? Is he your boyfriend?'

No reply.

'I know you can hear me, Mel. Have you been back to the bungalow with him before?'

A dance track boomed on the radio. Carmen turned it off.

'How old is he?'

Mel rolled her eyes.

'Mel, you have got to be careful. That guy is a lot older than you, and you were off your head last night. Anything could have happened.'

Mel pulled a face as though Carmen was paranoid and ridiculous and old and Carmen felt a flare of real anger – she would have liked to pull the car over and slap Mel's face.

'Mel, I am going to say something to you and you can just listen, OK? I know things have been hard for you –' Mel started to object but Carmen spoke over her – 'I know things have been hard for you and that is unfair, but you could ruin your life if you are not careful, and I am not talking about messing up some exams. He could have raped you, do you realise that? He could have done anything.'

'That's just stupid,' said Mel.

'How do you know? You were unconscious. You could have choked and died. Your mum came last night – yes, you didn't even know that, did you? We were shaking you and you didn't wake up.'

Mel looked out of the window.

*

Laura had arranged for a friend to do the school run so she would be there when Carmen dropped Mel off. She came out to meet them as they pulled up outside the house, which added to Mel's discomfort. She had her arms wrapped around herself as she stepped out of the car and, despite her best efforts, squinted in the sunlight. Laura kept a distance, didn't attempt to embrace her daughter, nor berate her. 'You'd better go up to bed,' she said, and Mel obeyed, skirting her mother slightly as she went into the house.

Laura turned to Carmen. 'Thanks for driving her,' she said. She was dressed in cords, a sweater and a neck scarf, freshly laundered and fragrant, back in control again. 'Would you like a coffee?'

It was said out of politeness, Carmen knew. Their brief intimacy of last night was over, and the last thing she felt like was half an hour of small talk, but she said yes anyway, partly because the coffee would help her get home, partly because she couldn't resist the chance to see inside the house.

She followed Laura through a gate into a courtyard garden laid out with herb beds, then through sliding doors into a huge, airy breakfast room. The original kitchen had been knocked through into a glass extension so the whole area was flooded with light. There was an oak table in the centre, an Aga built into the inglenook, a nest of sofas to one side with a giant flatscreen TV, a Labrador in a basket – Riley, she had met Riley before; he roused himself to greet her. 'Excuse the mess,' said Laura, but of course there was no mess.

Laura scooped ground coffee into a cafetière and Carmen

sat down at the table, clutching her handbag. It was so lovely, so grand – she'd had no idea, although she should have done. It was evident from the outside that this was a big house, but somehow she hadn't imagined that it would be like this inside. She thought of her scruffy little flat and that feeling of smallness started to kick in . . . Stop it, she told herself, stop it now. But she was so tired . . .

'I thought about what you said,' said Laura as she brought the coffee to the table on a tray with cups and saucers and milk in a jug. 'About Mel being upset about Zena.' She glanced towards the door, as though to check Mel wasn't in earshot. 'Did she say anything more? What it was about?'

Carmen felt cautious, instinctively. She didn't want to cause trouble. 'She mentioned a credit card.'

Laura put her hand on the cafetière. 'Did she say anything else?'

Carmen wanted to tell her, to find out more, but she was conscious that she could say something really tactless here, really put the cat among the pigeons. She had no idea how much Laura knew about what Zena had done. It may not even be true. 'No,' she said.

Laura poured the coffee, picked up her own cup and saucer. 'Maybe Tom has told you this, but I found out he was having an affair because he used our joint credit card to pay for a hotel room,' she said. 'Of course I saw the payment on the statement.'

So Carmen's caution had been justified. Laura still believed that Tom had revealed the affair by his carelessness. She didn't know that Zena had set the whole thing up deliberately so that Laura would find out. 'How awful,' she said.

'Obviously I had suspicions anyway . . .'

'Did you?'

'Oh God, yes.'

'Why?'

'Well, he was staying over in London more and more and buying new clothes –' her face showed her scorn – 'but I did what people do, I guess, and ignored it. Went into denial, or hoped it would burn out.'

'But then you saw the credit-card payment.'

'Yes, and I couldn't do that any longer. I was furious as much as anything that he'd spent seven hundred pounds for one night at some boutique hotel.'

'*Seven hundred quid?*'

Laura pulled a face. Exactly.

'And he wouldn't do that normally? If he was staying up for work?'

'No! He stayed at a motel, hundred quid a pop. It was stupid of him of course, to pay with our joint card, but I'm wondering if that is what Mel was talking about. Maybe Zena told her something about it.' She sipped her coffee. 'Do you think that might be what Mel meant?'

'Maybe.'

'Did she say anything else?'

Carmen shook her head. It wasn't for her to tell Laura the rest, that Zena had manipulated things so that Laura would

250

see that credit-card transaction, that it had never been Tom's error. 'Poor Mel, if that is true,' Carmen said. 'It must be hard to hear that – no wonder it's stuck with her. How old was she then? Twelve?'

'Yes, that must be right.'

God, what had Zena been thinking, telling her that? About Mel's own parents? Stupid woman. No, worse than that, cruel. Amy had said she wasn't cruel, but . . .

Unbelievable really.

Carmen left as soon as she had finished her coffee, drove back to the bungalow, where thankfully, finally, she climbed into the cool of the double bed and slept until late afternoon.

When she woke up, she rang Tom. He was at work but he could talk so she told him about what had happened, about the events of the night before. He interrupted her to say, 'Why the hell didn't you call me?'

'I didn't want to wake you.'

'What are you talking about? Don't you think I'd have wanted to know? I'd have come up.'

'What about work?'

'I'd have taken the day off.'

'I'm sorry, I thought it would be better to call Laura. I thought she might be expecting Mel home and worrying. And once I'd told her, I didn't see the point in waking you up.'

Tom didn't reply. She knew he was angry.

'I was just trying to do the right thing.'

'I can't believe you're only telling me now!' He was silent for a moment. 'What did Laura say?'

251

She told him the rest of the story, how Laura had come over, and how she'd driven Mel back this morning.

When she had finished neither of them knew how to continue. 'Hey, you never told me your old house is so stylish,' she said, trying to lighten things.

'It's not.'

'The kitchen's amazing. I didn't see the rest.'

'Well, Laura saw to that, the rest of the place is nothing special.' She could hear him fiddling with something on the desk. She didn't believe him. 'So how did you get on with her anyway?'

'She's nice. A bit guarded.'

'That's Laura.'

'What do you mean?'

'Just what you said, she's . . . guarded. That's the right word. Not cold, but always in control.'

'Why's she like that?'

'I don't know, the way she was brought up, I suppose. Boarding school. Not like you, spilling everything everywhere.'

'I'm not like that!'

He didn't answer. He was half joking but only half. He was still angry.

They sat in silence again.

'Do you think Mel's done it before?' said Carmen. 'Do you think she was at the bungalow that night the other week when she didn't go home?'

'Maybe. Listen, when are you coming home?'

She looked around her, at the bare walls of the bungalow, and had no idea what she was still doing there. 'Now?' she said.

252

'Oh good. Oh . . .'

'What?'

'Actually I've got to have a drink with a client, after work, I'd forgotten. I might be quite late.'

Carmen looked at the clock. It was nearly six. If she left now she'd hit rush hour. 'Maybe I'll come back in the morning then.'

But after she'd put the phone down Carmen started to feel strange. The quiet in the bungalow felt oppressive. She turned on the TV to shut out the silence but a game show came on, and the noise, the cheery voices, grated on her nerves. It's the booze playing out, she told herself, just a hangover, and now she'd slept most of the day her body was out of sync, reacting in a visceral way.

She looked through the list of recordings for something engaging. There was a crime series recorded in full here, which she'd meant to follow but never got around to. She settled down to watch.

It was gripping from the outset, but gruesome. A woman was alone in a house, preparing her evening meal, watched by the camera as though through the eyes of a stalker. The opening sequence was deliberately slow, played out in real time. Carmen watched the woman eat, and tidy her house, then run a bath and start to take her clothes off, as the eyes of the camera followed her from window to window. The tension built. Carmen heard the breath of the stalker come into the sequence, heard it speed up as the woman stripped, and then the action changed pace and he was running towards the house, frantic jerky movements. A jumper was placed over

253

a window and then a hammer – a pane was broken, he was inside. Carmen could hear a radio, the woman singing along. Then the hammer was directly in front of the lens, in a gloved hand – the man was creeping now, towards the bathroom. There was steam coming out, the sound of the radio, the woman still singing. The man entered the room and Carmen looked into the woman's horrified face as she turned and saw him, then the door closed and the camera view was of the door and there was only noise, the woman screaming where a second ago she had been singing. The sequence went on and on, it was unbearable, the woman's screams as she fought her attacker, graphic thuds as her body hit hard surfaces, a roar from the man that was terrifying, animal, then the woman's screams turning to whimpers, clinging to the last of life.

Carmen turned it off. Her hands were covering her mouth. When did TV drama get so bloody violent? That was like a horror movie! The screen was blank and the room was silent again, but Carmen's heart was pounding and thoughts rushed through her mind. The sequence had triggered something in her that had been just beneath the surface – something close to panic.

She shut her eyes but that didn't help, all she could see was that man in Brixton, that poor man lying on the ground, Tom pummelling his head. And then she wasn't looking at him any more, she was looking at Zena, on the floor, and Tom was pummelling her head, smashing his fists into her face.

Carmen opened her eyes but she couldn't shut the image out, it was in her head. She put her hands to her cheeks to stop it, pressed her fists against her cheeks – feel this, this is real. Shut it out.

The image faded but thoughts rushed through her mind: how can I go on with him? How can I be married to a man who murdered a woman? How could I even have thought that was possible?

Her breath came in gasps. All the calm of the weekend exploded in her brain, a nail bomb.

She sat up straight, tried to get some control back, but she was in full-blown panic now and she couldn't think straight at all.

What the fuck did he do to her?

Her senses were distorting. The bungalow was full of voices, whispers.

You know, don't you, Carmen?

It was Zena's voice, she could hear it in her head.

You know, don't you?

'No!' Carmen said it out loud.

One day he'll do it to you.

She couldn't stay here. She stood up, walked through to the bedroom to get her things together. Her legs were weak. As she reached to pull her bag out of the wardrobe her hand was shaking.

Carmen . . .

The walls felt tighter, as though they were closing in on her. She had to get a grip. She sat down on the bed, forced herself to breathe evenly, put her hand on her chest and counted the breaths, in, out, in, out. This was just a panic attack, she'd had them before when she was younger and she remembered the drill. She held her hand out in front of her and focused her vision on it, took shallow deliberate breaths. Gradually, slowly, the trembling reduced.

Carmen.

'This is just panic it is not real. This is just panic it is not real. This is just panic it is not real.' She repeated it till the voice faded away.

Silence.

She stood up. She had to get out, she couldn't stand these four walls, she couldn't breathe in here, but she was in no state to drive. She pulled on a jacket, picked up her keys and went out into the road. She would walk around, into the village or down to the beach.

It wasn't cold, but she felt cold. She pulled the jacket around herself, and walked, head down, with no direction in mind. She reached the end of the road, then followed the pavement right, and right again. Her breath was normalising; she could still hear it but it was getting easier. She rested for a minute against someone's wall. Silly to let herself get so worked up. The sky was streaked with red – the sun was setting inland but she couldn't see it from here, just the reflections in the sky. What was she going to do? She couldn't go back to the bungalow, the thought of being there made her feel sick, but she couldn't just walk round and round. She looked up. She was in the neighbouring street – she had walked down here just a few days ago with that woman Paula, with her shopping bags, talking about the way she had found Zena's body. She could see Paula's house from here – the lights were on. She could go there. Paula had said to pop in.

There was no answer when she rang the bell though she sensed movement inside, a door opening somewhere, a change in the light she could see through the frosted glass panels. She knocked, in case they hadn't heard the bell.

Someone was coming. It was Paula – she opened the door. She was in a dressing gown. Carmen realised then how late it must be, how inappropriate this visit was. Paula looked concerned. 'Is everything OK? Are you all right?'

'Yes. I'm so sorry – I just – I was alone at home and I thought I'd come round for that coffee. I didn't realise how late it was.'

Paula smiled then. 'Oh, don't be silly, I was just washing my hair. It's not late – it's only –' she twisted to look at a clock – 'it's only eight. Come in.'

'If you're sure.'

'Of course.' She turned and led the way through. 'I'm terrible – as soon as dinner's over I'm in my pyjamas these days, I think it's because of the kids. Oh, don't worry about that.' Carmen had taken her shoes off. 'Do you mind coming into the kitchen? Is that all right?'

'Of course.'

There was a man in there, sitting at the table, behind a laptop. He looked up. 'Shaun, this is the lady I told you about who lives in that bungalow behind, you know, Iris's old place . . .'

Carmen smiled at him. 'I'm Carmen,' she said, and he nodded but didn't smile or introduce himself.

'I'm just . . .' He indicated the computer.

'Of course, I'm sorry, I could . . .'

'Oh, he's just looking, aren't you, Shaun? Sit down, I'll put the kettle on. He's always stuck behind that. It's nice to have a visitor in the evening, makes a change.'

Carmen sat down. She was feeling a hundred times better already. 'Are your children in bed?' she said.

Paula laughed. 'At this time? Cheyenne's stopping over with my mum and Charlie – that's our boy – he's playing on his computer in his room. We shouldn't really let him in the week but . . .'

Shaun banged his mouse on the table. 'Bloody thing's frozen again.' He raised his eyebrows at Carmen in mock frustration and she warmed to him.

Paula put three mugs of tea on the table. 'I should have offered you wine, I didn't think, we're not big drinkers but . . .'

'Tea's lovely,' said Carmen.

'So you live behind,' said Shaun, pulling the lid down on the laptop.

'Yes,' said Carmen.

He sipped his tea.

'You knew Zena, didn't you?' Carmen said.

She didn't need to explain. He nodded, knew immediately who she was talking about, which meant that of course he had placed her as well. Paula must have told him about her, about meeting her on the beach. 'I knew her when we were teenagers.'

'What was she like?'

'You're interested in her then, are you?'

'Of course she is, it's natural,' said Paula.

258

Carmen felt herself blush. She had overcome the shame of being so obviously curious about Zena in her need for information, but hers was not a dignified position to be in.

He half smiled at her discomfort, but not unkindly. 'She was . . . a looker. That hadn't changed when she came back, though she was a bit Lady Muck.'

'How do you mean?'

'Well, she didn't want to speak.'

'To you?'

'Not just me.'

He had been hurt. Who else had Zena offended?

'Were you at school with her?'

'No, she went to a posh girls' school.'

'No, Shaun, it was Hamesdon, wasn't it?' said Paula. 'That's a normal school, just single sex, that's all. It's not posh. In fact it's quite rough.'

'I don't know, she seemed like that to me,' said Shaun.

'Like what?' said Paula.

He didn't explain.

'How did you know her then?' said Carmen.

'Just around. A lot of kids came down here in those days, hung out on the beach.'

'From her school?'

'Not really, no, she wasn't the sort who hang around with a gang of girls, she came more with boys.'

'Boyfriends?'

'I guess so, older boys. The boys with cars – that's what the girls liked. She was a funny little thing. She was a looker but she wasn't snooty – not then anyway. I used to call her Olive Oyl because she was so skinny.' He laughed. 'She hated that, used to punch me in the arm and she was strong, she could hurt. You could have a laugh with her.'

He had been fond of her, it was clear, and he had been hurt when she hadn't acknowledged him when she came back. Why had she done that? Had she just forgotten him? Probably that was it. Carmen realised there must be many people from her own youth she would struggle to recognise now. Zena was a person people remembered, but most people aren't. There must have been something about her. 'Did you go out with her?'

'Nah, we were just buddies, you know. But I tell you what –' he turned to Paula. 'Do you remember Barry? Barry Bighorn – with the Fiesta, you know . . .'

'Carl?'

'That's him. We called him Barry Bighorn,' he explained to Carmen.

'What about him?' said Paula.

'He adored Zena. It was a bit of a joke, he was completely in love with her for years and I'm not kidding – years, poor bloke, used to follow her around . . .'

'Did he get anywhere?' said Paula.

'Nah, she wasn't interested in him, poor old Barry, but she was nice to him, not mean.' He paused. 'She left home young, didn't she?'

'Yes. Do you know where she stayed?'

He shrugged. 'Just on people's sofas, I think, and then she

260

got a bedsit, signed on. It seemed quite daring at the time. We were all just living with our mums and dads.' He paused, sipped his tea.

'Do you know anyone she was close to then? Friends?'

He thought about it. 'I can't remember. I think it was mostly boyfriends, like I say. She was a man's woman. She thought like a man. That's probably why girls didn't like her and men did.'

'A tomboy?' It wasn't what he was saying but it came into Carmen's mind.

He laughed. 'I suppose so, in a way. A free spirit.'

A boy appeared in the kitchen doorway. 'I'm going to bed.' He stared at Carmen. It was her cue to leave. She was feeling so much better, so much calmer, from just being with other people, gossiping and soaking up the family karma.

Paula saw her out. She was about to close the front door when she said, 'Hang on,' and disappeared inside again. When she came back she handed Carmen a bracelet. 'I was cleaning Cheyenne's bedroom and I found this,' she said. 'I'd forgotten all about it, but that day on the beach, when we found . . . you know . . .'

'Zena's body?'

'Yes. Cheyenne had run ahead of me and when I caught up with her she was holding this. I never knew where she found it, I thought it must have been on the beach but . . . I think it might have been on her.'

'On Zena's body?'

'Yes. Cheyenne was there first, you see, she was only little, and I just found her playing with this. I'd forgotten about it, but I found it the other day in her room and I meant to give it to you, I thought your husband should have it.'

Carmen looked at it. It was good quality, heavy, not a piece of tat. The metal parts were tarnished, you could see it had been out in the elements. She thanked Paula again and left.

When she got back to the bungalow she sat on the bed and looked at it more closely under the lamp. It was a lovely little thing, quite expensive, she would guess, tightly strung with different materials, shining discs, polished stones, metal beads. She tried it on her wrist – it was a bit too tight, but she didn't take it off.

She lay down on the bed. The room was benign to her now, nothing oppressive about the walls, no sounds. Her panic of earlier had blown itself out and exhaustion had taken its place. She needed to think, she couldn't ignore what had happened earlier on; something fundamental had shifted inside her and the implications would be explosive, would rock her world, she knew all of that. She'd thought she could accept what Tom had done, that nothing need change, though she knew that was impossible. But she had no strength to confront it all now. It could wait till morning.

She pulled off her clothes and climbed under the quilt, switched the light off, but her sleep was not peaceful. She dreamed that she was in the sea, swimming, and she could see Zena ahead of her, in trouble, going under and bobbing up again, drowning. Carmen swam to help her, but Zena grabbed hold of her and pulled her down with her. Carmen was gasping, struggling for breath, panicking to get back to the surface but Zena wouldn't let her go. And then she saw – Zena was laughing at her, underwater, they were drowning together. Sometime during the night she took the bracelet off her wrist and dropped it into the bag that was sitting beside her.

Chapter 17

Tom reached across the table to take Carmen's hand but she pulled it away. She was shocked at how hard she was finding it to control her hostility, her anger. He'd suggested she come over to meet him from work, that they have dinner out, and she'd agreed. She knew this meeting was going to be hard and she thought maybe it would be better on neutral territory with other people around, that she would be cooler and the conversation clearer, but that had been a mistake because it was hard to formulate her thoughts in this environment, let alone talk about anything.

'What's the matter?' he said.

'Nothing.'

A waiter appeared beside them with a plate of rocket, zig-zagged with balsamic cream. 'In the middle?' he said, and Carmen nodded. Anything that could sit between them would be welcome at this stage.

The eruption that had happened inside Carmen last night had not abated; it had evolved, progressed. She had woken up in

St Jude's feeling turbulent and volatile and that had continued all day. Was this the end? She couldn't say that yet, but she wasn't scared to think it any more, to see that it was likely, probably inevitable. Sitting here with Tom, she knew she was no longer looking for reasons to stay, no longer trying to find ways to let him off the hook.

She stabbed the leaves with a fork.

'Mel went into school today anyway,' he said. 'That's something, I suppose.'

He had spoken to Laura. He had been telling Carmen about it when the salad arrived.

She cleared her throat. 'What are you going to do?'

He shrugged.

He pushed a piece of rocket around with his fork. 'Did Mel say something to you about Zena?'

'Did Laura say that?'

'She mentioned it.'

'God, why can't you just be straightforward and say so then?'

'Sorry, I didn't mean to not be straightforward. Carmen, what is wrong?'

But Carmen wasn't ready to say. She stuck her fork into the salad again. 'Yes, Mel did talk to me about Zena. She said that she hated her – which I found weird because I thought they were quite close.'

'Why did you think that?'

'Someone told me, I don't know, does it matter?'

Tom fiddled with his knife and fork. 'Did Mel say something else?'

'Yes actually, she did. She talked about a credit card, and about you and Laura splitting up.' She looked Tom in the eye. She didn't tell him the rest of what Mel had told her – about Zena having engineered the break-up. She wanted to see what he would say, to see how he reacted, what lies he would tell now.

'I knew you were upset,' he said. 'Why didn't you just tell me?'

'I am telling you. And I'm not upset about that.'

'What are you upset about then?'

The waiter, a young Italian guy, arrived at that moment and took the salad plate. 'Was that good,' he said.

Ignoring him, Tom reached across the table and put his hand over Carmen's. 'There are things I haven't told you,' he said. 'Things that maybe I should have done, I don't know . . .'

The waiter left.

Carmen looked at him. Was this going to be it then? The confession? Now that the moment had come she felt numb . . .

As though he could read her thoughts he said, 'It's nothing big, just . . . what you were saying, about Zena, they did have a falling-out, her and Mel. I didn't realise Mel was so upset about it, certainly not that it still bothered her.'

Carmen said nothing.

'I don't know why I didn't tell you, it's stupid that I didn't. I'll just tell you now.'

But still he took his time, fiddled with the napkin, chose his words carefully as he explained how Laura found the credit-card bill for the hotel room, how his marriage ended. 'It was on our joint account statement. She wasn't snooping – she just opened the statement the way she always did. I thought I must have made the most stupid mistake and paid with the wrong card – I couldn't believe I'd done it, but . . .'

The waiter appeared and put their meals in front of them, wordlessly this time. Carmen had ordered steak, rare, and she cut into it straight away. Tom ignored his food. 'What's all this got to do with Mel?' Carmen said.

'Because it turned out it was all Zena's doing. She was the one who'd booked the room, and she'd paid for it on my card. And she'd used the wrong one. I had a work credit card as well in those days and that was the one I'd always used before.'

'So Laura wouldn't see.'

He acknowledged it.

'Didn't you remember it was Zena who'd booked it?'

'Not at first. I did after a while but I still thought it was just a mistake, that she'd used that card by mistake. She certainly let me think that.'

'But it wasn't a mistake.'

'No. But I didn't know that till much later, and it wasn't me that she told . . .'

'Mel.'

He nodded.

'And that's why they fell out? Zena told her that she had done this thing and that she'd done it deliberately?'

Tom nodded.

'It sounds like you chose a lovely person to have your affair with.'

Tom looked pained again.

'I just don't get it though,' said Carmen. 'Why tell Mel?'

'I have no idea. It was so unbelievably stupid, she just ... I have no idea what was going through her head. To this day I have no idea.'

Carmen chewed on a piece of steak. 'How did it all come about?'

He shrugged, shook his head.

'Well, what happened? Where were you?'

'In St Jude's. They walked into the village to the newsagents ...'

'They?'

'Zena and Mel. They used to do that – they did get on well. They'd have an ice cream and bring back sweets for the other two. But that day Zena came back on her own, without Mel. She was acting like everything was OK, but she was obviously wound up and I was trying to find out what had happened and where Mel was and then Mel walked in and started screaming at Zena and sort of attacked her, so I shouted at Mel and she ran off.'

Something clicked in Carmen's mind. 'Oh my God, it was the day Zena died.'

'Of course. Didn't you realise that?'

'This was the row the neighbour heard.'

'Yes.'

She shook her head. 'Why the hell didn't you tell me?'

He lifted his hand to touch his forehead. 'I don't know. I'm sorry Carmen, I wasn't lying ...'

268

'Of course you were lying! You're unbelievable.' Carmen took a swig of wine. It was all about that day. 'Fucking hell!'

Tom was watching her, wary.

'So what happened then? Mel walked out, and what happened?'

'What do you mean?'

'Did you go after her?'

'I couldn't. I had Mercy there and she was just a toddler, and Jake – I couldn't just leave them. They were both upset. I remember Jake wanted to go and look for Mel but I wouldn't let him – he was only nine or ten. And remember I hadn't got a clue what had happened – I thought Mel was just being difficult. Then Zena told me what she'd said and I couldn't believe it – I'd had no idea.'

'What did she say?'

'Apparently Mel had said something to her about me and Laura and it had annoyed her. Zena admitted that – that it had got on her nerves – and so she'd told Mel "the truth".' He marked the quotes in the air. 'I asked what she meant and she said the way she'd made our break-up happen. And I said what do you mean, and she said that she'd deliberately used that credit card so that Laura would find out. I was . . . gobsmacked. And she was completely unrepentant about it, I remember, she couldn't understand at all why I was pissed off. She said she thought I knew. Maybe I was stupid that I hadn't realised, but I just hadn't. And then that she'd told Mel. I mean, what the hell was she thinking?' He was gabbling now, now that he was telling the truth, it was coming out in a torrent.

269

'Were you angry with her? About what she'd done with you and Laura?'

'Of course! But she just thought she'd done nothing wrong. She talked about how I'd wanted to leave and didn't seem able to do it and I think she felt that she'd just . . . helped things along.'

'Maybe that's right, perhaps you never would have left.'

He shrugged, shook his head.

'Do you think that? Looking back? Be honest.'

'I don't know.' He shook his head. 'Possibly. I was avoiding making a decision, I suppose. But – I couldn't believe it, I couldn't believe she'd done that. And that she'd told Mel – that was what I was most angry about. And she just didn't seem to think it was a big deal, she couldn't see why it was such a wrong thing to do.'

'Maybe it was her way of telling you.'

He shrugged.

Carmen thought about it. It wasn't hard to imagine how Zena would have done what she'd done with that credit card. Tom was shilly-shallying over leaving Laura. No doubt he'd made promises that he wasn't living up to, and after the five or six months that their affair had lasted in secret, it must have been tempting for her to give things a shove in the right direction. Zena was never going to settle for being the other woman, not unless it suited her.

She looked at Tom. 'Were you a bit flattered? That she went to those lengths to get you.'

Tom looked at her, cautious.

'Be honest.'

'Possibly, a bit.'

Carmen sat back in her seat. Her head was spinning with it all. 'I would never have done that.'

'You don't know what you'd do. I didn't think I'd ever have an affair.'

Carmen felt a need to get away. She excused herself and went to the toilet. She sat in the cubicle and tried to clear her thoughts, then took her time washing her hands, drying them. She reached in her handbag for lipstick and found the bracelet Paula had given her. Well, he could have that back for a start. She held it in her hand as she returned to their table.

'I wouldn't want you to be like Zena,' he said as she sat down. 'Surely you can see that. Doesn't what I am telling you make you see that? What's that?'

She had put the bracelet on the table between them. She told him Paula had given it to her. He looked at it. 'I remember this,' he said.

'It is Zena's then?'

'Yes.' He picked it up, turned it around in his hand.

'Did you give it to her?'

'No, I don't know where it came from, she always had it. How weird.'

He handed it back to her.

'What are you doing? I don't want it,' she said.

'Well, I don't want it either. It's – creepy.'

Carmen looked at the bracelet.

'Carmen, please, just get rid of it.'

She looked at him. It had affected him badly, seeing it, she could tell, but it was an unpleasant moment, his rejection of it. 'Please,' he said again.

She took the bracelet and put it back into her bag.

'Thank you.' He stared at the table. 'Shall I carry on? I can't remember where we got to.' She didn't help him. 'Oh yes, I remember, Zena had told me what had happened with Mel.'

'Did you have a row?'

He shook his head. 'Zena wasn't the type for thrashing things out, not if it was me who was angry – obviously it was different if she was.' He trailed off. 'From what I can remember, she just got changed into her swimming costume and walked out.'

'In the rain,' said Carmen, almost to herself. 'That's why she went swimming in the rain.'

He didn't reply.

'And that's why you weren't worried when she didn't come back. Because you'd rowed. You thought she'd gone off to the pub or something in a huff.'

'I just . . .' He broke off again. He looked at her. 'I know I keep saying this, but I didn't get Zena. I couldn't predict how she was going to act. I didn't know her like I know you, do you understand? Yes, you are right, she could have been out for the whole night and I have no idea if she would have thought it was normal to do that without telling me, but probably, yes.' He reached across, reached for Carmen's hand, but he stopped short. 'With you I'd know, I'd know that you would never do something like that without telling me. Do you understand?'

Carmen nodded. She understood. She knew what Zena was like now.

'It's me and you that matter, Carmen, me and you, not any of this.' He reached for her hand but she moved it away.

'Fuck.' Tom sat back in his chair. 'Fuck, fuck, fuck.' He banged his hand on the table. 'Go on then, what else do you want to know?'

Carmen paused and then she said, 'How dare you talk to me like that!'

'What?'

She stood up. 'How dare you!'

'I'm sorry, I'm just frustrated. Sit down, please, Carmen.'

'Don't ever talk to me like that again.'

'I'm sorry, I won't. Come on, please sit down and we can finish this.'

He was shocked, she could tell, at her reaction, and embarrassed that people were looking. He tried to smooth it over by talking. 'So, yes, that's it. Zena went off and then quite soon after that Laura came to pick the kids up – I told you that, didn't I? And she went to look for Mel while I stayed with Jake and Mercy.' He was watching her. 'Do you want more wine? I'm sorry, Carmen, I didn't mean to get angry . . . I just—'

'I hate your temper, do you know that? I hate it.'

'I know, but—'

'Do you know how frightening you can be?'

'I'm sorry, it will never happen again.'

What hollow words.

'I'll get us more wine,' he said, and went to wave the waiter over, but Carmen stopped him. She sat down again, sideways on her seat.

He gabbled on. 'Yes, and so Laura found Mel and they came back and then they all went home.'

'You didn't tell the police any of this, did you?' said Carmen. 'About what had happened with Mel and Zena. Why?'

'Why should I? It was personal. It didn't have anything to do with Zena going missing, did it?'

'Of course it did – it meant there was an obvious reason why Zena went off that day and why she didn't come back.'

He didn't reply.

'They knew as well, didn't they? They knew there'd been an argument. That's why they suspected you.'

He swilled the last of his wine around his glass.

'Why didn't you just tell them that it was Mel who was rowing with Zena?'

He tipped his head back and emptied his glass. 'Why do you think?'

'I don't know.'

'Mel was twelve years old. I didn't want the police questioning her.'

'You were protecting her.'

Of course. Of course. He was protecting Mel.

A chill passed through her.

They took a cab home. They sat in opposite corners in the back, both drained. When they got back to the flat Tom made a pot of tea and Carmen sat at the kitchen table.

He came and sat with her. 'Have I messed things up completely?' he said.

Carmen looked at him. He looked anxious, scared.

'Have I ruined things? Tell me, Carmen.'

'I don't know,' she said.

For a moment he was silent. 'I can't bear it to all go wrong. Not again.'

And then Carmen started to laugh. It just seemed so funny, his selfishness. As though his only concern was that relationship number three might be messed up and he would have to go through it all yet again, meeting someone else, putting down new roots, moving that pile of boxes to another flat . . .

'What have I said now?' he said.

She shook her head. 'Forget it.' But in a strange way it had warmed her to him more than anything else he had said. It was so human. She half smiled at him and it was enough to embolden him.

'I bet you don't always tell me the whole truth,' he said.

'I do,' she said.

'Carmen, I think all couples lie a little bit – it's natural.'

'I don't.'

But that wasn't true, was it? Carmen thought then about Nick, about Monday – and Monday night – in St Jude's. She thought about all the other things that she had done behind Tom's back – reading his emails, going to see Zena's mum and the police. She'd been lying to him for weeks. With cause maybe, but still . . .

She looked at him. She should just tell him now. What had

she got to lose? But instead, in a weird twist of her mind, she turned on Zena, gave away her secrets instead. 'Kieran told me something strange about Zena,' she said. 'I didn't tell you . . . I don't know why.'

Tom looked sceptical. He had no patience left with Kieran.

'He met someone who worked with her, a girl.' She paused. 'Tom, do you think it's possible Zena was having an affair? With someone else, I mean, while she was with you – someone at work? Before she died?'

He looked at her strangely. 'Who was this person? What did she say?'

The look on his face frightened her. Confusion. Anger. She regretted saying anything. 'Look, just forget it Tom, it's probably nothing anyway.'

He touched his forehead with his hand. 'Who was she? What did she say?'

'I don't know. It was just some girl Kieran knows who worked at the magazine for a while, but she was only an intern . . .'

'What did she say?'

She had to tell him now. And part of her wanted to hurt him. 'She said there were rumours about Zena and some guy.'

'What guy?'

'I don't know.'

'What did Kieran say?'

'Just . . . he was someone high up in the company. Look, forget it, that girl was probably just talking nonsense, it was probably nothing.'

But he was shaking his head. 'It won't have been nothing.'

He sighed, rubbed his forehead. 'I told you. I keep telling you and you won't listen.'

'What?'

'What a total bloody catastrophe she was. What a total fucking idiot I was. What a fucking idiot.' He hit his fist against his forehead.

'Tom . . .'

'Idiot.' He did it again, hit himself again. Then he covered his face with his hands and breathed hard, in and out, in and out.

Carmen didn't know what to do. She was scared. She sat and watched him, frozen, and slowly his breathing quietened and his body relaxed.

She'd wanted truth, here was truth, there could be no doubt about that.

They didn't talk any more. Eventually they went to bed. They lay down together, side by side, and somehow the huge emotion they were both experiencing spilled into touching, and an embrace, and then sex. They were gentle at first, soothing, but Tom became passionate as he was aroused, and held her tightly as he made love to her, buried his head in her skin like an animal.

The subdued mood carried over to the next morning. After Tom had left for work Carmen had to force herself out of bed, to shower and put on clean jeans and a T-shirt. She felt as though she was on the edge of a precipice, that there were no certainties left. Her mind darted this way and that, anxious, distracted.

The phone rang. It was Lucia. Carmen answered immediately, pleased for the distraction, but then regretted it because there was a weight in her mother's voice as she said hello and went through the usual greetings. 'Is something wrong, Mum?'

'I'm just lonely, that's all.'

Carmen felt guilt and resentment in equal measure, the same old cocktail. Her tone became brisk. 'You need to get out more, it's no good sitting in that flat all the time, anyone would feel crap. Go and see a friend.'

Carmen could hear Lucia's fingers drumming, a classic sign of tension, a bad sign.

'Listen, I'll be over at the weekend.'

Drumming. Drumming.

'Mum, I think you're getting depressed. Maybe we should make an appointment with the doctor.'

'So he can tell me I'm mad and give me drugs?'

After they hung up, Carmen raised her eyes to the heavens. She loved her mother, but sometimes she could feel like a burden.

She thought about Laura then. Laura hadn't burdened her husband or her children, she didn't pull on them, and look how she was rewarded. Maybe she didn't pull hard enough, maybe that was her mistake, since the wronged partner always has to be at fault somehow these days. Maybe Tom just drifted away, floated off . . .

. . . and got caught in a spider's web.

Mel too, Mel had drifted away. Had she got caught in the spider's web too?

But Mel had started to struggle.

Carmen reached for her bag and pulled out Zena's bracelet. She didn't want it. What was she going to do with it? She put it on again, but it pinched her, it was too small, meant for a slimmer wrist than hers.

There was something that tickled her too. She took the bracelet off and held it up to the light, stretched the elastic. There were hairs trapped between the discs – not hairs from an arm but longer, hairs from someone's head.

And suddenly Carmen thought, Maybe they got caught there when Zena reached out to push someone away from her. To defend herself. Maybe they got caught in a struggle.

She looked more closely. These were not Zena's black hairs, these were full red – there were six or seven of them, caught in this bracelet at the same time.

And her first thought was – Mel's hair is this colour. Red hair, Celtic – it had to be. Zena's hair was black, and Paula, who had had this bracelet for three years, was fair. So was her daughter Cheyenne – Carmen had seen her playing in the garden.

She thought about what Tom had told her the night before, how Mel had argued with Zena, how furious she had been. He'd said Mel attacked her – was it possible . . .? But Mel was a child, twelve years old when Zena died. Strong though, and tall. Zena was tall too, but slight.

A child who is angry will lash out – hard. Had it been more serious than Tom had told her? Had Mel found something hard and hit Zena round the head with it?

Carmen felt chilled. He'd almost told her, hadn't he? He'd

said that the reason he'd lied to the police was because he was protecting Mel. He'd said he didn't want them to interview her, but did that make sense? If they'd just had a row? He must have known how serious it was to lie to the police, what was at stake, would he take that risk?

It made sense if something much worse had happened, if Mel had injured Zena.

But no, it was unthinkable; if Mel had injured Zena, Tom would have called an ambulance.

But what if she was dead? How would Tom have acted then?

Was it plausible that he would have disposed of his girlfriend's body to protect his daughter? That he would have carried Zena through the streets to the sea?

But Zena died from drowning, not from the head injury. She was still alive when she went into the sea. Would Tom have carried her still-breathing body, and dumped her in the waves?

No, it was unthinkable, he would have called an ambulance.

Unless in his panic he'd thought she was dead? That Mel had killed her?

She went to her computer and googled DNA tests. She could have the hair tested for a genetic match. A page of firms came up offering DNA testing, paternity testing – that would be good enough, she just had to establish a match.

There was a chest of drawers on the landing that the children used to store their personal bits and bobs. Each of them had their own drawer. Carmen had painted them different colours – pale pink for Mercy, green for Jake, lilac for Mel.

Mel's was half empty. There were a couple of pairs of knickers, a romantic novel, a cigarette lighter – what the hell? – a dirty eyeliner, a hairbrush. Carmen held the brush up to the light. She held the bracelet up beside it. The hairs looked the same.

She had no idea how she should go about this, so she fetched a pack of new rubber gloves from the kitchen and used them to extricate a tangle of hair from the brush, which she laid on a sheet of paper and wrapped into a parcel. Then she carefully removed the hairs from the bracelet and folded them into a separate sheet alongside.

She taped them up, scribbled a note explaining that she was looking to see whether these two samples contained matching DNA, wrote a cheque for £150 from her personal account and sealed the lot up. Then she walked down to the post office.

On her way home a butterfly, pure white, crossed her path and she stopped to watch it. It landed on a rosebush, on a petal, and its wings flickered to keep it buoyant. She watched it linger there and then it flew off again, to another petal.

It was so simple and so beautiful, and she stood for five minutes or more transfixed by its movements. And as she watched her mind calmed down and it seemed to her suddenly that she had been caught up in some sort of overheated meltdown, a whirlwind of imaginings that had nothing to do with what actually happened to Zena and everything to do with the distance between her and Tom.

The butterfly flew away.

It's over, Carmen thought. My marriage is over. There's nothing to be done.

She texted her mother to say, I'm coming to stay, and then she went home to pack a bag.

Chapter 18

August, two months later

It was nine thirty. Carmen was early. She could have waited in the new deli that had opened up near the station, had a coffee, but she walked to the cemetery instead, past the woman selling flowers, through the wide gate and up the hill, to the plot they had paid a premium for with a view over the suburbs, out to the countryside.

'Hello, Dad.' She bent down and pulled out a dandelion that was obscuring the small stone that marked the place where they had scattered his ashes. Raymond Webb, beloved father and husband. 'How are you doing?'

She sat down on the grass, looked at the view. It had changed in twelve months – they had thinned out some trees. She could see further, but more houses, it was less peaceful somehow. It bothered her, which was stupid, since her father knew no different.

He used to bring her here as a child, for a walk after

Sunday lunch. Lucia hated fresh air so it would always be just the two of them. She'd liked it here, at least compared to some of the other places he took her for walks; they were always too adult, the pace always too brisk. If they went to the park the swings would be a grudging afterthought. He didn't really understand about children. He loved her, but he was impatient for her to grow up so their time could be spent in his world.

She'd been thinking about him recently, about her family, about family generally. He hadn't been a perfect parent, far from it, she could see that even more clearly now, the ways in which he'd let her down. But she had loved him and he'd loved her. She touched his headstone. She could have done with him around these last few weeks, someone to help her, someone to talk to, things hadn't been easy. But he was dust, useless to her forever now.

When Kieran arrived Carmen was making a daisy chain. He had brought flowers – a multicoloured bunch of carnations. 'Horrible, aren't they?' He dropped them beside the gravestone, awkward, embarrassed. Carmen reached over and put them straight.

He sat on the grass beside her. 'They've cut more trees down,' he said.

'Yes.'

It had become their habit to meet here on the anniversary of their father's death. Carmen had suggested it years ago, and now it was a ritual. She felt a wave of warmth for Kieran, for still showing up.

They strolled around the grounds. 'How are you doing?' he said.

'Fine.'

Kieran asked after Lucia and Carmen told him she was OK though not great. But the doctor had arranged for some counselling and she was enjoying the sessions, so hopefully that would help.

'At least she's got you there.'

'Well, actually . . .' And then Carmen told him that in fact she wasn't staying at her mother's place any more – that she had moved back into her flat.

'Really? Tom's gone? About bloody time – you should have never let him stay there, it's your flat.'

So then Carmen told him that no, actually Tom was still there, that she'd moved back in with him, that they were back together.

He stopped in his tracks. 'You're fucking shitting me.'

'Don't swear like that.'

'Jesus Christ, Carmen!'

'This is my decision, don't—'

'For fuck's sake, are you completely mental? Why would you do that?'

'Because I'm pregnant.'

It wasn't true. Well, it was true, but it wasn't the only reason she and Tom had got back together. But how could she begin to explain it all to Kieran who saw life like a child, all in blacks and whites?

Her hand rested on her tummy. There was no sign yet, but the baby was there, growing, waiting.

'You're pregnant?'

'Yes.'

'And it's Tom's?'

She rolled her eyes. 'Of course it is.'

'But he's a cunt.'

'For fuck's sake, Kieran, grow up. There were a lot of good things about me and Tom and I loved him. I love him still. Life isn't so simple – you of all people should know that. We've sorted things out, can't you understand that?'

He looked sceptical. He looked upset. She could understand – he'd done his best to be supportive when she'd told him she'd left Tom, and of course he'd never liked him. But that's life. She had no patience for it any more, none of it – Lucia had been the same way. But it was her life. They'd just have to get used to it.

'I really want this baby. I really want this to happen. Can't you just be happy for me?'

They carried on walking. He was taking it in, she could see that.

'You're going to be an uncle, you do realise?' she said.

And eventually he stopped being angry and even smiled about it. 'Uncle Kieran,' he said. 'Poor bloody kid.'

Chapter 19

Carmen was sitting on the beach at St Jude's. It was a beautiful afternoon, warm with a breeze. She'd set off for the village to buy milk but decided to sit down in the sun and she'd been there for half an hour or more, staring out across the North Sea. Long ago it had been dry land and our ancestors had migrated across it on foot, lived out there, hunted and even started to farm, trawlers still turned up fragments of their existence. Now where she sat was a frontier. Some of the houses on the edge of the beach flew Union Flags, as though the Dutch might be able to see them from their gardens: Keep out!

They'd seen a relationship counsellor, Carmen had insisted on that, an older woman. Not to talk about Zena – Carmen had come to see all of that as a red herring for what was wrong between them – but to talk about each other, themselves, their partnership. And it had been good. The counselling had helped them to see many things more clearly, like the great similarities in their backgrounds, and how these had shaped them. Carmen hadn't recognised any of that before – she had focused only on their differences. But both she and Tom had a father who was distant and actually absent for large chunks of their childhood and subsequent life. And both of them had a mother who, for very different reasons and in very different ways, had prevented them from saying what they thought, openly. Who had unwittingly trained each of them for a life of subterfuge.

Carmen felt more confident than she had for years. Her relationship was built on firmer foundations, they were going to have a baby, the future shone ahead of them.

Her phone rang. It was Tom. 'Hi, darling,' she said, 'I'm just—'

'You fucking bitch!'

She was so shocked she couldn't speak. She could hear his breath, he was panting with anger.

'What did you think? That I wouldn't find out?'

'Don't talk to me like that! What are you even talking about?'

'I'm talking about you and I'm talking about Nick. I'm talking about you and that . . . wanker – in my house, in MY fucking house.'

Carmen's stomach turned over. She could hear his fury, and her fear made her angry too.

She pressed the red button and cut him off.

Shit. Oh shit oh shit. She dialled him straight back.

'Tom . . .'

'Fuck you.' He cut out on her this time. The line was dead.

'Bastard,' she said to the phone, but she knew she was in the wrong, completely in the wrong. Why hadn't she just told him during all of these weeks about meeting up with Nick? During all of this time of peacemaking and clean slate? What an idiot!

She had to sort this out now. She called his number again, but it went to voicemail, so she tried again but the same thing happened. He'd turned his phone off. She left a message. 'Listen, Tom, it's not what you think. Please call me back, let me explain, he just . . .'

Then she panicked and rang off.

She needed to think before she talked to him. She needed to find out what he knew. She didn't want to make things worse by telling him too much – maybe he didn't know Nick had stayed the night, maybe he'd just heard he'd been up there.

God, what am I doing? she thought. Just tell him the truth, tell him all of it. I have done nothing wrong, I'll just tell him the truth and he will see . . .

Oh shit oh shit oh shit.

He had never been angry with her like this. She had never heard him so angry, not with her.

She felt scared suddenly.

She looked around her. The beach was empty and she felt exposed in the open space. She walked back to the bungalow, slowly, her hand across her belly. They had spent the weekend there, just the two of them, and it had been so beautiful, they were both so happy about the baby, about being together. Tom had caught the train to London early that morning and she had stayed because they'd made an appointment with a landscape gardener – they were finally going to tackle the scrubby yard at the back of the bungalow. The meeting had gone well – the woman had drawn up some ideas, it was going to be lovely.

She started to cry as she walked. It would be OK – it had to be. She just had to tell him the truth, he would see she had done nothing wrong. God, he'd lied enough to her.

She called his mobile again, from the phone at the bungalow, but it was still turned off. She tried his work number, but it went straight to voicemail. She emailed – 'Tom, you need to call me, this is not what you think. I love you and I have done nothing wrong.'

She reached instinctively to call Kath, to tell her what had happened. She wanted reassurance that everything would be OK, that what she had done was not so bad, but she didn't go through with the call. She was ashamed to tell Kath about Nick. It sounded so bad, that she had invited him up, that she hadn't told Tom, that he had stayed the night.

She didn't know what to do. She should be setting off soon, to be back in London when Tom got home, but she wasn't sure if she should continue with their arrangement or not. She sat down on the sofa. She had to stay calm for the baby, not get too upset. She breathed, in, out, in, out. She was cold. She pulled a blanket over herself.

She fell asleep.

When she woke it was getting dark and for a moment she was happy, then she remembered what had happened. She reached for her phone, hoping to find a message or a missed call from Tom, but there was nothing. Of course not, it would have woken her.

It was gone nine, six hours since they'd spoken.

She tapped out a text – 'please call'.

She was scared now. Tom had never been unreachable to her before. During all the difficulties of the past weeks she'd been the one turning her back, he'd only ever reached for her.

What have I done?

The curtains were open and the orange street light threw the shadow of the rose across the room, on to the wall, the way it had the night she'd sat here with Nick. She remembered the way he had touched her . . . she mustn't think about that. Nothing happened, she told herself, I have nothing to feel ashamed or guilty about, I have done nothing wrong.

She heard footsteps outside, someone was coming up the path. Maybe it was Paula – that would be good, someone to distract her. The door between the living room and the hall was open and from where she lay she could see through to the front door, at the side of the house. Her eyes rested on the frosted glass panes at the top, she waited for a figure to appear, for the bell to ring, but nothing happened. She strained to hear something more. She was just about to move, to tell herself she had imagined it and to stand up and turn on the light, when a shadow passed across the glass.

There was someone out there.

Tom. Had Tom come here? Driven up?

Suddenly she was terrified. Her body went rigid. She waited, for a key in the door. Seconds passed and nothing happened. He must have gone around to the back.

She ran to the front window, looked for Tom's car. It wasn't in the street or the drive and for a moment she felt relief, but then she thought, That means nothing. Her mobile was in her hand. Should she dial 999? She tapped out the numbers, her finger rested on the green call button, but she felt stupid. What if it was a trick of the light? The shadow of an animal? What if she had imagined it?

She waited, taut, listening and watching. The lights were off, no one knew she was here. What if whoever was out there smashed their way into the back? Or forced the front door? It was obscured, around the side – she'd never liked that. She looked for ways to get out. The windows in the living room were casements, they opened fully and there were no locks – there were no locks on any of the windows. If she could get to the catch, she could get out.

That helped. She waited, silent and still. Nothing happened. She started to believe she had imagined it. It would have been a cat or a fox, the shadow a trick of the light.

Then she heard a noise at the back of the house. This time she didn't think, she just ran out of the door and down the drive, and she was standing in the street in her socks. The front door stood wide open, she hadn't picked up her keys. What now? Call the police? Her phone was in her hand, but already she was questioning herself again.

There was no one out on the street. Part of her was glad of that because she was already feeling stupid again. What was wrong with her? But she was still frightened, too frightened to go back indoors. She needed to see another human, someone normal and everyday whom she maybe recognised a little and

292

could say to, 'I know I'm being ridiculous but I thought I heard something . . . probably just imagination – but would you mind . . .?' Someone to come with her and look round the back, look through the house, check it over so she could go back inside and bolt the doors and forget all about this.

She looked at her neighbours' houses either side. Both were in darkness like her own. There was a light on a couple of doors up, but it was no one she knew, even by sight.

She scanned the cars in the street, looking for Tom's Audi but it wasn't there. Of course not, he wouldn't do this, of course he wouldn't. She touched her belly – their baby inside. He wouldn't do this, she knew.

She didn't know. She was frightened.

She remembered the police liaison officer she'd met, the guy who'd talked to her about Zena's death. He'd been kind to her and she'd liked him. He'd given her his card and she'd put his number on her phone. She could call him, but what was his name? She scrolled through the list – Andy, that was it.

She dialled before she could change her mind.

He was nice about it. She apologised, said she knew how stupid she was being but she'd heard a prowler and now she was standing in the street and daren't go back inside. He didn't laugh at her. He said he was nearby and would come over.

She felt better immediately, and foolish of course. He was there in ten minutes. She was sitting on the wall, hoping the neighbours wouldn't look out and come and ask if she was OK. Thank God he wasn't in a marked car. 'I feel really stupid,' she said, as he got out.

'It's no problem. I'll take a look. You wait here.'

She watched him stride up the drive, round the back of the house. He was wearing jeans, he must have been out, not working, and she felt even worse. After a minute or two he came back. 'There's no one there and I can't find any sign of an attempted break-in.'

'I'm sorry,' she said.

'OK if I check inside?'

'Oh, would you?'

He went in and again she waited. She saw the lights being switched on around the house. A woman walked past and looked at her socks.

Andy came out again. 'It's fine. Come with me.'

'I'm so sorry,' she said as they went inside. 'I was sure I heard something but I must have imagined it. I could have sworn I saw someone.'

He was opening the doors to show her each room. He had left the lights on all through the place. 'Don't worry about it, you did the right thing.'

When they had finished he stood with her in the hall. 'Are you OK?'

'Yes, I'll be fine now, thank you.'

But it wasn't true, she wasn't fine.

'I'm pregnant,' she said. 'Maybe that's made me a bit ... over-cautious. It's early days – just a few weeks.'

'Congratulations.'

At some point he had taken his jacket off. He pulled it on

again. She was terrified suddenly of him going, of being left here on her own. 'Can I make you a cup of tea?' she blurted.

He smiled apologetically. 'I can't, I need to . . .'

'Of course.'

But he didn't go. They stood together in the hall. 'You should improve your security,' he said. 'You haven't even got window locks.'

'Tom says we don't need them here.'

'Tell him he's wrong about that.'

She half smiled.

'That time you came in . . .' he said.

'I'm sorry about that, I've felt bad about it ever since.'

'Is everything all right? Now?'

She looked at him. He meant more than he was saying, but she didn't know what exactly. He had thought about her since they had met, and she knew he was concerned, and knowing those things affected her strangely. She heard herself saying, 'I don't know,' and sank into a chair.

He took his jacket off again. He asked her some questions. Was she feeling faint? Ill? Where was Tom? Why was she here alone? She found herself telling him that they'd rowed. She apologised again, said she was being stupid, she had no idea why she was telling him, wasting his time.

He asked her if there was anywhere she could go, somewhere she felt safe. Not back to the flat, somewhere else, with a friend, and no, not here. His obvious concern both frightened and reassured her. He was saying don't go home, don't go where Tom is, and it validated and underlined her fears.

She was glad to be told. It was a relief to be let off the hook. She didn't want to go back to her flat. It was her home but it didn't feel safe, and Andy must be able to see how she felt, or must suspect there was a real danger.

I am scared of Tom, she thought. And I am right to be scared of him.

Andy stayed with her while she rang Kath, while she told her that she and Tom had had a massive row and asked if she could stay at theirs. Kath was angry, with Tom not with her. 'How could he argue with you now?' she said. 'Of course you can come.'

Andy waited while she got a few things together, and was patient while she faffed. He made sure she locked the place up properly, watched her drive away. Carmen felt she had never been so grateful to anyone in her life.

Chapter 20

Carmen sat in pyjamas with Kath and Lily and a selection of toys on Kath's thick-pile living-room carpet. Kath and Lily were still in their nightclothes too – it was the school summer holidays so Kath was off work. Carmen had arrived late the night before and was only now explaining what had happened. How she'd met up with Nick and somehow or other she hadn't told Tom, and how he had found out and was furious.

'Oh, how ridiculous. But why didn't you just tell him at the time?'

'It just – didn't come up. I don't know, maybe I felt a bit strange about it. It didn't seem like such a big deal . . .'

There had still been no word from Tom.

'How is Nick?' said Kath, handing Lily a piece of buttered toast. There was a tray with tea and breakfast things beside them on the floor.

'Fine.'

'What did you do?'

'Nothing much, had lunch, hung out.'

297

'Did he take you somewhere swanky?'

'Not really.' Carmen sipped tea from a pretty mug. This, of course, was where it got a bit more sticky. 'Actually, we met up in St Jude's. He wanted to meet in London, but I happened to be at the bungalow when he was over so he came up.'

'That's a long way just for lunch.' Straight to the point – nothing got past Kath.

'Well, for the day – or it was meant to be that, but he missed his train home.'

'He stayed the night?'

'Yes, but not with me.'

'In a hotel?'

'No, in the bungalow but not in my bed.'

Kath slotted a pull-apart puzzle toy together. 'No wonder Tom's pissed off.'

'Kath, nothing happened.'

'Yes, but you wouldn't like it, would you? If he did that to you.'

'Nothing happened – I swear it. It was the night I told you about, when Mel came round drunk. You believe me, don't you?'

'Of course.'

It didn't sound like it.

Carmen was about to say more when they heard the front door go and Joe came in. He'd worked the night shift and looked tired and fed up, but he mustered a smile and a hug for Carmen. 'How are you doing?' He went to Kath and kissed her and ruffled Lily's hair.

'Everything all right?' said Kath. 'Any news?'

'Not yet.'

'Is something happening?' said Carmen.

Kath looked at Joe. 'Tell her,' he said. 'I don't mind.'

'Joe's been put on warning for redundancy.' Kath picked up Lily's toy again so that she avoided Carmen's eye.

'No!' said Carmen.

'Shit, isn't it?' said Joe. 'We'll find out in the next couple of weeks.'

'I can't believe it!' said Carmen. 'Kath, you should have told me.' She reached over and squeezed her friend's arm.

'I'm going to have a shower and a kip,' said Joe. 'Sorry, Carmen, I am knackered. Will you be here later?'

'Probably,' she said.

'You staying for lunch?'

'Yes.'

When he'd gone Carmen reached over and put her arm around her friend. Her shoulders felt stiff beneath Carmen's arm, tense. She was seriously worried, Carmen knew.

They dressed and took Lily out in the buggy, walked to Crystal Palace and around the dinosaur park, where they used to hang out as teenagers. Even though she lived nearby Carmen hadn't been to see the dinosaurs for years. The fresh air and exercise did them both good, and by the time they got back they were feeling more cheerful. Joe was up and had cooked macaroni cheese for lunch. They sat together at the kitchen table with Lily in her high chair and Joe told Carmen that he had ideas already, that he had been talking to a colleague and friend whose job was also under threat about setting up a private investigator agency. They would both get a good pay-off, enough to see them through the first year.

'That's a great idea,' said Carmen.

'If there's a market for it,' said Kath.

'There is,' said Joe, irritated.

'You don't know that for sure,' said Kath.

'I know there's lots of work out there.'

'I'm just making the point, it's not just us any more. We need security.'

'There's no such thing these days,' said Joe. 'I'm doing my best, OK?'

To change the subject as much as anything, Carmen told Joe how things were with her and Tom.

'You need to speak to him, don't you?' said Joe. 'Just explain.'

'He won't talk to me.'

'He has to sometime,' said Kath.

And then Carmen thought, What if he doesn't? They'd been through so much – what if this was the last straw and he just walked away now? And she felt so bleak that she started to cry. 'I'm sorry,' she said, wiping her eyes. 'It's just – horrible.'

'You'll sort this out,' Kath said. 'Of course you will. What's he going to do – let you have this baby and never speak to you again?'

'You are telling the truth that nothing happened with Nick?' said Joe.

'Of course I am!'

'That baby's not his, is it?'

'Joe!' said Kath.

300

'There is no way on earth the baby is Nick's, OK?' said Carmen.

'Well, that's good, because it would be a bit obvious,' said Joe, and then he laughed.

'Joe!' snapped Kath.

Carmen picked at her food.

'You're very hormonal,' said Kath. 'It's not as bad as you think. Joe, can't you do anything?'

'What can he do?'

'Can't you talk to Tom?' said Kath.

He shrugged, unsure about that.

'Oh, would you?' said Carmen.

'Well ... I need to go to Canning Town this afternoon. I suppose I could try to meet him for a drink in Canary Wharf after work?'

'Oh, thank you!' said Carmen.

'Don't get too excited, he might not want to.'

Carmen's mobile rang and her heart jumped, but it wasn't Tom's number, her screen said 'international'. She swallowed her disappointment and took it, but the line was bad and the man's voice at the other end so thickly accented that she struggled to understand what was being said. She almost hung up but a sincerity in the caller's tone told her this wasn't just another marketing call, so she signalled an apology to the others and went into the hall and shut the door. 'Sorry, I just can't understand what you're saying. Who is it?' He tried again – it sounded like Genevieve but it couldn't be that – and then she got it; it was the genetics company she had sent Mel's hair to, and the strands she had found on Zena's bracelet, weeks before. But they had written to her to say the sample was unusable – she told the man this.

'Well, that letter was correct. The sample you sent us is not suitable for a paternity DNA test because there had been a great deterioration of the material.'

'Exactly, that's what the letter said.'

'However, even with material in this condition we can test for a mitochondrial DNA link.'

'Sorry?'

'Mitochondrial DNA is non-nuclear DNA that is passed down the female line only. We can determine from it a shared female ancestry.'

Carmen was confused. The original idea had been to find out whether the hair in the bracelet was Mel's hair, the same as the sample from the hairbrush. 'So are you saying that test would show whether the two samples come from the same person?' she said.

'No, it would not, or not definitely. What it would show is whether the hairs came from the same person or from two persons who were closely related through the female line, such as siblings of the same mother or a grandmother or indeed a great-great-grandmother, but it would not be able to show which of these was the case.'

'What about a brother and sister? Would it show that?'

'Yes, indeed – a brother and sister of the same mother.'

She thought about it. It all felt like ancient history and yet her curiosity was piqued.

'We could do the mitochondrial match test at the same price as the paternity test.'

'OK, that's fine, yes, please, then do that,' she said, still half confused, and rang off.

The phone rang again immediately. It was the same man. 'Mrs Cawton. Actually I hope you can forgive us but I can tell you that we have already done the test I have just described.'

'But—'

'In fact we had already done so by an administrative error. I do apologise and I can assure you the result would have been destroyed if you had not given consent, but your approval does mean I can give you the result immediately.'

Carmen's head was spinning.

'I can confirm that there is a mitochondrial link between the two samples.'

'So they come from the same person?'

'That is one possibility, but it is not certain. As I explained to you, this positive result means that they may come from the same person or they may come from two persons who are closely related via the female line. As you say, siblings are possible.'

She thanked him and hung up and for a moment she felt excited and then she thought, So what? It was almost certainly Mel's hair and there would be an innocent explanation. It had probably got caught there when she was with Zena sometime, before they had fallen out – maybe Zena had her arm round her, or even lent her the bracelet. Kath asked her what the call was about and Carmen said, 'Nothing.' She had real problems to worry about now.

After lunch Joe went upstairs to sleep, and Kath went to settle Lily for a nap. Carmen washed up the lunch things and then turned on the TV and found an old black-and-white film. Kath came back down and said, 'That is just what I fancy,' and they watched together, lying top to tail on the sofa with a blanket thrown over them.

During the adverts, Kath said, 'Is something going on you haven't told me about?'

'What do you mean?'

'With Tom.'

Carmen sank deeper into the sofa. She should have told Kath more about what was happening before now, but she hadn't wanted to talk about it. Kath did find out at one point that Carmen was staying with her mother, but Carmen had said it was because Lucia was feeling low. 'We've been having some counselling – it's hard to explain.'

'Has he got off with someone else?'

'No – no, it isn't that. It's just . . . Oh, Kath, I just don't want to talk about it, do you mind? To be honest, it's all been resolved anyway. Just – end of the honeymoon stuff, it's nothing serious.'

'Really?'

'It's nothing specific I could put into words even. We're fine now – or we were until this.'

Kath squeezed her foot.

They carried on watching the film, and then Carmen said, 'Kath, do you think I've got bad taste in men?'

'What do you mean?'

'Well, Nick wasn't exactly perfect . . .' She broke off.

'No one is, are they? And Tom's completely different to Nick anyway.'

She didn't understand what Carmen was getting at, which was understandable since Carmen wasn't sure herself. Just those old doubts resurfacing . . .

'It sounds to me like Tom's the one who should worry about always going for the same type,' said Kath. 'You, Zena . . .'

'I'm not like Zena!'

But Kath was smiling. 'I was joking.'

'I know but . . . I don't want to be compared with her, that's all.'

'She was just a person, Carmen, just trying to get on with her life like the rest of us. Don't turn her into some demon.'

Joe left around three and texted at five thirty to say he was meeting up with Tom after work. Kath said that would probably mean a late night, since Joe wasn't working the next day, and suggested that Carmen sleep there again unless they heard otherwise. That suited Carmen, and while Kath was settling Lily for the night, she went out and picked up a takeaway. She'd intended to get a curry, but on the way she passed a fried chicken shop and bought from there instead. Tom would never eat fried chicken, but Kath was delighted. Tastes of their youth.

They ate out of boxes in front of the TV, the way they used to on a Saturday night when Kath was single and Nick was away and they were too knackered from work to go out, which meant just about every other weekend. Sitting there now,

Carmen realised how that time had slipped into history without her really noticing, a past era. What would it be like if she was single now? Very different, that was for sure. Even more different soon, with a baby. Carmen shied from the thought of it, from the loneliness.

Joe didn't call or text and there was no word from Tom. Kath was yawning by nine and by half past was falling asleep, so they went to bed. Kath had put Lily in their room so Carmen could have Lily's. She was sleeping on a futon beside the cot.

Even with the window open, the small room was hot and stuffy. Carmen abandoned her pyjamas and lay naked on top of the covers, looking up at Lily's mobile, four sheep following each other round and round. The tangerine glow of the city filtered through the thin curtain. She could have pulled down the blackout blind but it would have shut out any air. Besides she didn't really mind; it was brighter here than at her flat but she was used to it. Every so often a car with the stereo pimped for Saturday night thudded past, the noise invading, unlawful entry. Lily would grow up with that, the city laid down in her DNA, as Kath and Carmen had before her, an immunisation against any urban setting.

Another stereo thudded by. She knew she would never sleep like this and she was very tired now, so she surrendered to the inevitable, got up and closed the window, pulled down the blackout blind. That was better, quieter, and the room was almost pitch black, but she felt claustrophobic, and the heat was unbearable. She closed her eyes and encouraged her mind to feel enclosed in the small space, for it to feel womblike.

She fell asleep.

She couldn't say what woke her, but she sensed it had not been long, that she had still been in the first stage of deep sleep. Immediately she was wide awake. Something was not right.

There was someone in the room with her. Another human.

'Kath? Is that you?'

There was no answer.

'Who is that? Joe?'

She waited.

'Tom?'

There was no answer.

She could hear breathing.

Cortisol flooded through her and every muscle in her body stiffened, but she didn't move. There was no fight or flight, she was frozen. She could scream and Kath would hear, she told herself, and the thought reassured her.

But what if something had happened to Kath?

'Who is that?'

No answer.

Her hand resting on her thigh reminded her of her nakedness and it suddenly seemed supremely important to put on some clothing. Her hand slid along the cover, searching for the pyjamas she had discarded earlier – the top was somewhere here, near the pillow, she thought. She found it and examined it with her fingertips, trying to make sense of it, of the holes in the material where her body and head and arms should go, but she couldn't do it in the dark, she just couldn't work it out.

She was sweating, her heart pounding.

Put on the light, she told herself. See who is here. It doesn't matter that you are naked.

But where was the light in this strange room? It must be by the door, she would have to stand up. Then she thought about her phone – it had a torch. She groped around for it and found it, but her grip was slippery and it clattered on to the lino, flashed into life, and as it did so she saw him.

It was Tom, sitting on the edge of the futon, inches away from her.

It was only a moment, an instant in which their eyes met, then the light from her phone cut out again.

'Jesus, you frightened me,' she said into the dark. 'What the hell are you doing?'

He didn't reply.

'Tom, say something.'

She could smell the booze on him now. She reached for the phone – she needed to be able to see him, to see how drunk he was, his mood. She got on her hands and knees, scrabbling around for it. She sensed movement, he was moving.

'Tom, you're freaking me out, just say something, can't you?'

She felt newly conscious of her nakedness, acutely vulnerable. Her hand connected with the phone – at last. Her fingers fumbled to find the button. Thank God, light again.

He was sitting by the wall now, but in this tiny room that meant he was just inches from her. He was looking at her, his face a mask. There was no love there, no recognition even.

'Tom. What's the matter with you? Oh, this fucking phone!' The light had gone out again. Carmen had pulled her pyjama top to her body, instinctively covering her breasts and front with it, but she put it down now, in the dark, to fumble with the phone. Somehow she managed to find the torch function. There was light.

Tom's head was bowed now, as though he had fallen asleep sitting there. He looked so strange, in his suit, sitting on the floor, so huge in this tiny room. He was very drunk, she realised. 'You really scared me! What are you playing at?' She pulled her pyjama top on. 'How come you're here? Did you come back with Joe? How long have you been sitting there?'

He looked up, looked at her with those same eyes, so cold, as though she was a stranger, as though she was someone he despised.

She shivered. *I will not be scared of you.* 'Are you still angry?'

He rolled his eyes, almost imperceptibly.

'Tom . . . stop this, please. Didn't Joe explain? I did nothing wrong. Nothing happened. I know I should have told you and I'm sorry, I am so sorry but . . .'

He was shaking his head, the same scorn, the same disbelief.

'It's your fault too! You were lying to me, endlessly.'

'You can't pin this on me.'

'You lied!'

'I didn't spend the night with—'

'Neither did I! He got stuck there. Tom, I would never be unfaithful to you. I have not been unfaithful to you. I never even wanted him there. As soon as he came I realised I'd made a mistake. But everything was so weird . . .'

He was looking at the floor again. He was listening at least.

He was here and he was listening. Maybe she just had to go through this.

'Things were really crap, don't you remember? There was all that stuff . . .'

'Your paranoia!'

'You lied to me! Over and over again!'

He put his head in his hands.

She went over to him then, touched his arm, but he pushed her hand away.

She sat down on the edge of the futon. 'I don't know what to say, Tom. I don't know what to do.' She paused. 'I love you, that's all. I can't force you to believe me, but it's true, nothing happened.'

They sat there like that for a while, and then he reached out towards her and took her wrist, and she flinched because she didn't know what he was doing, but then he pulled her towards him and hugged her and relief flooded over her.

'I was so angry with you,' he said. He put his hand on her face, gripped her jaw. 'So angry! Don't ever—'

'Let go!'

He held her like that a moment longer, then he hugged her again.

She sat in his arms, let the tension flow from her.

'We're going to have a baby, Carmen.'

'I know.'

'That makes me so happy, have you got any idea how happy that makes me? We're going to have a baby.'

After a while Tom undressed and they lay down together on

the futon. He stroked her hair and then he touched her pyjama top. 'Why don't you take this off?' he said.

She felt vulnerable, raw. She wasn't ready for sex. 'Tom . . .'

'For once, just – can we not have a conversation about it?' She understood that he needed to make love, and although it wasn't what she wanted right now she let him pull her towards him, let him undo the buttons on the pyjama top. He pushed the quilt out of the way so they were both lying on the top sheet, exposed. He was naked.

'Where did you . . .?' she started.

'Shhh.' He put his hand over her mouth and held it there. And then he rolled on top of her so that all his weight was on her. She felt his knee pushing her legs apart. She didn't like it, she didn't want this, not like this – she struggled and he whispered, 'Shh – just let me' and his fingers were inside her. She struggled – against his body, against his hand over her mouth, and as she struggled she couldn't breathe and so she stopped struggling. And then he was pushing into her and rising up on top of her and he freed her mouth but pinned her shoulders to the bed with his arms as he thrust into her.

He came quickly, violently, shuddering and gasping, and it was over.

He collapsed, his weight on top of her. It had all happened in seconds.

Carmen was so shocked she couldn't speak.

He rolled off, on to his back, and almost instantly he was snoring.

Carmen lay in the dark and cried. She was in some sort of

311

shock. When Tom woke at six and saw she was awake and her face was smeared and red from crying, he couldn't believe that he had caused this. He was mortified at what he'd done. He said he'd thought she was OK about it, that he'd never have done it otherwise. Her fury came out then and she punched him and he said he was so sorry. He knelt beside her and begged her to believe it was a mistake, just miscommunication, the booze making him not read the signals.

When she was calmer he went downstairs to make them some tea. Carmen pulled up the blind and opened the window. The day was going to be hot, already there were clear blue skies and white sun. She lay down in a triangle of light on the cotton sheet, her belly in the hot sun, her head in the shadows. She felt tranquillised but unnaturally, by the tears and the trauma.

They talked. It was Mel who had told him about Nick of course – she'd been more aware that night at the bungalow than Carmen had realised. Tom said she had told him in innocence – she hadn't been trying to make trouble, she was just curious to know about this man friend of Carmen's – and maybe that was true.

'And you assumed the worst?' said Carmen.

He bowed his head.

'Why didn't you just ask me about it?'

He shrugged. 'Maybe I'd been waiting for something to go wrong.'

'What do you mean?'

He paused. 'Sometimes I feel like things just won't be allowed to work out with me and you. That I don't deserve you and I don't deserve to be happy so it will go wrong.'

She shook her head. 'Tom, what are you talking about?'

'Zena. Laura. What I did to Laura and the kids. When Zena died, I thought that was my punishment, and then these last months I've thought . . .'

'Tom, that's so superstitious.'

He shrugged.

Carmen felt irritated suddenly, that even this had become a drama about Tom. 'It's not all about you,' she said.

He stared at his hands. 'You don't want to hear what I'm really feeling, do you?'

'That's not true.'

'You can't handle the truth.' He put on a fake movie voice. 'You can't handle the truth.'

After Tom went off to work Carmen went back to the flat. She felt exhausted and bruised, but she thought, At least it's all out now, at least it's all over – the worst has happened and now we can move on, with everything in the open at last. But she kept crying for no reason, and angry feelings kept bubbling up inside her. She told herself she was tired and went to bed to rest, but that was worse, she just felt depressed.

She thought she would feel better the next day, but it was the same story. She had no energy to do anything and she kept crying without explanation. She felt violated, abused. She felt scared.

313

The next morning Carmen woke at 5a.m. and she looked at Tom sleeping, she knew she had to get away from him.

How could she deal with a man who behaved like that? Whose responses were so extreme? He'd been punishing her, she could see that now. She dressed without bothering to be silent, so maybe she was provoking a showdown, but Tom didn't wake up anyway.

She got into the car and drove aimlessly until she found herself beside a park. She left the car and walked across a wild meadow to a bench. The August heat was rising but the pink air was still cool, the birds were in full song. A man in reflective gear was collecting rubbish. He nodded a silent greeting as he emptied the bin beside her, then drove his little unit to the next stop.

The woman who ran the kiosk in the park arrived in her car and unloaded a tray of pastries. Carmen held them while she unlocked the cafe. She asked if it was too early for a takeout, and the woman obliged – made her a cappuccino and refused to take payment. It was a small act of kindness, but it felt like an omen.

There was someone she needed to talk to. She picked up her coffee, walked back to her car and drove north.

Chapter 21

Laura was gardening when Carmen arrived. She waved as the car pulled up. Carmen had rung ahead, said she was in the area and could she stop off for a quick chat, and Laura had been welcoming and friendly. Things had been different between them since the incident with Mel. Now Laura invited her in and made her a herbal tea – 'I assume you're off the coffee.' Tom had told her about the pregnancy and reported back that she seemed genuinely pleased for them both. When she discovered Carmen hadn't eaten, Laura made her up a plate of bread and cheese and salad.

'Listen, I don't know if you're interested, but when you said you were coming over . . . I've put a few things together,' said Laura. She fetched a box that she had packed, some of the children's old toys, and with it a carrier bag containing a brand-new packet of animal sleepsuits. 'I found these packed away – please have them if you don't mind hand-me-downs.'

'And you bought these?' Carmen held up the sleepsuits.

Laura smiled. 'I couldn't resist.'

Carmen was really moved. 'That is so kind.'

'Well, we're all part of the same family now, aren't we?'

Carmen felt tearful again. She had to get a grip.

'So, how are you?' said Laura, and it took Carmen a moment to realise that she was referring to the pregnancy, not the issues more pressing on Carmen's mind, and so they talked about morning sickness, and appointments with the nurse, and gestational diabetes, which had apparently been a problem for Laura, and it was cosy and pleasant.

It was Laura who eventually brought the subject round. 'Was there something in particular you wanted to talk about?'

Of course it felt inappropriate now, to talk to Laura about Tom. But she had come all this way for her advice. She had not forgotten that night in St Jude's, when she and Laura had sat in the kitchen after midnight drinking tea, and Laura had talked then about Tom, had shown a willingness to do so. She knew him better than anyone.

'When we talked before – that night with Mel . . .'

Carmen stopped. Laura looked at her.

'It's about Tom,' Carmen said.

Laura waited, but Carmen couldn't continue. And eventually Laura said quietly, 'Do you think there's . . . someone else?'

'No,' said Carmen. 'No, it's not that at all. I'm just scared he's – not a good person. I don't know . . . Maybe it's just being pregnant.'

She stopped. She looked at Laura, appealed to her.

'Has something happened?' said Laura gently.

Could she tell her? Could she really confide in this person?

She wanted to so much – she needed to know what Laura thought, what she had experienced. 'It's just . . .'

She stopped. Mercy had appeared in the doorway dressed in a nightie and dressing gown.

'I'm so sorry, Mercy's got a cold. She's meant to be at my mother's today with Mel and Jake, but she didn't feel well enough,' Laura said. 'Mercy, go back to bed, let me come up to you in a few minutes.'

'I'm hungry,' said Mercy.

'It's OK,' said Carmen. 'Hello, Mercy.'

'Hello.'

'What do you want?' said Laura. 'Bread and cheese like Carmen?'

The little girl nodded.

Laura walked around the kitchen, preparing another plate.

Mercy sat down beside Carmen. 'Am I going with you to the bungalow?'

She said the word deliberately – bung-a-low – as though it was a proper noun. Carmen ruffled her hair. 'Not today.'

'Tom mentioned you might be selling it to buy somewhere bigger in London,' said Laura.

The idea had been mooted, either that or sell Carmen's flat, or maybe they would keep them both and let them out. Lucia had bitten Carmen's head off when she'd told her that. 'So some poor sod can pay your mortgage? Is this what you've become?'

'Whatever happens, it won't be for ages,' said Carmen. 'I'm not even going to start looking until after the baby's born. And with prices the way they are . . .'

317

Laura put a plate of food in front of Mercy. 'Will you stay in the same area, do you think?'

'I don't know,' said Carmen. 'I'd like to. Tom wants to move north of the river to be nearer to here, but prices are even worse in north London.'

'You should stay where you know people – you're the one who'll be at home with the baby.'

Carmen acknowledged it. Tom had more or less agreed to this anyway.

'How much would a house in your area cost now?'

'I don't know. A lot – it's all a bit crazy.'

'Roughly, for a three-bedroom terrace, say. Half a mil?'

'No, more. Maybe even double that.'

'Really? Good grief. Oh well, Tom will find the money.'

There was a slight edge to her voice. However good relations had been between her and Tom, money was always a sticking point. 'I'm not so sure,' said Carmen. 'It's a hell of a lot.'

'Just tell him it's what you want,' Laura said. 'He'll have money you don't know about. I used to work with them, remember; they all have secret money squirrelled away. "Just-in-case money", they used to call it.'

'What do you mean?'

'They do it when they get married. Keep a bit tucked away in case things don't work out. Just push him – he'll find the cash.'

Carmen felt herself bristle. What was Laura doing here? Was she trying to reassure her? Having a moan about her own situation? Or was she trouble-making? Carmen didn't know. But of course her thoughts turned to the hundreds of thousands in those transfer documents. When they'd discussed buying a house she'd asked Tom about that, whether he'd bring that money back now, and he'd said maybe, depending on whether they decided to sell St Jude's and her flat, how much they got for them. He'd been perfectly open about it. But what if she hadn't chanced upon that letter? Would he have been open then?

Were there other accounts she didn't know about?

'It's nothing personal,' said Laura. 'It's just pragmatic. The fact he married you shows he loves you – a lot of them won't even do that in case they have to pay out.'

I should leave, Carmen thought. It felt all wrong now to talk to Laura about her other concerns, she would just have to work those out for herself. She was about to get up and make a move when the doorbell rang, and Laura excused herself to answer it. 'I should be going anyway,' said Carmen, standing up.

'Oh, hang on with Mercy, would you? I'll only be a second,' said Laura as she left the room.

Mercy had picked up Laura's phone and was playing with it, her bread and cheese untouched in front of her. 'Don't you want your food?' Carmen said.

'I don't want Daddy to sell the bung-a-low,' said Mercy. 'I like it.'

'Well, we probably won't,' said Carmen. 'I like it too.'

'I like the beach.'

'It's nice, isn't it?'

'Do you remember the day when Jake killed the seagull?'

'Yes,' said Carmen. 'That was horrible, wasn't it?'

'I hated that.'

'I hated it too. It was horrible, wasn't it?'

'Yes. That poor seagull.'

'I know,' said Carmen. She reached out and stroked Mercy's arm. How strange children were, the way they stored disturbing things up and then they came out like this, like a little well of poison beneath the skin, erupting.

'Do you think it went to heaven?'

'Yes, I do,' said Carmen.

'Mel had run off. She didn't see it.'

'That's right. Gosh, you've got a good memory.'

'I remember everything,' said Mercy. 'I remember when Daddy still lived here, even though people say I can't because I was so little, but I do.'

'That's amazing.'

'I remember having breakfast in my high chair and Mummy and Daddy were sitting at the table.'

'Mercy, do you really remember that?'

'Yes.' Mercy pulled the crust of her bread, coiled the soft white centre like a Swiss roll. 'I remember when Mel ran off before.'

'When was that?' said Carmen. 'From here?'

'No, from St Jude's. You were talking about it with Daddy, I remember that.'

Instinctively Carmen turned to look at the door. She could hear the murmur of voices in the hallway. 'What do you remember?' she said.

'Mel arguing with that lady, Daddy's old girlfriend.'

'Zena?'

'Yes.'

'Do you remember Zena?'

'Yes.'

'Did you like her?'

She shrugged. 'Mel liked her. But they fell out and Mel ran away.'

'Can you remember anything else?' said Carmen. 'What happened to Mel? Did she come back?'

'Yes.' Mercy laughed, a sort of fake laugh, exaggerated.

'Was it funny?'

'Yes.' Mercy laughed again, louder, almost shrieking.

'Why was it funny?'

'Because Mummy went swimming in her clothes. She came back and she was all wet.'

'It was raining,' said Carmen.

'Mummy had been swimming in the sea, Daddy said. He gave her some of Zena's clothes to put on. Mummy was all wet, all her clothes and her hair.' She laughed again.

How strange, thought Carmen. How could that be right? Laura had been out looking for Mel, why would she go into the sea? And fully clothed? What's Mercy remembering?

And then like a 3D puzzle, the pieces fell into place in Carmen's mind. Of course. Of course it was Laura. Laura went looking for Mel and found Zena. And then somehow, some way, they ended up in the sea, Laura fully clothed, Zena dead.

Carmen felt Laura pass behind her, come to stand by the counter. 'What are you telling Carmen?' she said.

'About that day when you went swimming in your clothes,' said Mercy, and squealed again.

Carmen smiled and shrugged to indicate that she hadn't the first clue what the child was talking about. 'Who was at the door?' she said.

'Gardener.' She was looking at Carmen.

'Listen, I really need to get going,' said Carmen, and stood up.

'No, please, wait a moment,' said Laura. She looked at Mercy, to indicate to Carmen that she wanted to talk in private. 'Mercy, you can watch TV now. Go on into the living room.'

Mercy leaped off her chair. 'Bye-bye, Carmen.'

And she was gone.

The two women were alone.

Carmen had no idea what to do. Did Laura realise that she had worked out what Mercy's words meant? She must at least suspect, clearly she did. Instinctively Carmen felt that the best thing was to play ignorant, but she could feel her cheeks were burning, hot and red, and Laura was watching her. She felt then the depth of Laura's composure, the self-control that had taken her to leadership of a team of lawyers while she was still in her twenties. She must have been as horrified as Carmen by the turn events had taken, and yet she hadn't missed a beat. She was controlling the situation, not Carmen.

In an effort to change that, Carmen met her gaze. 'What is it?' she said, as though Mercy had never said what she had said.

Her words seemed to jolt Laura and she stopped staring at her. Her gaze shifted instead to her hands, spread out on the smooth wooden work surface in front of her, and Carmen's eyes followed. Laura had big hands, Carmen realised for the first time, she had never noticed before, strong hands, big fingers, the bone and sinew visible underneath, hands that worked in a garden, in a stable, hacking through woodland, not hands that worked at a keyboard like her own white slender fingers. She remembered now what Tom had told her, after Jake had killed the seagull, that Laura could despatch an animal if she had to. Of course that was true.

Carmen felt frightened suddenly. 'Listen, I really need to get going,' she said again, and stood up.

'Please just wait a moment. I'm sorry, Carmen . . .'

Laura broke off. Her tone was apologetic, not threatening, and Carmen looked her in the eye again. She had misread her response – Laura wasn't in control, she was unsure, she didn't know what to do. She was frightened like Carmen. Her skin, always pale against her red hair, was white. 'Listen, I won't say anything,' Carmen said impulsively, but the shock that registered on Laura's face told her immediately that she'd made a mistake revealing herself, she should have played dumb, let the situation slip away. 'I don't know what's going on,' she said quickly, but it was too late. Whatever uncertainty there had been in Laura's mind was gone. She knew for sure that a disaster had occurred. Now she was working out how to deal with it.

'It was an accident,' said Laura.

For a moment Carmen became passive. Her knees went weak. She sat down again.

'I tried to . . . talk to her.'

323

The two women looked at each other across the kitchen counter.

'You don't believe me, do you?'

'Of course I do, I—'

'I tried to talk to her about what had happened with Mel, but she walked away,' she said. 'She slipped on the shingle and fell against one of those wooden things, banged her head. It was an accident. Do you believe me?'

She looked at Carmen. Carmen nodded. 'Yes.'

'I had to take care of it, I had to sort it out.' She looked at Carmen. 'You don't believe me.'

'Of course I do, I . . . do.'

Laura looked down at her hands again and Carmen followed her gaze. Those strong hands, laid out in front of her. *All the perfumes of Arabia* . . . She was lying, Carmen knew it. 'I'm so sorry, Laura, but I really have to go,' she said, and stood up. 'Everything's going to be all right, you've got nothing to worry about.' She picked up her bag and the things Laura had given her.

'You can't tell anyone – no one must find out. You understand, don't you?'

'Of course I understand, no one will find out, I'm not going to say anything,' said Carmen. She turned towards the conservatory doors.

'No, come the front way,' said Laura, and stood up. 'The gardener's working out there, I'll show you out the front door.'

Every instinct in Carmen's body told her not to follow Laura, to leave the way she had come, through the door she could see with her eyes, not to turn into the house, but she went along with her, through the kitchen door into a grand hallway with a curved staircase. She could see the front door, it was ahead of them. They walked towards it side by side, they were nearly there, when Carmen felt a shove that caught her by surprise and forced her into a tiny room. The door slammed behind her and Carmen heard the lock turn.

For a moment she was completely dazed. And then she thought, What a fucking idiot I am.

She banged the door. 'Laura!' she shouted. 'What the hell are you doing? Don't be stupid, let me out? Laura? Mercy?'

She shouted out for a minute or more and then searched through her bag for her mobile, but it wasn't there. Mercy had been playing with it. She'd left it on the counter in the kitchen.

How ridiculous. She looked around her. She was in a small study. There was a desk, papers, lots of file boxes on shelves on the wall. There was a phone on the desk. She grabbed it and afterwards she thought many times, Why didn't I dial 999? But somehow in that moment she still hadn't grasped the full danger of the situation, and instead she rang Tom's number. And it took an age to engage, the way his bloody mobile always did. And then he didn't answer. Of course he didn't – it was Laura's number that came up on his screen; he never answered to Laura, always rang back in his own time, when he'd listened to her message and prepared himself. His phone clicked into voicemail and she hissed into it, 'Tom – I'm at Laura's, I know what happened – with Zena. And now she's locked me in this little room by the front door – oh for fuck's sake answer this call . . .' And then she realised that the phone was dead, the handset she was holding said 'disconnected'. The base unit was blank. She clicked the handset but there was no response. The power had been on, but now it was cut. When had that happened? How much of what she had said had recorded? Any of it? Enough to let Tom know?

That was when she got scared. That was when she thought, Laura's killed once, she will kill again if she has to. If she feels threatened. She knows I don't believe her. Carmen's hands moved to her stomach; she felt acutely aware of her pregnancy. God, why hadn't she dialled 999? They would have logged the number, they would have come looking.

She heard the front door shut and looked out of the window. Laura was marching down the path, towards her 4 × 4, pulling Mercy, who obviously did not want to go with her. Too late Carmen banged on the window, but Mercy was being strapped into the car by then and couldn't hear her, couldn't see her. If Laura could hear her, she didn't show it.

They drove off. Laura was driving too fast. They were gone. She was alone.

What now?

She tried the phone again – it was dead, there was nothing. She tried the desk lamp, which was out of action too. She tried the overhead light – that was working; Laura must have tripped the fuse for the socket circuit in this room.

She checked the windows. They were leaded and fitted with thick security glass so there was no chance of breaking one. Each had a solid lock. She looked around, ran her hand over the windowsills and the ledges by each lock, over the desk, tipped out the pen tidy, checked the drawers, but there wasn't a key in sight. Not like at her flat where the keys sat beside the locks, the only hope of them not getting lost. She checked each fitting in turn just in case it had been left unlocked, climbing on to the table for access, but the only one open was a tiny casement at the top that measured only a hand's width and was just for ventilation. It could be of no use to her.

Carmen turned around, scanned the tiny room. She was trapped here, that was clear, with no means of communicating and no way out. As she started to accept this she felt that what she needed more than anything else was to sit down. She needed to think, and her pregnant body needed to rest.

She clambered down from the desk and sank into the office swivel chair, but it was uncomfortable. There was a battered leather armchair in the corner by the filing cabinet, buried underneath a pile of coats and clothing. She pulled them off. The chair was a ruin, old, lumpy and too upright, but she sank into it. She felt cold, despite the warm day outside – it was probably the shock. She pulled a coat over herself and tried to focus.

What now? What was Laura doing? What was her plan? Did she have one or was she just getting Mercy out of the house?

What about the others – Jake and Mel? They would be home at some point, they'd help her, there was hope – but then she thought, Would they? Against their own mother?

Don't be silly, of course they would.

Would they?

They hadn't helped Zena . . .

She needed to focus but it was hard, her brain cells were shot, they kept dragging her towards numbness, towards sleep. How could her body do this to her now? Sleep meant death. Was it some weird prehistoric tribal survival thing – if it comes to a fight, don't try to carry the woman who's pregnant and risk everyone's lives? Let her sleep, let her die peacefully.

She had to stay awake. What had just happened? She had to work it out. She made herself think about Mercy's words, to pin them down. What had she said? Mummy was wet, Mummy had been swimming in her clothes. She never said Mummy killed Zena or hurt Zena – did she know that? No, Carmen was sure of it, Mercy had no idea, she was just repeating a strange thing that had stayed with her, that she had found funny and disturbing because it wasn't right somehow. Like the seagull. Things she needed to talk about and to process because they weren't right.

Mercy had not understood the meaning of what she had seen, but Carmen had. It was just too strange a detail – Mummy swimming fully clothed. Laura swimming fully clothed. Laura could have tried to explain it away. What Mercy had described might have happened on a different occasion, a different set of circumstances. Mercy was only, what, three when Zena died. Hardly a reliable witness. It might not have happened at all. It might have been a dream. Stupid, stupid Carmen for letting on that she knew.

The DNA. The red hair in the bracelet. Of course, that was Laura's too. All that complicated explanation they had given

328

her – about the maternal line, the DNA passed from mother to child. The match was Mel's but the hairs had been Laura's. Why hadn't she thought of that? She'd considered everyone but not Laura.

It didn't matter – none of this mattered now. What mattered was that she was here, trapped, pregnant and vulnerable. Laura had killed once to protect her child, she would do it again.

I need to protect myself, Carmen thought. She looked around for a weapon, something she could use.

Would Tom have got her message? Had she said enough before Laura cut the power for him to be able to work out what was happening? Would he come and fetch her? Rescue her? Would he even bother to pick up the voicemail, if he saw the call was from Laura's phone? Yes, yes, he would – he always did in the end, and it was from the landline so it could be Mel or Jake calling him – but maybe not until he got home, got away from the office. That would be too late.

Carmen panicked. She realised suddenly and completely the grave danger she was in. Laura had gone out in order to get Mercy out of the way. Why? It could only be because she had realised Carmen didn't believe her story, didn't trust her to keep quiet about what she knew. Laura had decided she had to silence her. She was going to kill her. She was preparing the way.

Carmen felt her panic build so that she wanted to scream, but what would be the point? There was no one to hear. Oh let me get back to London, just let me be back in London, Carmen thought. I will never again complain about you, London. She thought about her flat, her neighbourhood, her neighbours, the people who nodded and said hello when they saw her in the street, the way they lived so close, so many packed into every block, always someone through a wall or a floor to hear, to be interested. People say that Londoners walk by, that they never speak, but that isn't true, she thought, people stop to look and comment and join in if you want them to, that was her experience anyway. If she was in London now she would scream and someone would hear and come.

She was getting overwrought. She couldn't handle this, this waiting for Laura to kill her. To kill her baby. Her arms were wrapped around her stomach but it was a futile gesture, she knew that. If she died here, her baby died. If she bled to death, her baby died. She knew the animal feeling that all parents must know, that they would gladly die to save their young, but she didn't have that option. They would both die here. It was unbearable.

She started to cry.

She couldn't stop. She couldn't handle this, this waiting to die, this waiting for her baby to die. She thought about those images you see of women in disaster zones, cradling babies who are dead or dying. She felt the true agony of it for the first time. She felt the brotherhood with all life that parenthood can bring to life, but it was too late for her.

She heard her phone ringing, distantly, not in the room of course, because it wasn't here, it was in the kitchen. Was it Tom? Had he got the message? Was he calling her? She felt a prick of hope. It had to be him, it must be. When she didn't answer he would realise, he would come.

The ringing stopped. She heard the voicemail bleep. He had left a message. It was him, it had to be, not Kath or Kieran or her mother or some insurance salesman, it had to be Tom. He must have picked up her message, he must be coming.

And then Mercy's words came back to her, when she was telling her about Laura arriving soaking wet. She'd said, Mummy had been swimming in her clothes. She'd said Daddy told her that. She'd said, 'Daddy gave her some of Zena's clothes . . .'

She felt sick. It was obvious – why was she being so stupid? He knew, of course he knew, more than that, he was complicit. Why hadn't that clicked until this moment? She wasn't thinking straight, what it all meant. Tom knew what Laura had done, Tom had always known. That's why he'd lied to her, over and over and over again. He wasn't protecting Mel, he was protecting Laura.

Was he part of it? Had he encouraged it? Her brain wasn't working right, she couldn't compute this. Her mind wasn't clear. Was he part of it? Had they planned it together? 'No!' She howled it, her hands around their baby. Was he part of it?

Had she done the worst thing she could by calling him? No, what difference could it make? Laura would call him anyway, wouldn't she?

Was she being mad? She couldn't think any more.

She looked around. She had to find something to protect herself and the baby. The odds were against her, overwhelmingly, but she couldn't just give in, she must fight and she must win. She found strength again to get to her feet. She scanned the room, the top of the desk, the stack of trays with papers, pens, a few books. She pulled open a drawer to search more thoroughly – stationery; another – files, photographs, sticky tape; the last – filled with junk, more files, a glass paperweight, heavy – she brought that out, it might be useful, she put it in her pocket.

There was a low filing cabinet beside her chair. She opened the drawers, they were hung with lever files; she flicked through them but it was just more paperwork. She tipped some on to the floor. Nothing but paper. Nothing in between, nothing behind – why should there be? Nothing she could use.

There were shelves above the chair. Pots and margarine tubs, more files. She worked through them, pulling some off to get to others. She went through the coats she had tipped off the chair earlier on. Nothing there, but behind them in the corner, lying by the wall, she found a pair of walking exercise poles, with a tapered end. Not a spike, but surely some use if she thrust it.

There was nothing else. The room was chaos. She sat back in the chair but upright now, ready to fight. The paperweight was in her pocket, resting against her leg, the sticks were by her side. She would fight. She was ready.

She waited. There was no clock in the room, she had no way of knowing the time.

She had a plan now. She would attack as soon as the door opened, scream and thrust the stick, aim for the soft belly with the point, it was her only chance. If she could, she would use the second one too.

She needed the toilet. In the end she crouched and peed

in the waste paper bin. What choice did she have? She would throw it at Laura when she came back.

She waited. Her thoughts started to fog, sleep tried to claim her. She fought it off. Her mother kept coming into her mind: Lucia who in this moment appeared to her as a tower of strength. Depressed or not, Lucia would fight for her life, Carmen knew that without any doubt. She would kill without compunction if she had to, Carmen was sure about it, had always been sure, there was something savage about her. She would fight to save herself and she would fight to save her child, and Carmen must do the same.

She thought about Lucia as she would be now, in her flat, the place cosy, padding around in her long dressing gown and her slippers, preparing something for her supper, something simple but delicious – even if it was sardines on toast, it would be delicious; there would be olive oil and a twist of lemon. Lucia, there, with no idea that she was here, that her only daughter was in danger like this, might die this very day. Her daughter and her unborn grandchild, her bloodline, annihilated.

In the end it was sleep that defeated Carmen. She was so exhausted that she didn't hear the crunch of tyres on the drive outside, or the footsteps on the path, or the front door opening, or the lock in the door to her own room turn, or the footsteps on the carpet. She awoke only when the light went on, and of course for a second she was disorientated because she was so exhausted and it was so bright, and she was looking into a face and it was Tom's face above her, leaning over her, and she said, 'Tom,' and he said, 'What the fuck have you done?'

And the look on his face, the tone of his voice – without any time for thought, every nerve in her body, every sense and instinct, screamed, He isn't your friend, he is your enemy, he is the enemy, and without knowing that she was doing it she lifted her hand and with all the force she could muster she smashed the paperweight into the side of his skull.

Chapter 22

Nine months later

Carmen sat on a blanket on the pebbles at the top of the beach and stared out to sea. Rosa was asleep beside her. Barely a minute went by when Carmen didn't peer over the side of the buggy to check her, this perfect creature, swaddled in a crocheted cotton blanket that Lucia had produced from a suitcase and that apparently dated back to her own babyhood. The air was good for her, you could see that, Rosa's cheeks were pink, like a china doll's.

Carmen was still adjusting to the little privations of early motherhood. She would have liked to walk to the water's edge, to throw pebbles and sit where the waves crashed at her feet, that was what she'd imagined she would do when she planned her trip here, but of course there was no way she could manoeuvre the buggy down the shingle. For now, for the next years, maybe for the rest of her life, she would not be the focus of her own existence. That was sinking in, day by day.

It was a small price to pay for the depth and pain of love that had accompanied Rosa's birth and that somehow continued to hold her suspended above the horror of these last months.

She must start to confront it all sometime, the emotional cost. Maybe today would be the beginning of that. She had chosen to come here on the anniversary of Zena's death. Tom had no idea, no one did, but it had been important to her, she'd planned it for the last month, set off early this morning and brought herself and Rosa on the train loaded down with all the paraphernalia that went everywhere with her these days – nappies, wipes, mat, toys.

She'd thought about where she would sit. This was the place where Zena liked to swim, where she had almost certainly left her clothes that day, in a bag to protect them from the drizzle. Carmen looked over her shoulder, back towards the bungalow, along the beach road, and imagined Zena striding down here, indignant after arguing with Tom, maybe penitent or maybe not, maybe genuinely not understanding what all the fuss was about. Or angry that he hadn't sided with her. Or perhaps she just couldn't care less.

Did she realise, as she walked, how wrong she had been to confide in Mel like that? Carmen still couldn't comprehend that – why had she done it? To even think it would be appropriate to tell her that, to not realise that a twelve-year-old who says she hates her mother will violently defend her if anyone else should dare criticise her. Was it a mark of things having gone wrong for Zena that she didn't see that?

Carmen thought about Zena's family. Her mother, Amy,

who'd seemed so empty and lost, her father who'd walked away. Did Zena just not understand what it meant to be part of a normal family, to have parents and siblings you are passionately attached to even while they're driving you up the wall? Carmen had thought at one point how similar her background was to Zena's, but she'd been wrong.

So Zena had miscalculated the outcome, but still there was that question: why had she done it – such a cruel, pointless act? Tom had said she was provoked because Mel had been talking about Laura. Was it competitiveness gone mad? Was it not enough that Zena had won Tom's love from another woman – did she need to be acknowledged as the victor even by his children? To win those children too?

She hadn't seen the danger. Amy had told Carmen that Zena was fearless, had never grasped that things could hurt her. Was that some genetic kink?

There was another strand in Carmen's thinking too that disturbed her. Amy had told her that men were chasing Zena even when she was twelve, thirteen years old. Zena was so beautiful, and people assume that must make life easier, but is it really such a blessing for a young girl?

Who knows? Carmen wasn't a psychologist, she didn't have any answers, but it made her sad. That was the strange thing about Zena; when Carmen thought about her, she just felt sad. She kept thinking of that little girl on the beach, diving into the waves, immune to fear, grabbing life as it passed. Zena was someone who took what she wanted; she could be selfish, but she was bold and brave as well. And yet when Carmen thought about her she felt as though she was a victim. Which of course, at the end of the story at least, she was.

Carmen wished that she had known her. Perhaps they could have helped each other. In a strange way Zena had helped her, to regain her confidence, to find herself.

Mel had been dazzled by Zena and Zena's life, what twelve-year-old girl wouldn't be? But when it came to it, when she heard how Zena had forced her parents' marriage apart, she had been angry, and she had run away.

But not as angry as Laura, when Mel told her.

Because that's what happened. Carmen knew the whole story now, Tom had told her it all. When Laura came to the bungalow to pick up the children, and Tom told her that Mel was upset and had run off, Laura went looking for her, and found her along the beach road, crying, and Mel told her everything – of course she did, because that's what twelve-year-old girls do when they are upset, they tell their mum. Everything that Zena had said to her. The way she'd said it – confiding, bragging almost, as though they were two urbane women discussing their love lives. How when Tom was shilly-shallying over leaving Laura she'd had this great idea and used a credit card that she knew Laura would see so that she would find out about the affair. That she'd made it happen.

And Laura was angry. She was angry for Mel – that Zena had dragged her children into this so inappropriately – and she was angry for herself. Divorce, betrayal – these are everyday events – but Carmen, who had lived through the separation from Nick, knew that didn't lessen the depth of the pain.

Laura had been impeccable, a tower of strength and maturity. But then Mel told her what she told her. And while Mel, distraught at what she had heard, was telling her, she saw Zena on the beach, walking towards the sea in her red bikini, and something snapped. She sent Mel on ahead and went to confront Zena, but rather than trying to talk to her the way she told Carmen she had done, she had grabbed Zena's hair and smashed her head against the wood of the groyne and they fought until Zena stopped moving. Then she dragged her body into the sea and walked back to Tom's house.

Did Mel know what had happened? She had never spoken about it, but she must have had suspicions. Jake too – they were old enough to realise how things didn't add up, to draw conclusions. They saw their mother come back to the bungalow fully dressed but drenched from head to toe. They saw their father help her by giving her clothes – Zena's clothes – just hours before they learned that Zena had disappeared, and soon afterwards that she was dead. Carmen had witnessed small moments between Jake and Mel when they seemed to be protective, to share a secret. She couldn't begin to think about the implications of all of this on them, but it was Tom's problem to deal with, not hers.

Tom protected Laura. Of course he did. When Laura came back she told him what had happened and he gave her Zena's clothes and told her what to do, and later, when they had driven away, he went down to the beach to make sure there was no evidence. Hours later he rang the police to report Zena missing, and when suspicion fell upon him, as of course he knew it would, he let it happen. He would have gone to prison for Laura – he would have taken the rap, he'd told Carmen that. Because their children needed her more than they needed him and because it was all his fault. All his fault.

Carmen had blooded his head with the paperweight, maybe fractured his skull. Nine months on he still had headaches, but he wouldn't go to hospital, he didn't want to involve the police. Things were bad enough already. After Laura had locked Carmen in the study, she had taken Mercy to join Mel and Jake at her parents' house. Then she had driven to a wood, walked along a path, sat down beneath a tree and cut her wrists. A couple out walking found her and saved her life, and she was at her parents still, recovering. Tom was on long-term leave, living back in the old house with the children, doing what he needed to do.

About Tom, Carmen knew two things, and these she had told him. The first was that she couldn't be with him any more, that it was over. He had held her hand through Rosa's birth and stayed with her in the days afterwards, but he had moved his pile of boxes and his grandfather's armchair and his other things out of her flat, and that was permanent. They still saw a lot of each other because of Rosa, and in a way they were closer than ever because – finally – there were no secrets between them, but there was no going back. He would be a part of her life at least until Rosa was grown up, and they'd be great co-parents and hopefully friends, but there couldn't be more. Apart from his brutality that night at Kath's, he'd looked her in the eye and lied too many times.

It hadn't all been one way. Tom had been shocked when Carmen told him the true extent of what she had done behind his back, how she'd been to see Amy, and Ross, and searched his computer. She'd asked him about that download from the forensic website and of course she'd been right – he'd looked it up ahead of the police finding Zena's body, trying to prepare a defence for when the inevitable came. He told her he'd planned to deflect the blame on to himself if it came to it, and she believed that; she understood the depth of his guilt over betraying Laura and leaving his children, his belief in this as some sort of rightful retribution. In that old-school way, you could call him an honourable man. She sympathised with them both.

And so the other thing she had told him was that she would share the burden of this secret and not go to the police with what she knew. It was a huge decision, but in Carmen's eyes it was the way Laura had said – they were all tied together now. Her, Tom, Laura, all the children including Rosa, Zena too in a funny way – they were family, and they would be for life. This was the right thing to do, she was sure, for them all, but especially for the children.

She wasn't scared that Laura would harm her. Even that day, when Laura had realised what Carmen knew, when Carmen was cornered, Laura had only hurt herself. Laura had killed Zena in anger – it was a completely different matter to kill in cold blood.

Carmen looked out to sea. Zena's mother had watched her daughter in those waves and feared that she would meet a violent death and she had been right. She had wanted to keep her safe, but life had happened to them both, twists and turns they could never have anticipated, and Amy had had no power to protect her.

Carmen thought about Mel and Jake and Mercy, and what lay in the future for them now. She looked at Rosa, asleep in the buggy beside her, and the size of the task ahead of her felt overwhelming. A good-enough parent – they say that's all you need to be – but she knew that was not as simple as it sounded. One mad summer, one fit of unbridled rage, and the shockwaves can ripple for generations, ruining lives, embedding in DNA, poisoning hope.

'Hello.'

She looked up and the sun came out. It was Andy, her policeman friend. He was smiling and something about his presence was so wholesome and straightforward that the gloom could not persist. He'd emailed her, after that night at the bungalow, to see if everything was OK, and she'd replied, and somehow that had carried on, occasional emails, chatting about this and that. She'd told him she was coming down today, and asked if he wanted to meet her here on the beach, and he'd said yes, that he'd bring lunch.

He looked into the buggy, smiled. 'She's lovely,' he said. It was the first time he'd met Rosa. He took off his coat and pulled a foil-wrapped packet from the pocket. 'I hope you like cheese and pickle.'

'You made them?'

'Yes, is that OK?'

'Of course, I really like that, that you made them.'

He lay his coat beside her, the other side from Rosa, and sat down on it. He lifted the foil and placed the sandwiches between them.

They chatted and sat in silence and looked out to sea, ate the bread and cheese and fed bits to the gulls. There was a real comfort in seeing him. She felt as though somehow, somewhere, she had moved closer to his world, no longer quite a civilian. But she could never tell him about any of that.

He knew she and Tom had broken up. 'What are your plans?' he said.

She shrugged. 'Live.'

Raise Rosa. Keep the past at bay. Try to let the sun keep breaking through. She was going back to work of course, back into journalism, telling people's stories. Maybe try to do some good.

Live, that was the main thing.

Acknowledgements

Thanks to my agent Felicity Blunt, who saw the potential in this book, and nurtured it and me. Also to Stefanie Bierwerth and the team at Quercus for choosing *Undertow* and putting so much expertise behind it. Thanks to my family and friends for their support and encouragement along the way, and particularly to those who read it and gave me feedback – Nicola S, Paul B, Una M, Nina K and Clare G. Also a special word for Anne R and Suzy G – you know what for. Thanks to my wonderful children, and first and last to Nev, for supporting me in my dream – I love you and I couldn't have done it without you.